The Reunion

by
DNI Bradbury

authorHOUSE®

AuthorHouse™ UK Ltd.
500 Avebury Boulevard
Central Milton Keynes, MK9 2BE
www.authorhouse.co.uk
Phone: 08001974150

First published by AuthorHouse 4/8/2008

ISBN: 978-1-4343-7853-8 (sc)
ISBN: 978-1-4343-7854-5 (hc)

Printed in the United States of America
Bloomington, Indiana

This book is printed on acid-free paper.

I dedicate this book to my family
and all my friends.
They know who they are.
The friends in the story are fictional.
I thank goodness my friends are real.

D N I Bradbury

The Reunion

"And say my glory was I had such friends"
(W B Yeats: The Municipal Gallery Re-visited 1939)

They met each year. Once all together they ate and chatted their way through copious amounts of food and drink. Girls in the nineteen fifties they had all reached 'a certain age' with no more than a few emotional bruises from lost lovers and were all respectable and comfortable. Well, at least, this is how they portrayed themselves, until now.

This is the story of Beth, Lucy, Ronnie, Maddy and Liza.

CHAPTER ONE
Introductions

Beth

"Full many a flower is born to blush unseen, and waste its sweetness on the desert air"
(Thomas Gray: Elegy Written in a Country Churchyard 1751)

The day started out as many do in early June, bright and sunny and full of hope. Hope that the day will be full of warmth with a gentle breeze and good company. The journey to the sea would take about an hour and a half. She had packed her part of the picnic with great care. She loved to cook and had carefully planned the wine in the cool bag that would accompany her special chicken dish which was so full of flavour and goodness and grapes and taste that she salivated at the thought of her friends' delight when they saw it, let alone when they tucked into it. She was happy as she packed the boot of her tiny car. Her travel rug had been her mother's and every time she looked at it she remembered the tiny bird-like lady who had brought her up, loved her, tended her when she was sick and been the ball and chain from which she would never be free. How did you balance the life you wanted to live against the one of familial devotion topped up with acute barbs of emotional blackmail? She physically shook herself and decided not to dwell on the past but just live for today. Today she would spend with her friends, reminiscing

1

about their school days. Current situations did intrude but did nothing to dispel the bond of affection that held them together.

She had never married. Her one and only offer of marriage had been tempting but then he had immediately wanted her to give up her job and move with him to Manchester. Manchester held a very good job with a global chemical company for him and absolutely nothing for her. She had a very well paid position with the local bank and liked her life. To her shame she remembered using her widowed mother as an excuse for vacillation. As time went by and he went north their passion turned to indifference and petered out. She briefly thought of the irony in the situation. Her excuse for staying had become reality. She found as the days turned to years she and her mother had become increasingly co-dependent.

The journey this year was to the wonderful Dorset coast. They had all decided last year not to go on meeting at their homes. A picnic had seemed like an excellent idea, hence the gathering at Lulworth Cove this year. The roads were not too busy and she had an uneventful drive. Parking in the, as yet uncrowded, car park she realised that her bag was a bit heavy and she felt encumbered with her beach paraphernalia. However, not one to give up she struggled and carried and cursed under her breath and made it to the beach. She looked round and discovered that she was the first to arrive so she picked a spot halfway along the cove under the cliffs where she spread out her blanket and towel and settled down to wait against a rock. She sat and sighed and gazed blissfully at the sea.

Lucy

"Stone walls do not a prison make, nor iron bars a cage"
(Richard Lovelace: To Althea, From Prison 1649)

It was always difficult on the days when she had to go out on pleasure. John was so mean that she was made to feel guilty about any money spent on 'luxuries'. He kept tight hold of the purse strings and gave Lucy an allowance for household spending. The meagre sum was supposed to run the house and clothe the family. John kept the rest back for himself and his golf. His golfing set were aware of his meanness and made sure that he was embarrassed into buying a round occasionally. In fact part of their sport was to see how many different ways there were to get a drink out of the tightwad. Lucy had very little money of her own as she had given up her clerical job to be at home with the children and was now so under confident that she managed only a part-time job with the local drop-in centre for homeless people. Poorly paid and difficult emotional work it gave her a sense of purpose but little remuneration.

These annual reunion days were a high light of Lucy's year. She was able to remember when she had a future and could hold her own in any conversation. She had been a talented artist and had hoped to go to college. Unfortunately she had met and fallen in love with John and very quickly had a child. This was followed by a series of miscarriages and then two more children. John and his domineering mother had blamed Lucy for the miscarriages. The thought of leaving him had occurred to her often but as the years went by she lost her self esteem and belief that she had any entitlement to a life other than that of suffering and martyrdom. Her children had long since got fed up with seeing her suffer and had been unable to jolt her out of her doom. They were all living far away as they could not bear to see their mother in such a lonely place. One was in Scotland, one in Australia and one was in perpetual motion in China.

Today she was determined to enjoy the early summer day and take a fair picnic contribution to her friends. She had hinted over the years about John's mean streak but usually she made a joke about it and said everything was all right really. She would have been amazed to realise that not one of them was fooled by this pretence. Out of her hearing they all wished she would leave him and be the happy, witty girl with whom they had shared much fun and laughter at school. She carried the small hamper with her as she boarded the bus. It took her to the station from where she caught her train into Dorset. From here she would be picked up by Veronica and together they would drive through the luscious Dorset countryside to Lulworth Cove. It wasn't such a long journey but as she had never learnt to drive it was the only way she could get to join in. John had told her she was too nervous to drive safely so she had long ago given up on the idea. John didn't offer to drive her to the station as he had a golf match that morning and wanted to get ready. He hadn't mentioned that his golfing partner was, as usual, Cynthia.

Veronica

"I keep such music in my brain No din this side of death can quell;
Glory exulting over pain, And beauty garlanded in hell."
(Siegfried Sassoon: Secret Music)

She took the bend in her Mercedes as fast as she usually did. She had two speeds, fast and even faster. She revelled in her love of speed. She took a few risks but had only ever had one accident. She was a very capable woman who ran her own business. When she left university she had quickly realised that she did not want to work for anyone, she wanted to be her own boss. She was not afraid of hard work and started to provide promotional material for local businesses. She was clever and creative and personable and gutsy. She was successful. 'Ronnie' had married later than her friends. She had been a forceful woman and so scared off many a suitor. However, one day, she had taken on a new client and during the course of the contract sealing lunch her new client's father had dropped by and, despite the fifteen year age gap they had fallen desperately in love.

George and Ronnie had been blissfully married now for twenty years. He was in his seventy third year and she was in her late fifties. The bliss had been tempered by the adoption of a beautiful boy who was their pride and joy. Perhaps they had loved him too much. The pain was unbearable when he was killed in a road accident at the age of eight.

4

The tragedy had touched not only their lives but that of the woman who had run him down. She had been temporarily distracted by her children who were playing in the rear seat of her car. Like many young children on their way to school they had been animated and unruly. The outcome was unimaginable suffering to both families. The woman never recovered and became an alcoholic finally taking her own life a few years later. Ronnie and George had weathered the desperate trough of despair and emerged as loving as ever to each other but their joy and fun loving way of life would always have a hollow ring. The pain behind the smile never really went away.

George's daughter from his first marriage, which had been a comfortable and loving coupling, felt the exclusion from their grief. She was a good person who loved her father and indeed tried to love Ronnie. Ronnie did not make this a very easy thing to do and so they lived their lives drawn together by a shared love; and a determination on the part of Jane to be part of her father's new life.

All these years later Ronnie was still outwardly the amusing, urbane and critical friend she had always been. Very good company and intensely loyal to her band of friends she had not missed one reunion. Today she picked up Lucy from the railway station and they motored along down to Lulworth with a wonderful sense of adventure and camaraderie. It was on these days that they could all forget some harsh facts of their lives and go back to the hopeful, funny, gauche teenagers they had grown to love. It would be a difficult day for Ronnie this year. She knew she was expected to be strong and frightfully amusing but the news about George had shaken them to the core. The clinic had only recently confirmed his diagnosis and it had rocked Ronnie's world to its foundations.

Glancing at Lucy in the passenger seat Ronnie mused on her friend's life. She looked as though things had got no better over the intervening months since they last met. They made an oddish couple as they walked together down to the cove. Lucy was shorter and now very thin whilst Ronnie was, and always had been, tall and statuesque. Her figure was not fashionably gaunt but she was very comfortable with it and had suffered no lack of confidence because of her size.

Madeleine

"A robin redbreast in a cage puts all heaven in a rage"
(William Blake: Auguries of Innocence 1803)

The brightest of all the friends, academically, she had three failed marriages behind her but she travelled hopefully in the vain hope that she would find the perfect partner. A solicitor by profession, 'Maddy' lived in Surrey with three cats and a dog. One of her brief flings with matrimony was doomed from the start because he thought he was more important to her than the animals. He didn't understand that he was equally important, not more so. None of her group agreed with her, to them rather fanatical, fixation on animal welfare and rights but they were extraordinarily fond of her so they accepted her for what and who she was. Acceptance was the key to all their stories and helped to explain their deep bond.

She had driven down the night before the reunion and stayed at a local hotel. As she considered the hotel and its service she thought how provincial it was. These rather condemnatory thoughts were quickly followed by self chastisement as she realised how 'Surrey' she had become. It was something about herself that she did not much care for. Perhaps she would move right away and bury herself in the country somewhere and find that peace for which she so longed. Increasingly she had been worried about her long term future and how she would manage on her own. Gregarious by nature she hated being alone. Perhaps she could open an animal sanctuary. She wouldn't be alone then. Maddy had made a comfortable living as a solicitor and now had no worries on the financial front. Her savings had been further enhanced by the death of her parents, quickly, one after the after, with only six months separating the two funerals. The legacy of their deaths was a substantial sum of money and a lifetime of memories, both good and bad. Long ago she had managed to shake off the bad and remember only the fun. She and her brother were close emotionally but not geographically. He had emigrated to New Zealand many years ago and only occasionally came back to visit. So it was that the arrangements for both parents' final farewells had been left to Maddy. This had left her rather worn out and tired with her current life.

It was Maddy who had missed more of the reunions than her friends. Somehow the frantic life of socialising, marrying and working had been more important than her schooldays companions. She was now remonstrating with herself about how she had neglected this great band of people. Maybe they hadn't achieved what she had achieved. What was that anyway? Social position and wealth did not make up for family loyalty and happiness the like of which she had not found despite her sometimes desperate search. She saw in her friends a warmth and completeness which she envied. Well, not all of them. She certainly did not envy Lucy. What a bastard she was married to, better to be alone for ever than be shackled to such a cruel man. Perhaps she would encourage Lucy to break free. She doubted whether anyone had ever encouraged Lucy to do anything. Lucy's parents had been negative about her abilities compared to her sister who had succeeded in the sciences and gone on to become a research chemist. This was much more laudable than art. What good was that? Maddy had never liked going round to be with Lucy in her house. They had lived in adjoining streets. When they had got together it was usually at Maddy's house where there had always been a welcome and a home made currant bun waiting to be eaten.

Maddy drove the short distance from her hotel to Lulworth Cove and parked near to Beth's car. She recognised it by the plethora of stickers in the windows exhorting the world to be compassionate about world peace. Although she had been the closest over night to their appointed place she was the last to arrive.

Liza

Liza had been a very quiet girl in school. She had lived in a world of make believe and fantasy. She had always longed to wake up one morning and find out she had been adopted and was really a princess and had been found at last by her rightful parents. They would have been king and queen of a distant country with lakes and mountains. They would have loved her. She devoured the stories of Hans Anderson and The Brothers' Grimm to a point where her reality and fantasy had become indistinguishable. Her natural parents had actually loved her but they had been so busy trying to scrape a living that Liza had sometimes felt neglected. She had a lively imagination but found it difficult to empathise with her parents' troubles. She had been a self centred child for whom her family felt great warmth tempered by irritation. Constantly she had written in her secret diary which she had kept hidden and locked. Her family heaved sighs of exasperation and prayed that she would find her way in life without too much heartache. They knew that the trouble with great aspirations is in the reality that, for most people, they are not realised.

Liza's dreamy quality perfectly complemented the rest of the group. There was bossy Ronnie, hardworking Maddy, creative Lucy and solid, good old Beth. They all formed the basis of an eclectic but wonderful team.

Shortly after leaving school Liza had thrown up all her ambitions to be 'discovered'. No longer interested in becoming a poet or an actress or a singer she had taken up a job in the civil service and moved to London. It was from here that she met and fell head over heels in love with a Welsh farmer. He had been in London to watch a rugby match. They had literally fallen over each other in Trafalgar Square. One thing led to another and they married. They now lived in Devon where they seemed to be blissfully happy. She had worked extremely hard alongside him and they had prospered. Their family business had incorporated farming, tourism, cream teas and an art gallery that sold local art. Their eldest son was now running the business with his father and so Liza and Edwin could afford to take more time off and enjoy what they had worked for over the thirty three years they had been together.

Occasionally Liza would refer to Edwin as her prince. This was the only indication that she had such a past of romantic longing. She no longer wrote a diary, she no longer dreamed her life away wanting what she could not have. She had what she had and so that is what she wanted. That was the best way to be. The other way lay disappointment and regret. Some people are born to take risks and others settle for what comes along. Liza was a settler. If you tell a child often enough that her dreams are childish and unsustainable then in many cases she will eventually believe that she is in the wrong to have such thoughts. Liza was one such child.

CHAPTER TWO
The Picnic

Once Beth had sorted out the picnic area she sat on the beach and waited. It was only ten thirty so she knew that the others would not come at least until eleven or perhaps later. She enjoyed the sea. The light dancing on the water was almost magical. She shivered slightly as the early summer sun was not over hot yet. She put her fleece round her shoulders and continued to sit and look at the cove. She breathed deeply. She casually wondered why it was that the sea gave off such a wonderful smell of homecoming. Just to breathe in made her feel complete. There were some small rowing dinghies pulled up on the shore waiting for holiday makers to come along and row in the comparative safety of the sheltered water. Rocky in places, the twin headlands reached round forming nearly a perfect circle as if to embrace the space within. Although there had been some incidents where careless people had gone out beyond the entrance and needed to be rescued generally it was thought to be a safe place. Perhaps they would take a boat out later. She smiled as she thought of her friends in the boats and their likely antics. What a joy to be here and anticipate the chatter and news that was always the measure of their 'get-togethers'.

Liza was the next to arrive. She had made good time along the coast road from Devon and had enjoyed the freedom that driving alone can bring to a busy, buttoned down life. She spotted Beth who had settled somewhere in the middle of the great sweep of the cove and shouted a greeting. Her voice was taken by the sound of the sea and so she had to shout several times before Beth finally heard her. "Hello Beth, how are you? What a glorious day. Aren't we clever picking today after the rain of the past few weeks? Did you have a good journey down?" She plomped down on the beach and hugged Beth who was half standing half sitting struggling to get up to greet her friend. "It's so nice to see you. You're looking well. The journey was fine and yes we are very clever with the weather." They paused for breath and Beth then asked after Edwin: "How's Edwin, and the family?"

Liza leaped in with, "Oh he's fine, bit heavier than when we last met but he does love the cream teas too much." Having dismissed her prince she looked at Beth and asked, "How are you? You're looking a bit better than last time. Not so sad."

Beth struggled to find a light enough answer, "Oh you know how it is. Time is a great healer. So they say. I don't know that I always think that but…" She tailed off and Liza smiled at her and gave her another hug. "It will get easier. I promise you. When Mum died I thought the whole world had turned on its head. She had been so lovely, especially when the kids were born. Now, well I still cry sometimes but Edwin jokes me out of it and I just get on." Beth felt temporarily sorry for Liza as she imagined the practical, huge man her friend had married. He loved Liza still with all his heart but had no idea of her buried dreams. He thought, as her parents had done, that she had 'grown out of all that romantic nonsense'.

They paused to look round at their surroundings and drink in the luxury of being at the seaside in the middle of the week. Their gaze was drawn to two figures, both laden with bags, hampers, blankets and hats, as they staggered along to the waiting pair. Lucy and Ronnie were laughing and exaggerating their burdens as they finally made it to Beth and Liza. Everything was flung down in an untidy pile there then followed hugs and 'How are you?' was bandied back and forth until everyone had established that they were all well and that their journeys had been trouble free. Lucy had recovered sufficiently from Ronnie's driving to venture, "You're lucky we are here at all. Ronnie overtook an army lorry on a bend and well, the language, you can imagine. The army were quite restrained but Ronnie's language, phew. She must have her guardian angel with her today. Thank god as mine seems to have given up on me." The weak smile that accompanied this was an attempt to make light of her desperate home life. They weren't fooled but it was too soon for heart to heart exchanges yet. That would come later. They all knew this and so busied themselves arranging the picnic and blankets to sit on and sun hats and sun cream and giggled their way through the next quarter of an hour.

It was nearly twelve noon when Maddy finally arrived at the beach. She walked with grace and poise even though she carried a huge hamper and bag which was bulging with rug, hat and sun cream. What also made it difficult was the enormous photo album that she had stuffed into her bag at the last minute. They all made their way to intercept her journey along the shingle and carried various items from her suntanned arms. It was with great joy that they now finally busied themselves with the ritual of sorting out who had brought what and how much savoury there was to go with the sweet things. They were all sufficiently aware of the need to eat fruit and be healthy but this was one day when there was never an apple in sight. The worst offender was Maddy herself; she always brought the most delicious desserts full of cream and raspberries, strawberries, black cherries, peaches and more cream. Meringue was usually buried somewhere under the pile of cholesterol laden creamy fruit. It was difficult to find but great fun trying. Maddy never brought savoury and she never made the desserts herself. She knew a rather famous patisserie near her home and they were used to her regular orders of extravagant naughtiness.

The happy band all sat down and talked and joked about the most insignificant things. The weather-beaten old man who was looking after the boats, his helper who was in his twenties, and incidentally the other man's grandson, the family with the large dog and a myriad tiny children, the sedate couple with matching sweaters all came in for comment from the group who were mostly kind in their comments. The inconsequential chat was suddenly brought to an abrupt end when one of their number revealed a secret that she had not meant to mention until later.

"That one over there, he's a bit long in the tooth for me, I think I've had enough of stroking a certain person's," Beth paused realising she had their attention "ego." As this comment came from an unexpected source, Beth looked up to see astonishment on all their faces.

"Well you're certainly in the running for dark horse of the year" Maddy chimed in. The others laughed and spluttered. It was Lucy who decided to seize the moment and ask Beth to explain herself.

"Just who have you been seeing that would cause such a comment?" Lucy directly confronted Beth. Beth slowly looked round the whole group who were, to a woman, staring at her and grinning. Very deliberately she got up and handed out plates to the rest and opened the chicken dish and indicated all the rest of the savoury food with a flourish of her long spoon and in a voice full of triumph explained, "Let's eat as it is well past one o'clock now and while we are enjoying this gorgeous feast I'll tell you my story, so far." Liza, rather quizzical now spoke what the others were thinking, "I thought we knew your life history." Liza paused and reflected, "Just like we think we know all our stories. Does this mean you've been leading two lives?"

Lucy piped up before Beth could answer and offered, "You all know for instance that my husband is a sod of the first water. He's mean and a bully. He's been having an affair for a year now and thinks he's been very clever about it." She drew a deep breath then ploughed on, "Sorry Beth, to jump in but if I'd waited I wouldn't have found the courage again."

Beth and Ronnie both made accommodating noises, "Don't worry."

"It's all right, carry on." Liza and Maddy stopped eating and stared at their friend. Maddy encouraged Lucy to continue her unburdening. "Lucy, darling, we've known for ages you've not been happy but we've never really confronted you about it."

"Yes," interjected Liza, "Rightly or wrongly we thought you should be the first to broach the subject but we've all spoken to each other about you and hoped and prayed that you'd leave the bastard."

Lucy smiled and then burst into tears. "This is such a relief, I can't tell you." Spluttering Lucy carried on, "She works with him and they play golf together. They're probably in a bunker now messing about." Pausing to take a deep breath she grabbed the nearest hand which happened to belong to Ronnie, "You're such nice people, anyway I've been to a solicitor and he says I've got every chance of walking away with a fair sum." Suddenly she laughed, "He has no idea and on Friday he will be served with a notice saying I want a divorce. By then I will be in Scotland with Amy." Lucy's daughter had married a lovely Scot who hated his father-in-law. They lived near Dundee and had welcomed the idea of Lucy staying with them while she sorted her life out.

Ronnie squeezed her hand and gave her a hug and the rest of them whooped with joy and relief for her. Liza got up and danced a rather wobbly, creaky dance of delight and they all laughed. They looked at Lucy and suddenly she seemed ten years younger. "Come on," said Beth, "Let's eat and try to imagine the old skinflint's reactions, what joy. I'm so pleased Lucy, you deserve so much more." They all tucked into the food with renewed gusto.

"Gorgeous chicken, Beth."

"Lovely quiche Liza, home grown courgettes?"

"Who brought the salmon? Such a treat, wild Scottish smoked. Mm."

Maddy burped and went pink as she apologised. And so it went on for a while as they satisfied the inner woman. There was a renewed lightness about the group now. They all had a greater or lesser secret to share but they agreed that Lucy's was the best news ever.

Ronnie on the other hand had the worst news to impart. As she didn't want to burst anyone's bubble following Lucy's news she kept it to herself for the moment. Ronnie heaved a heavy sigh and patted her ample tummy, "I've got to walk off the first course before I can attempt the instant heart attack pud that Maddy's brought. Any one for a stroll?"

Beth got up and stretched herself like one of Maddy's cats, "Yes I'll come. Need to stretch my legs then we can enjoy the gateaux." No one else made any attempt to move so the two of them strolled off together.

"Well old Lucy's a dark horse. She never even mentioned anything to me on the way down. You'd think she'd have given some sort of clue."

Beth thought for a moment then ventured, "You know Ronnie you're a bit larger than life sometimes." As she struggled to find the right words Ronnie jumped back in with, "What do you mean? I know you're not trying to be offensive but sounds like a bit of an insult to me."

Immediately she said, "Sorry Beth. If I think about it I do know what you're trying to say." Yes, it's difficult. Meeting up like this, it's always a reality check. We none of us can pretend to be anything other than what we are. We've known each other too long. Although it doesn't mean we all tell the entire story all the time" They carried on struggling to walk casually on the shingle, turning over the odd ankle and avoiding the tar that is found on most beaches at the tide mark.

Beth turned and looked out to sea. "You also drive so fast that it's tricky to do anything but hold on and hope the road is clear of other cars." The smile she gave Ronnie took away any sting from the remark. As Ronnie was well aware of her tendency for speeding she acknowledged this with a grin.

Beth carried on, "I've been seeing someone. Since Mum died I felt the overpowering need to be with someone and so I joined an art class."

"Oh Beth that's so good to hear. Was he another artist or the teacher?"

"Well," Beth took another of her sighs and said, "actually he was the life model." Laughing she carried on, "I saw all he had to offer before I even knew his name." Ronnie had stopped in her tracks and stood with her mouth open and her hands on her hips. "Who is... what's his...?" Beth laughed so hard she bent over and couldn't continue for a while. "Ronnie, I have never seen you so stuck for words. He's a retired estate agent and very well off and very well endowed." The silence grew as Ronnie took this in. Beth continued, "He was doing the art thing as a favour to his friend who runs the course, they've known each other since college. He thought it'd be a laugh."

15

Liza, Maddy and Lucy saw the other two stop and laugh and wondered what had caused the two such pleasure. Maddy observed, "If Beth is telling Ronnie about her secret love life she'll jolly well have to repeat it. We are not going to miss out on such brilliant news."

"Her mother was very difficult you know. She became a right ball and chain to Beth." This last came from Liza, "I wanted her to come for a holiday to the farm but her mother kicked up such a fuss she decided not to risk it."

The other two murmured agreement. "She was always dying from some new disease she'd read about. Funny when you think she had cancer all along and it went undiagnosed."

Lucy continued for Liza, "Yes she complained so much to her GP that he thought she was just an old lady making a fuss and so sent her away with more pills. God knows what for."

"Oh girls I can't wait to get away. It's such an adventure. Amy's been a godsend over this business. Angus too is a sweetie. I hope he doesn't find me a nuisance after a while."

Maddy and Liza both said in unison, "Course not."

"Anyway," continued Lucy, "I'm going on holiday, one of those trekking hols to Egypt. It will be marvellous to be on my own and free."

"Gosh Lucy you have thrown off the shackles."

Maddy was overcome with admiration for her hitherto downtrodden friend. "What made you even begin to get the confidence. That bastard took away every little bit of self worth you ever had."

"Well Mad, it was you last year. You may not remember but you said you were thinking of retiring and setting up a sanctuary and I realised, like a blinding flash that I needed a sanctuary. My home was certainly no place for me and I couldn't conceive of another thirty years doing the same thing in the same amount of misery. So I've organised my new life and taken the opportunities presented by those endless golfing days when he's been out with bitch-woman." As she drew breath the others smiled and Liza touched her arm in a friendly caress. The touch was an affirmation and an approval.

"I can't get over it. She's actually done me a favour. I've got photos of them together."

As the other two gasped she carried on like an unstoppable tide, "No I didn't engage a private detective but someone was showing me a series of pictures of a golf presentation and they were unaware of the camera. He, my husband, was holding her bottom and kissing her shoulder. Snide, conniving bitch. She was leaning in to him in an intimate way that he has never shared with me since the first few years of our marriage."

As she watched her friends' reactions she added, "The photographer was actually being kind and I have met him a few times for coffee since."

"How did the photographer know who you are and who …?"

Maddy's question was interrupted by Liza who said, "Was that the chap you told me about on the phone who came to the shelter and took an interest in the work you were all doing there?"

Lucy's grin said it all. As she whispered "Yes" she hugged her knees and swayed back and forth in a moment of personal caress.

It was during this last exchange that Ronnie and Beth came back. "Hello, hello, more news on the Lucy front?"

"We just heard something about a photographer. Tell us more."

Liza repeated all the conversation as Lucy was dreamily gazing out to the mouth of the cove and seemed to be in another place. Ronnie playfully pushed Lucy and said, "Oh well done you." She reflected for a while then said, "You know Lucy, you're going to be ok. You have a new found strength. If you feel at all like faltering please give one of us a call and we will be there for you."

The rest chorused, "Absolutely, Luce." "Of course you must Lucy." "Any time you like, day or night." "We're here for you, of course we are."

Maddy had had enough of Lucy's news for a while, "and what were you two laughing about so much that you nearly fell over?"

17

"Beth was explaining how she met the man of her dreams." Ronnie's exuberance was starting to sound a little false but the rest ignored that as it was much more exciting to hear about Beth and her new man. Beth explained all that she had told Ronnie and added that she was seeing him but not thinking seriously long term stuff with him.

Whilst the group were listening to Beth, Ronnie wandered a little way towards the water's edge and sat on a rock contemplating the wavelets as they harried the rock and the rock pools nearby. It was Liza who came to fetch her and ask her to tell the others what was upsetting her. "Come on Ronnie. You are keeping something quite dark inside you. Please come and share it. You'll be grateful that you did." As they walked back she added, "We all care you know."

"Yes," sighed Ronnie, "I know you do, you as much as any Liza. You are a very caring person."

Ronnie wiped away the tears that had gathered in her eyes and spoke to the sea knowing she had the undivided attention of her friends. "There's no way to wrap this up. George has less than six months to live." Great wracking sobs were all that followed this statement. Ronnie cried openly now and was wrapped in a bear hug by Liza. Maddy and Beth stood up and put their arms across her shoulders while Lucy pulled a clean linen handkerchief from her handbag and softly wiped Ronnie's face. They had all met George on numerous occasions and had liked him so it was that within a few minutes they were all crying. After a while Ronnie calmed down and the tears gradually subsided. "I've kept it inside me for so long that it is a blessed relief to let it out. George is upset at letting me down but is so tired he actually looks forward to not fighting any more."

Sometimes silence is the best response and this was one of those times. It was a very powerful endorsement of their mutual affection and sympathy.

The afternoon wore on with no more startling revelations. They decided to leave the remains of their picnic and take out two dinghies. All of them considered a breath of sea air and some rowing practice would ease out the tension of the day and restore some levity to the reunion. None of them could remember such a day for the life shattering confidences shared between them. Platitudes would not help Ronnie and Lucy needed absolutely no encouragement to talk, yet again, about her exciting plans. Beth was now considered to be a dark horse and was no longer the butt of sympathy. Rather it was with some renewal of energy and life that they embraced her secret love affair. Almost as though it gave them all hope that their lives, hitherto ordinary and sometimes safe, could at a sweep of a paintbrush be transported to a more exciting level. In her mind Maddy was genuinely pleased for Beth and Lucy. She had led a life of extraordinary fulfilment and was now quite happy to put herself out to grass and wait and see what happened. Deep down she believed it would be no more 'safe' than it had always been. Something always turned up for her to encourage her to take a new path. She had rarely turned fate down.

Of all of them it was Liza who was most troubled by her reactions to Beth and Lucy and their changes of circumstance. On the surface she was happily married with a good business and a lovely and loving husband. Their financial circumstances were comfortable and they had four great children all of whom had gone off to follow their own path. The eldest son had now returned and was a key figure in the running of the family business. Just occasionally she let her guard slip when she was alone and dreamt of some adventure, some change in her orderly and comfortable life. It was at these times that she felt most disloyal to her husband purely because he was so steady and didn't deserve any aggravation. She was plump with a womanly figure that many people would be proud of. Liza dressed well although a little bit country. It was Maddy who dressed with the city edge that had a sharpness about it that spoke of success and achievement in a commercial sense. Liza's clothes came from tried and tested tailoring dynasties whose ancestries could be counted back to the seventeenth century.

CHAPTER THREE
Boat Trip

The rather nice old man let them have two boats for an hour. He looked rather quizzically at the assortment of middle aged ladies and wondered if any had ever rowed before. In case they needed help he gave them all a quick lesson and indicated to his grandson to standby should any of them get into difficulties. Ronnie was an expert sailor and was used to the water so she took the oars in one boat. (As she started to row she reflected how it was now probable that she and George would no longer enjoy those lovely sailing holidays round the Mediterranean islands that had been a feature of their year ever since they met.) Beth and Lucy got into the boat with her which left Liza and Maddy to take out the second. The latter pairing was not the match made in boat heaven as neither had rowed before. Both of them had been used to having had a companion to do that sort of thing for them while they looked on admiringly. Surprisingly it was Liza who took the oars. She looked at Maddy's delicate arms and manicured hands and decided that her own time on the farm had given her muscles in days gone by that had never quite gone away. Maddy on the other hand had hardly done any physical work. A successful solicitor she could afford to engage a cleaning firm for her house and a gardener for her lawns which were as well manicured as her long fingers. It was only because the old man had had little business that day that he let them out without more thought. He needed the money as he was helping fund his grandson through agricultural college.

Ronnie struck out towards the mouth of the cove with even strokes. Lucy and Beth dangled their hands in the still cool water and they giggled and chatted and laughed. Liza made less headway with their boat and struggled to get the oars in time with each other. However she stuck at it and they gently and slowly made their way across the cove. They did not wish to go anywhere near the entrance as the sea outside the sheltered waters looked a bit choppy. Ronnie, on the other hand, fast and dangerous Ronnie, Ronnie who liked the thrill of danger, thought she'd scare the other two by going close to the mouth and give them a view of the choppy sea beyond. When they had then been sufficiently alarmed with a flourish she would whisk them back inside the cove and return the boat. This was a rather desperate way of her trying to regain control of a life that was sliding out of her grip. The currents were in opposition to Ronnie's plans that day and so when she tried to turn the boat they were caught up and thrust out beyond the shelter of the headlands and out into open sea. Up to now Beth and Lucy had gone along with the adventure. They pretended to be frightened and half encouraged Ronnie in her devilment by pleading with her to turn back. This is how Ronnie received the cries of her companions anyway. They would say that this was not the case.

As the calm water of the cove gave way to a buffeting swell outside the confines of the bay the silence and fear in the little jolly boat was palpable. Lucy stared at the receding headland with horror. She was a poor swimmer and had an awful fear of drowning. She became rigid and uncommunicative. Beth remained outwardly calm but berated Ronnie for her foolishness. Ronnie's answer to this criticism was to flash back, "Later Beth, chastise me later, let's just try to keep calm and get this boat back somewhere safe." She struggled with the oars against the sea and then pleaded, "You two, look for somewhere where p'rhaps I can row to safe harbour." As this elicited no reply she shouted, "Now, look now, for god's sake we're being pulled out. Try and help me." Short of fashioning oars out of thin air they weren't quite certain how to help but they duly looked towards the vanishing coast and like all sailors in peril, they

21

prayed. Beth saw the young man on top of the cliff and waved at him. He waved back and shouted something back to them but they could not hear above the sound of the sea and the wind. They were cold now and very quickly, much more quickly than any of them would have imagined, they became rather desperate.

As Liza and Maddy returned their boat to the waiting boatman they looked round to see where the others had got to. The hour had gone surprisingly quickly and they had enjoyed their time together. They had discussed Maddy's plans to move west and look around for a suitable place where she could give sanctuary to animals that had need of such care. She thought that she would concentrate on dogs and maybe donkeys but her plans were as yet an idea rather than a concrete intention. Liza was encouraging and said she would keep an eye out for a suitable smallholding in her area. "I don't always agree with your stand on animal rights you know." Liza informed Maddy in a rather tight voice, "but I do admire your commitment so if we can agree to differ I'll help you as much as I can." She paused and then thoughtfully said, "We all eat meat and so we can't be hypocritical about some of the things you say."

Maddy blushed and said, "Yes I know what you mean but I've given up meat for over two years now."

"OK lets not talk about it any more and we'll see what can be done." Secretly Liza did not believe Maddy would pull it off but she kept that to herself.

"Where are the others?" This cry came from Maddy as Liza was talking to the old man. "Ay, my grandson's called for the life boat and he's away to help lookout from the top of the cliffs." The old man looked distressed and angry, "What's your friend doing going out so far. I told 'm not to go near the mouth." His gaze never left the entrance as he wished and prayed they would be safe returned. He had tried to call them when he saw what they intended but his words were carried away by the wind. His grandson had run along the shore trying to catch their attention but to no avail. "Women of your age, should know better." This was an unkind chastisement to the two who had not strayed from the path of 'sensible'. The reality and serious nature of the predicament took a strong hold on Liza and Maddy and they started to shake. "You'm got any hot drink in that there picnic of your'n?" The old man was compassionate enough to notice that shock was setting in. He was weary of people not respecting the sea. Year after year he had seen tragedy averted and tragedy triumph as people played with the might of the sea. They often lost the wager. He knew that no one masters the sea but that the more you understand its vagaries the more respect you gave it.

The younger man waved from the cliff top and started running back down the cliff slope to his grandfather. It had been only twenty minutes since Ronnie's boat had gone out of sight. To Liza, Maddy and the old man it had seemed as though hours had passed. They all stared at the entrance to the cove and gradually there came to their view a bright yellow in-shore life boat trailing behind it a bedraggled dinghy. Inside the life boat inflatable were three very wet and sorry figures. They had all been given life jackets and were being spoken to firmly and fairly by the life boat crew. "Bloody idiots." "Should know better at your ages." "Waste of valuable resources." "What on earth possessed you?" These were just some of the comments that assailed their ears as they sat in the inflatable on their short journey to the shore. Mixed in with the chastisements were solicitous and kindly concerns for their well being. Ronnie considered that they had got off lightly. She knew it was her fault but felt also that she had been encouraged by the others. They demurred but were too shocked to think rationally. Beth, in her newly awakened state of physical attraction thought that the mature coxswain was rather a dish and wondered if he was married or 'spoken for'. Once you wake up the sleeping tiger it is hard to make her go back to sleep.

It was now five o'clock and time had come to pack up and start to go home.

All their names and addresses had been given to the rescue crew and the old man had been pacified to some degree by a promise to make

23

good any damage to the boat. Shamefaced the group walked shakily back to their area of the beach and sat down on the blankets. They rubbed their limbs, snuggled into dry towels and spare rugs and opened a flask of coffee which had fortuitously been included by Liza. Subdued they sat for a while in silence.

Shivering with both shock and cold the rather sorry group threw wan smiles at each other. Ronnie was the first to break the silence, "Sorry girls, I've been a bloody fool." Before any one could reply she continued, "I'll never forgive myself for putting you through that. Life's shit sometimes." With that she burst into tears for the second time that afternoon. Beth had been most alarmed by the experience but she had also had a lifetime of caring for other people, namely her mother, so it was she who went straight to the heart of the matter, "Do you want to talk about George's illness, Ronnie?"

"Yes you're a damn fool, you've driven too fast all your life and now you've nearly wiped us out." Lucy seemed inclined to blame and not forgive. She was on the threshold of a new life and had nearly had it taken away before it could begin. After her outburst she looked round at the others and sighed while tears, silent and unceasing, ran down her thin cheeks. Stunned into silence once more the others looked on with increasing embarrassment. Lucy acted. Now she had decided to be strong she would continue to be so. However this did not mean being hard and uncaring so she got up and went round to Ronnnie's part of the blanket, sat down and put her arm round her. "You do you know. Drive too fast. You'll kill yourself one day."

Ronnie shivered, "We'd hate that. You've lost your precious son and now you're about to lose George. We love you Ronnie, don't take you away from us as well." Maddy spoke for all of them when she interrupted, "Ron, hun, you do drive like a maniac but you're our maniac and we wish you'd stop and think. Take the train occasionally. You know. Slow down. Life sucks but all is not despair. Remember old Smelly Porter the English mistress. What did she tell us? Something about only by despairing could the great poets give their best work."

"Oh god Maddy. How do you remember all that stuff?" Lucy had never liked the nicotine ridden woman who had made her life hell for seven years.

Maddy continued, "She also said such rubbish as their genius was all important and that they could be excused their immorality because of it." Beth carried on the discussion, "We do that now with Hollywood types and supermodels. They get away with all sorts because they're rich, famous or beautiful."

"Footballers too," said Liza, "Anyway," this with great emphasis, "what about it Ronnie? Do you want to tell us?"

Ronnie stopped crying and sat up. "It'd be a relief." She took a deep breath and stared out to sea just as she had when she first broke the news to them earlier in the afternoon. Not looking at her companions made it easier for her to think clearly about what had happened to her husband and try to make some sense of it. He had been losing weight for some time and now they knew why.

"He has an aggressive form of stomach cancer that they have found too late to do anything with." The pause grew longer as she struggled for the right words. "George has, at most, six months to live." Through sobs she tried to explain what George had proposed, "He … he wants, no, he asked me to … to help him die." There, the words were out of her mouth. They hung on the sea air like little sharp knives of reality. Each word had been laboured and studied. She knew what she said and yet perhaps had not quite realised the enormity of what she had been asked to do, until that very moment. In a detached unreality she wondered if she had not wanted to come back from the rowing trip this afternoon. Perhaps she had been so tied up with her grief that she hadn't cared who perished with her. She hoped that that was not the case but, for as long as she lived, she would never be certain.

Beth asked, "What was your answer?" As this question elicited no reply Beth prompted her, "Ronnie? What did you say to him?" Dry wracking sobs were followed by a very quiet, "I told him I would if he was suffering too badly."

She laboured on, "I love him so much, we've been soul mates since we met. I can't bear to see him in such agony."

She paused, "Even now the pain is unbearable at times. His eyes plead with me and I say, soon my darling ,soon. But I don't know if I have the courage to carry it out." She lapsed back into her dreamlike state, "We watched our lovely boy die in the ambulance. His light went out and took a large piece of me with him." Body shaking sighs took hold of her again and she continued, "Have I the strength?"

Beth interrupted her reverie with, "Have you the right?" This was said with such quiet conviction that all knew where Beth's morality led her in this vexing question. What had never been shared by Beth with anyone, not even her closest friends, was a moment of such despair with her increasingly demanding mother that she had wondered, no it had been stronger than that, what would happen, if she slipped a pillow over her face and 'let her go'. It was from this experience that had taken Beth to the very edge of such an awful abyss that she had confirmed within herself the sure knowledge of right and wrong. Maddy and Lucy both considered the question redundant as they were firmly of the opinion that human kind should not play god. Both of them regularly attended church and believed in their own version of god. Had they ever discussed their spirituality they would have discovered that each had a very personal god that would seem to an outsider to be completely different one from the other. Maddy had never, certainly not in recent years, been tested by desperate circumstances and even though Lucy had it had never occurred to her that physical violence could free her from her daily torment.

Liza offered a different outlook. The romantic had lived with the practical for many years, death of animals during her married life had sat quite happily beside her love of life and she could not bear to see suffering in any being, human or otherwise.

"There are ways, abroad you know Ronnie. There are people who will help you. Clinics with professional people who offer an alternative to an ugly, painful or lingering death."

"Liza you can't be serious." A horrified Lucy broke the moment of shocked disbelief that followed this announcement. Liza looked at Lucy and very deliberately repeated her conviction, "Yes. Yes I think I am."

For the moment there was no more to be said. Ronnie's distress was so overwhelming that they decided not to pursue their disagreement on euthanasia. It was one of the most profound arguments they had had since school when they discussed and vehemently disagreed endlessly on many subjects. Perhaps it was easier back then. It was all supposition and 'what ifs'. Now it was real with people involved whom they loved and cherished. For a moment each one longed for the days when life was ahead of them and none of this pain was real. Adolescent pain was nothing compared to the reality of life with all its complexities.

Five 'fifty something' women had girlishly walked onto the beach that morning with a song in their hearts and the promise of yet another fun day full of chatter and laughter. Although each one carried their own burden they still had dreams and wanted the respite of re-living their school days when the future looked bright. A future that each one could visualise would be full of family and achievement and sunshine and light. Their childhood and adolescent experiences were all quite different and not without pain but there was escape through growing up, escape through as yet unknown relationships and careers. It was five very different people who staggered off the beach. All were still in various stages of shock and were coping in their own ways. Ronnie had withdrawn into herself and was no longer very communicative. She had aged and her face looked all of its years and no vestige of any youthfulness remained.

Maddy had suggested that they all repair to her hotel for afternoon tea and to freshen up. She thought they could do with the respite from the intensity of the day's revelations. Gosh, when had they had such a reunion? Beth and Liza had readily agreed to accompany Maddy back to her hotel. Lucy was more reluctant as Ronnie had expressed her intention to get back to George as soon as she could. They tried to persuade her that she needed a rest and time to get over the varying shocks of the day but she insisted that she would go. Lucy had to rely on a lift back to the station and Beth offered to take her after tea. Although Lucy was concerned about Ronnie she really did not care for another ride at breakneck speed with her. So as they got back to the car park all was settled. Ronnie hugged them all and thanked them for their company and their support. She bade them a tearful farewell and got into her car. As she drove out of the car park she stopped and looked round and waved at them. She smiled and then took off in her usual fashion and was soon out of sight.

CHAPTER FOUR

Tea

The Majestic Hotel was half an hour away from Lulworth Cove and the friends were soon settled in comfortable surroundings waiting for their tea and scones to arrive. Marjorie and Alfred were in their sixties and had run the Majestic for thirty years. As a young couple they had decided to sell up in London and find a place where their children could grow in relative safety amidst spectacular down land countryside. Dorset had not disappointed them and their family had grown and prospered. Now the children had gone to forge lives of their own and it was just the two of them left and they were content. Ironically their children had all moved back to live in London where they felt their true roots to be. Grandchildren came for the holidays sometimes and all was merriment and laughter. There were also huge sighs of relief and an embracing of quietude when the boisterous youngsters went home again. Marjorie had wanted to keep the original nineteenth century features of their hotel. Alfred was more inclined to make sweeping changes but had given in to his beloved. He had to admit that with hindsight Marjorie had been right. Modern bathrooms and en-suite facilities together with a very modern kitchen had been his only insistence but they had done nothing to spoil the Victorian splendour of the original bedrooms and reception. The result was a warm and welcoming interior with two comfortable but cluttered lounges and bars.

The Victorian conservatory made a splendid afternoon tea room and it was in this sunlit haven that the four friends were finally sitting.

They were all trying to steady their nerves in their own ways. Maddy was exaggeratedly efficient while Lucy was visibly shaking and pale. Liza was indulging in silent dramatic gestures and Beth was withdrawn and more than unusually quiet. Maddy had briefly explained to Marjorie and Alfred what had occurred that afternoon with regards to the boating incident and let them believe that the shock was all down to that. Alfred immediately brought them all brandies which acted as a marvellous restorative.

"I've been saying a silent prayer for Ronnie and George." Lucy quietly dropped the idea into the quiet reflection that seemed to presently surround the group. "I wonder if my prayer alone will help and just thought I'd see if it could be a joint effort." Lucy felt rather embarrassed by her own boldness. Maddy encouraged her by her own, "Yes, me too. Anything will help." Beth took in the deepest of breaths and said, "Not sure what will help. I'm worried that Ronnie may not make it home." She had the group's attention now. "Did you see the way she stopped and smiled at us as she left the car park?" Falteringly she carried on, "it was like a farewell." Beth's tears started up again. "What a bloody awful afternoon." Liza exploded and started to shake again. "I'm going to ring Ed and ask him to come and fetch me. He can bring Tom and then he can drive my car home." She staggered to her feet and her plump little body shook as she tried to stem her own tears now coursing down her cheeks. She took her mobile out of her bag and went out into the garden where she could be sure of a signal and a bit if privacy.

The remaining three sat and stared at the brilliant white tablecloth. For the moment talk seemed unnecessary and somehow inappropriate. They sipped their brandies and sighed. The sighs were deep and audible as though they were trying to get new life back into their bodies. Alfred who had been keeping an eye on the friends decided that now was a good time to bring in the tea. Gratefully they all fell on the welcome intrusion. When pain is so deep it can be a relief to engage in ordinary everyday activities. Chatter gradually came back to them with inane comments such as, "Shall I be mother?" and "Milk first or do you want to do your own?" "There was a debate on TV the other day about whether you put cream or jam on the scone first." "Must have been a slow news day." Liza came back and sat down. Very quietly she took part in this ritualistic drinking and eating of tea, "Ed's coming for me. He should be about an hour. Tom's coming to pick up my car."

They toyed with their food and it was only Lucy who made any inroads into the jam and cream. All the tea was drunk and they asked Alfred for another pot. The evening sun went low in the sky and a beautiful glow settled on the conservatory. Maddy decided to stay another night and persuaded Lucy to join her. She rang her friend who was looking after her menagerie to make sure he would be able to stay at her house for another night. She had failed to tell her friends about this latest man in her life but she decided he would keep for another time. She assured Lucy that she would get her back in time to avoid John and do all she had to do before he came home and found her gone for good. Lucy rang John but there was no reply from their home number so she left a message saying there had been some problems but that she was all right. As she rang off she considered how he would react when he heard her message. He would be angry at her absence and worried in case she had spent any money that he had not authorised. She rang him again and this time he answered, "What on earth have you done now? How much is this hotel costing?" Lucy interrupted him with, "Its all right Maddy said she would pay for me. I'll be back about ten o'clock tomorrow." Lucy then did a very brave thing, she hung up.

John was apoplectic. It was only the thought that Cynthia could come round that night that calmed him down. Lucy would have to be taught a lesson. As he debated how to punish his wife, he would consider what to do and take his time over it, but first he must ring Cynthia, god she was insatiable. He would take the pills the doctor had given him, they kept him horny all night. It would be unfortunate for Lucy that the next day he would feel wiped out and so decided to come home early from work.

Lucy came back to the table and said, "Its all right I've told him that I'll be back at ten. I hung up on him, he'll be livid." She smiled a wan smile and then drank some more tea. "It must've been the brandy. I've never felt so brave."

"Well done, Luce. We'll have a good night's sleep here then I'll drive you all the way home. No point you taking the train. Then we can have a good natter when all this seems a bit farther away." Maddy gestured towards the sea or at least in the direction that she thought Lulworth might be. Liza turned to directly face Beth, "Beth. Do you really think Ronnie will try something silly on the way home?" Beth answered with studied calm, "I don't know but her smile seemed to me to be a final farewell." Her friend's face took on a haunted look so she tempered it with, "I may be wrong. I just get feelings sometimes and... well ... she loves him so much I don't think she can bear his pain." Silence descended again so Beth sat upright and poured yet another cup of tea and brightly said, "Look, I'm just being fanciful. She'll probably be home by now and all will be well." Beth knew the words she spoke were false but she did not have the energy to cope with her friends' anguish as well as her own.

It was by now getting late and Beth had an hour's drive before she reached home. She stood up and one by one went round the table and hugged her friends saying a personal good bye to each one. "Lucy, best of luck with your new life. You deserve every bit of happiness you can find. Let me know how you go on" Lucy assured her they would be kept up to speed with developments. "Liza, take care and I'll be in touch soon. Perhaps if the offer is still there I'll come to stay one week end." Liza immediately replied, "You'll come for the week and no less. Anytime you like."

"I'm so glad you made this one Mad. I think it's been momentous and none of us should have missed it even though it's been, well sort of tragic. Let me know how you go on with your searching."

"Of course Beth. You take care too and have fun with your art." Maddy accompanied this with a wink. As an after thought she added, "We all need to carpe diem. You just don't know what's round that next bloody bend." Silently Beth thought that might be prophetic as she once again imagined Ronnie and her fast car and her anguish and her last smile. "OK then. Talk to you all soon. I love you lot." With that Beth departed. She got into her car and started the journey home.

As there were now just three of them left Marjorie came into the conservatory and asked them if they wanted an evening meal. Liza declined as she explained that her husband and son were coming to fetch her. Maddy and Lucy decided just to have an omelette and a salad. After all they had eaten extremely well down on the beach before the unfurling story of the afternoon got in the way. As Marjorie made her way to the kitchen to prepare the supper two tall and well built men appeared in the reception. Alfred greeted them and then took them through to the party in the conservatory. Liza's face grew bright when she saw Edwin and Tom and she flung herself at Edwin then burst into tears. He hugged her as though he would never let her go. "Come on Mum, let's get you home." Tom took charge and guided his parents out of the room. Liza turned and went back into the room and gave Maddy and Lucy a final hug and then went to Edwin, took his hand and walked away.

"Phew," said Maddy, "What a day!" She and Lucy had repaired to the dining room. Marjorie had put Lucy in the room next to Maddy's who had been given her old room back from the night before. They had freshened up and somewhere Marjorie had found some toiletries for Lucy's unexpected night away from home. Lucy was still wearing the same clothes that she had been in all day but Maddy had changed into a fresh top and felt better. "Do you fancy a bottle of wine, Luce? My treat."

Lucy felt she had to say something about money, "Look Maddy I know I haven't any at the moment but I will pay you back when I'm settled."

"Nonsense. I'm happy to do it. Mum and dad left me pretty well off and I love an adventure." She looked thoughtful and then added, "I know it's been a bad day in many respects but at least we were together when all this stuff came out." Lucy opened her mouth as if to speak when Maddy continued, "and its no use pretending that some of today's news wasn't good. Look at you. You're finally going to live the life that you deserve. I know it won't be easy at first but now at least you'll have the chance to be yourself." Lucy screwed up her face and she suddenly seemed older again.

The pale grey tinge had come back, "Mad I'm so scared. He's started being physical as well as tormenting my mind. I know he's taken away my confidence and he's a bully but I never thought he would hurt me in that way. Usually he can't bear to touch me." She shivered. "One evening he came back from a golf do and he, he …he raped me." Lucy shuddered and heaved an enormous sigh and continued as though she had mentioned nothing more innocuous than the weather, "That photographer chap I mentioned, well he's taken to, sort of, talking to me when he can. He seems to like me. If it wasn't for him I wouldn't have had the courage to do what I'm doing." She reflected for a while then added, "Why do we need to have someone else tell us what we can do? I never dreamt I would end up like this. The children were right. I should've listened to them." Lucy looked directly at Maddy and asked her, "Will you come with me tomorrow and wait while I finish my packing? I've nearly done it all and then I'm getting a taxi. It's a lot to ask I know but just now I think I need a bit of your confidence as well as mine."

"Oh Lucy, you idiot, of course I will." Maddy grasped her friend's hand and quietly asked, "Do you want to talk about it? The rape I mean." Lucy shook her head and very firmly said, "No. No I don't. He hurt me Mad, so badly. I'm not ready yet." Lucy stopped and then thought that she could carry on, "Normally, when he wanted to … make love, that's a laugh, to um … use me in that way," Lucy blundered on, " he would attempt some kind of … oh I don't know … a kind of gentleness, it was always a bit scary when he went like that. That night he was … he was in a rage about something I s'pose." Lucy suddenly stopped again but this time she didn't carry on. She could explain no further. Lucy sat dry eyed, this Maddy found rather more worrying than floods of tears. Maddy was increasingly alarmed for her and so decided to bring in

34

reinforcements. Things had become much worse with Lucy than any of them had realised. "Tell you what I'll ask my friend, the one who's looking after the animals, to come too."

Lucy was puzzled, "Why do you..?"

Maddy interrupted, "because my dear he's a policeman. He's special branch actually, and he will do anything for me, at the moment that is. He'll be a good insurance in case John comes back unexpectedly." Maddy began to enjoy herself. She was looking forward to helping poor creatures who couldn't help themselves and at this moment Lucy was just such a creature. She ruminated for a while then said, "I'll tell him to bring Nimbus with him. You've never met my new acquisition. He's lovely and huge and somewhere between a Newfoundland and a wolfhound. God knows what his parentage is." Before Lucy could object Maddy had called her new friend on her mobile 'phone and asked for and received the news she wanted. "Yep, that's settled. He'll be down tomorrow morning about eleven at your place. OK?" Lucy felt as though she had been swept along by a tidal wave, "Wow, I suppose so. Thanks Mad, you're a real star." They finished the evening with coffee in the lounge chatting to Marjorie and Alfred. The hotel was quiet that mid week night and so the four of them had a night cap and all went their separate ways to bed. The morning would bring fresh hope and excitement but for now, tiredness took over and they slept.

CHAPTER FIVE
Aftermath

i

As Beth drove home she went back over the day in her mind. What a long time it seemed from this morning. All her thoughts then were on whether her friends would like the chicken recipe she had found. How futile it all seemed now. Then she changed her mind. No it wasn't futile. It was the small everyday stuff that kept everyone sane, everyone on track. Cooking and her art class had been her saviour when her Mum died. She missed her terribly. She didn't miss the person her mother had become but she missed the lovely woman she had been before the selfishness of her illness had taken her over. 'Oh Mum, you would have loved to see me with my new man.' She reflected on the mutual attraction between her and Ben. He may be many things, she thought, but of one thing she was sure. He made her laugh.

ii

Ronnie floored the accelerator pedal and shot off on the country roads to find the A31. This would take her back towards Hampshire and then she could get on the M27 and really put her foot down. What a day! She had nearly killed her friends and herself into the bargain. What on earth was she thinking? She should not have told them about George and his horrifying request. As she pondered this she recollected the conversation when George had asked her to help him die should the pain get too much. She had queried how she would know, "Darling, how will I be able to tell? I can't kill you. I love you too much." He had come back as quick as a flash, as though he had rehearsed the argument beforehand, "If you love me that much you won't want to see me suffer." He looked a little petulant and then immediately regretted it. "Oh my god, Ronnie my darling girl. What have I done? I promised myself I would not try to persuade you. What a rat I am."

"Yes you are a bit aren't you? Emotional blackmail." Ronnie had reflected out loud about the selfishness of an all consuming disease. George had felt so bad that he had walked away and they had not broached the subject again. It was, however, a wall between them. Daily they carried on as before. This was a thinly veiled pretence as underlying each conversation, each touch; each glance was the knowledge that the request was unresolved.

iii

As Edwin drove through the evening to their home in Devon he stole occasional glimpses of his beloved Liza. He knew he was not always the romantic she once so longed for but they had been happy. They had worked hard and were now reaping the benefits of that labour. She sat in the car in a daze. A sort of frozen look that was typical of shock. He had gleaned something of what had occurred at the reunion but certainly not all. His anger rose as he thought of the possibility that his Liza might have been unlucky enough to be in the same boat as Ronnie and the thought of what might then have happened to them was unbearable. Life without his sweetheart was unthinkable. He was a practical farmer and matters of life and death are renewed daily in that line of work. He had long ago tried to be as ethical as he could and still be commercial in his life. Sometimes the balance was wrong but he carried on as best he could. Liza had embraced life with him as she had loved him very much. She still did but he realised there was a part of her that remained

37

unfulfilled. He had never known how to reach out and be part of that longing.

Half an hour into their drive home Liza suddenly spoke, "Its been a lovely and a horrid day all at the same time." With this revelation she burst into tears and slumped further down in the seat. Edwin pulled into the next lay-by and took her in his arms, "Love, I don't really understand what's gone on today but let's get home and I'll make you a nice hot toddy and we'll sit and you can tell me all about it. This lonely lay-by is no place for this and anyway Tom will be wondering where we are." He kissed her on her forehead with great tenderness and started the car for the rest of the journey home. Liza relaxed somewhat after this brief but loving interchange and the rest of the journey went without incident.

iv

Maddy and Lucy breakfasted well on Marjorie's full English breakfast. Alfred amused them with his version of the morning's national news, "Good morning ladies, the government is in disarray, the monarchy is safe, for a while, the USA still unfortunately has an idiot for a president and the French still don't like us. Oh and we lost the one day international yesterday at the Oval. All's well with the world and the 'sun has got his hat on hip hip hip horray'." The last few words were sung whilst he did an arthritic skip out of the room. Maddy roared with laughter and Lucy grinned and chuckled. They ate their breakfast smiling now much more relaxed than the previous evening. Because of this they were able to talk about the events of their rather disastrous reunion in a more rational tone. Lucy started the first serious conversation of the morning that did not include passing the butter or the coffee pot, "Is it very selfish of me, Maddy, to be scared about what I'm doing? I'm very worried about Ronnie and so sorry for her predicament but just at the moment it's sort of at the back of my mind."

Maddy reassured her, "Lucy we all have to live our lives. Bear will be down to help in case we need a stronger presence."

38

Lucy looked puzzled, "Bear? Who or what is...?"

"Oh," Maddy paused, "I didn't tell you. This new chap, he's called Bear because he can't very well use his name that his stupid parents gave him. He's a public school type and they called him, wait for it, Rupert." Maddy could not contain her amusement and she laughed until she cried. Lucy smiled and felt vaguely sorry for the small boy who must have had to defend himself because of that name. The two friends drove away from The Majestic Hotel feeling emotionally nourished as well as very full gastronomically. Marjorie and Alfred really were very nice people. Maddy would return. She had found the hotel to be a haven of understanding and while the two Londoners were running it she would return regularly to partake of their wisdom, compassion and respite from a weary world.

Lucy had no thought in her head that morning other than how she would get through the next twenty four hours. She had allowed herself to become a victim for so long that she doubted whether her bid for freedom would work. Thank God for Maddy. Of course she also had Bill to thank as well. If he hadn't brought his camera to the homeless shelter to do a feature for the local paper she would not have met him and they would not have become friends. He was married to a woman who adored him and so there could be nothing further than friendship. She knew enough of misery in a marriage not to break up someone else's that had a chance of sorting out their differences. He had at least instilled in her a new confidence that had enabled her to make the move she desperately sought. In a lucid moment or two she did wonder why she had become such a weakling as to need someone else's approval but that way lay all sorts of issues that she did not have the energy to go through. That would be for another time when she felt more in control. The journey back to her detached, estate, anonymous looking house took a little over an hour and a half. The house had that abandoned feel as they drove up to the garage. Lucy let them in and set about making Maddy a cup of tea whilst she mentally went over all she had to do and what likely time scale was hers to command.

"What can I do to help Luce?" Maddy wandered into the sitting room carrying a hot mug of tea. Lucy was about to ask Maddy not to spill her drink as John was very particular with furniture and possessions when she stopped, "Maddy, John doesn't like…," she paused, smiled and relaxed, "Sod what John doesn't like. Do what you will with your cup; I don't think I care any more." They exchanged smiles and set about gathering Lucy's, rather meagre in Maddy's eyes, belongings and stacked the bags and suitcases by the front door. Bear arrived soon after most of the activity had ceased and Lucy marvelled at the tall, rangy man holding the massive dog on a lead walking up the front path. "Wow, Maddy. He's gorgeous." Her girlish grin widened as she added, "your bloke's not too bad either." Maddy pushed her playfully out of the way and went to let Bear into the house. "Hello darling" Maddy kissed Bear briefly on the mouth and then bent to stroke Nimbus. She didn't have to bend very far as he was a very tall hairy bundle of playful dog. "Been good?" She asked and Bear nodded. "All set?" Bear inquired after introductions had been made. "Yes, let's get out while I've still got the guts. My daughter is expecting me to be on the late train from King's Cross so I'm getting the noon train from here." Bear picked up the heaviest case and went out of the door saying, "Right let's get going and we'll have you safe and sound in no time."

"Safe from who and from what?" John hovered on the threshold as he observed the activity. His voice was quivering with anger and his fist was balled into a fighting weapon. Maddy started to say, "Safe from you and…" but Lucy stopped her and said in a trembling but determined voice, "I'm leaving you. I've had enough. You and Cynthia can do what you like. Let me pass." John stood his ground until Bear firmly held his arm and manoeuvred him out of the way. "After you, Ladies," Bear gestured them out side and they gratefully made their escape. Bear flashed his police warrant at John who stopped trying to free himself so he could take a pop at Bear and froze on the spot. "Who the bloody hell are you and why are you here?" Bear strong armed him to the sitting room and made him sit down. He looked at the puce and by now very

40

sweaty, face and said very calmly, "Your wife is leaving you, you will be served with a notice soon to that effect and you will not harm her or try to stop her." As John made to get up he actively encouraged him down again and said, "Do you understand?"

"No. I don't understand. Who are you?" John's voice was now rather weak and trembling. This bully ran true to type and his cowardice began to show. Bear was used to unsavoury characters in his line of work but Maddy was disgusted with John's behaviour. Not once had he asked Lucy about yesterday and how she was.

All this time Nimbus stood in the hall grumbling slightly because he had smelt food and he was perpetually hungry. John did not appreciate this and so decided that for the moment he had been out manoeuvred. Lucy sat in the car shaking and breathing heavily as though she had been in a physical fight. "Its all right Lucy, we're here and we'll get you away." Maddy was very concerned at the change that had come over her friend with just that brief encounter with her own husband. The realisation of what she had gone through to get to this state made her very angry. Bear came down the path with Nimbus under control and put him in the back of the Range Rover. He bent down to tell Maddy he would follow her to the station and then they would drive home in convoy. "Right let's get going. He's in shock but I'm sure he'll cope. Eventually." Bear climbed into his driver's seat and prepared to follow Maddy's rather up to the minute Lexus. Lucy had settled down in the passenger seat and looked exhausted. Maddy patted her arm and they set off. "Let's get you on that train and away from all this misery. You'll be all right you know." Lucy suddenly came to life, "I never thanked Bear for his help. What would we have done without him? Why was John home in the middle of the day?" Maddy's voice sharpened slightly, "Stop thinking about everyone else. Stop being a martyr and start being a person again. People will get compassion fatigue and then you'll feel worse." Lucy busied herself with powdering her nose and looking out of the window. Maddy wondered if she had gone too far but considered that her friend would need to toughen up if she were to get to Scotland and then through the next few weeks unscathed.

Ronnie had driven like a woman possessed until she got onto the M27. There was the usual light mid-evening traffic made up mostly of lorries with a sprinkling of private cars. Anyone following her through the beautiful Dorset countryside could have been forgiven for thinking she was drunk as she drove with a reckless disregard for anything. Usually fast she now went up a gear and inhabited the truly dangerous zone. Had this anonymous person continued to follow Ronnie onto the motorway they may have thought she was hell bent on destroying herself and anyone in her way. As she topped 100 miles an hour she attracted the attention of the Hampshire police. It was some moments before she realised that she was being asked to stop, eventually she pulled over to the hard shoulder where she turned off the engine and just sat in her car staring ahead. The two police constables got out of their patrol car and walked determinedly towards the rogue driver. They had spotted that she was an older woman and were surprised but not unduly worried about confronting her. The first constable knocked on the driver's window and asked her to step out of the vehicle. Ronnie continued to stare ahead and took no notice of any attempt to communicate with her. The second policeman was radioing back to his sergeant for assistance when after a very long delay and unsuccessful coercing Ronnie still had not opened the car door.

Something snapped in Ronnie's consciousness and she looked round as if for the first time she realised where she was. She saw the two constables and wound down her window. They had passed the tolerant stage of their efforts and were now in very officious mood. Thus it was a very brusque, "Now then Madam get out of the car." She noticed the lack of courtesy but did as she was told. "I'm sorry officer, I've had a …" She was interrupted,

"Do you know how fast you were going? We made it 97 miles an hour. Not only is that illegal, it's dangerous and not just for you. You should know better at your age." That was the second time that day that she had been told that as she was a certain age she should act in a certain way. Fleetingly she thought of a retort about still feeling and hurting even though she was obviously in her dotage but thought better of it.

"I am sorry officer. I was wanting to get back to my husband and lost track of how fast I was going. He is ill you see and ..."

"Well then how would he feel if you didn't get back at all. Going that fast you could well have an accident and he would be at your funeral." The second officer was more sympathetic , "Now then madam, have you had an alcoholic drink in the last few hours?" He considered that she hadn't as she displayed no signs, she just seemed preoccupied and anxious. He took control and most unusually for the twenty first century took the compassionate route, "We will let you off with a caution this time. Remember though that we have your registration and will be checking up on you and verifying your story." The reality was that this checking had all ready been completed. They knew who she was, where she lived, who and what her husband was and also what he had wrong with him. Fortunately for Ronnie she and George were well known in their local community for charitable work and had mixed with several members of the local constabulary on many occasions. It may have helped too that George belonged to that rather powerful group of men who profess charitable intent and limit their association to the worthy and the successful. The young officers advised her how to get back into the motorway traffic safely and followed her for several miles before turning off and resuming their other duties. Ronnie continued to drive home within the speed limit, chastened and contrite.

vi

Edwin handed Liza out of the car as though she were a porcelain doll. He felt her fragility was both physical and emotional. He had pieced the events of the day together from snatches of conversation that his wife had dropped into the exhausted silence of the homeward journey. Soon she was sitting cosily before the kitchen range having had a restorative bath and changed into her night clothes. She looked like a cuddly pale

43

blue teddy bear in her towelling robe and fluffy unsophisticated slippers. Edwin made her a hot drink into which he had put a tot of brandy. As she sipped at her cup she gradually told the whole story to Edwin and Tom who had been following his parents very closely on the way home. It wasn't the shock of Ronnie's dilemma or Lucy's determined bid for an escape that alarmed them but the awful thought that had Liza gone in the boat with Ronnie she might well have not come back to them. The transient nature of life, even though they were inured to it day after day on the farm, hit them both like a stone. Life without this woman, this wife, this mother was almost unbearable to contemplate.

Edwin spoke, his voice a hoarse whisper as he tried not to ruffle the calm that had descended on Liza after her outpourings, "You, my darling, are going to rest all day tomorrow then we are going to plan that second honeymoon we've spoken of for so long. It must've been five years since you first hinted that'd make you happy. Sorry I've been a bit slow. Tonight's crystallised for me how much we need to seize the day. Forgive me love?" His Welsh lilt was a caress and she smiled, "Of course I do. That sounds nice. I'm too tired tonight but tomorrow we will think where we'd like to go. Oh Edwin, and you Tom, I'm so lucky. The others, well, they've all got such problems." Her sigh was full of compassion for her friends. "I'm off to bed now. It's so nice to be home. Thanks my beauties." She turned to speak to Tom. As she did so she put her hand out to caress his cheek, "You must seize the day as well. Don't let one failed marriage put you off from seeking another. Go seek you daft idiot. They're not all like Imogen."

It had been a long time since her ex daughter-in-law's name had been mentioned by any of them. The separation from their grandchildren had been traumatic. Only now, three years on, were they gaining access to the two boys who had been the light of their son's life. Imogen had found herself unable to forgive Tom's lack of restraint when confronted by a delectable sales rep from their regular horse feed firm. Her many illicit liaisons were not considered of consequence when her father's legal firm were engaged to represent her interests at the subsequent acrimonious divorce.

CHAPTER SIX
More Consequences

Lucy's Journey

Maddy drove Lucy to the railway station and they parked in the car park. Lucy started to get out of the car when Maddy stopped her. "Lucy, have you bought your ticket?"

"Er no I, um, hadn't thought beyond getting away. I'm sure there'll be no problem though."

"Too right. How do you fancy another further adventure?" Maddy laughed as she said, "I've been thinking that I could do with a run in my new, well newish car. Why don't I drive you up to Amy's? It'll be fun." Lucy didn't want to go with Maddy. Lucy didn't want to go with anyone. She was reeling from her meeting with her husband. She thought she would get away from the house before he came home. She thought she would be well on her way to Scotland. Now he was hot on her heels and she was sure he would try to stop her. Maddy had driven quickly to the station but John had known a quicker way through the back streets and was even now waiting in the car park for Lucy to turn up. Now Lucy had a crisis of confidence, a confidence which had only recently been allowed to surface and was still paper thin. "Maddy, John's here. Look. Over there. Do you see him? Is Bear on his way or are you meeting him somewhere else?"

Maddy slowly turned her head and yes, sure enough, there was John looking at them. He started to get out of the car. As John walked very slowly across the car park Lucy sat mesmerised. Her limbs felt like lead and she could hardly breathe. Maddy too watched in fascination as the two of them became locked onto each other as a cat will stare at its prey before pouncing. Maddy had to break this but was uncertain how to proceed. At that moment Bear got out of his car and followed John at a distance of about twenty yards. He had been disturbed by the man's attitude to his wife and decided to follow him. When Maddy and Lucy had driven off Bear parked round the corner and waited for what he felt was the inevitable, John's pursuit of his 'possession'. Bear had interviewed many a suspect of domestic crimes and one of the overriding traits was a need to be in control. John and Lucy's marriage was over, everyone knew that now but John had been under the impression that he was in charge and he would leave Lucy when he was ready, never the other way round. He was boiling mad and he had been humiliated in his own house by a stranger. He still couldn't make out who he was and where he had sprung from but that could wait. Now he had to get Lucy back so that he could leave her. Cynthia had given him an ultimatum, marriage or nothing. She so wanted the lifestyle that she considered her right and John had been very attentive and she wanted what he could give her. Observers would say that they deserved each other. John's arrogance was both his armour and his Achilles' heel. He cloaked himself in his self belief which cocooned him from any external influences.

As John walked across the car park the one thing in his head was to subdue Lucy. He could see her staring at him like a rabbit in the headlights so he knew he was going to win. So absorbed was he that he did not notice Maddy's increasing agitation as she tried to get Lucy to look away from the advancing menace and talk to her. None of them had taken any account of the figure that shadowed the errant husband. As John reached the side of the car where Lucy sat, spellbound, Maddy leaped out of her side of the car and spoke in a voice of studied calm, "John, what do you want from her? She's told you she's leaving so let her be."

"Mind your own bloody business, this is between Lucy and me, she'll see sense if I talk to her. I s'pose she's told you a pack of lies about me. Well I never hit her, she fell." He cast around in his mind for a foul slur that he considered would wound her, "Drunk as usual. What I've had to put up with, you wouldn't believe." This last was uttered in a voice designed to get public sympathy. Lucy's face was ashen and her mouth slightly open as she listened to this final indignity. The words came out very slowly as every utterance needed a renewed breath, "You pig, you mean bastard." From somewhere Lucy found the physical strength to get out of the car and face him. A feeble attempt to slap his face was badly executed as it gave him a chance to grab her arm and twist it away. He smiled as he inflicted the pain, "Let her go." The command came from behind him and was accompanied by a powerful hand gripping his shoulder. Bear had seen and heard enough, truth to tell he had believed only half of Maddy's story about her friend but seeing this man and woman together told him all he needed to know. The power balance between them was way off with Lucy the victim and John the aggressor. Bear was sufficiently wise in the ways of human emotions to understand nothing is that simple or clear cut but evidently this was a relationship that had deteriorated beyond redemption.

John still held Lucy's arm, still gripped it tightly to inflict pain and still did not understand who this man was who kept interfering with his life. "Who the hell are you? This is my wife and I'm taking her home. She's sick and needs her medication." "I'd... d... don't take any medication I... I...I'm going John, you're hurting me let me go. Oh please God let me go." Bear squeezed John's shoulder so hard that he had to release his grip on his wife. "I'm here on unofficial business. Special branch. I can call on my local colleagues who I'm sure would be delighted to take you in and ask you a few questions." John turned and looked Bear fully in the face. He was lost for words and backed away. He realised he was beaten, for now. He started to walk away without saying any more but could not resist one last jibe, "I'll see you in court. You'll get nothing from me. You ungrateful bitch." Lucy stood erect and said in a determined voice, "Goodbye. You and Cynthia deserve each other."

John's face was a picture. He thought he'd been so clever and that his poor apology for a wife had no idea. "How did you …?"

"I have my sources. You've not been as discrete as you imagined." She turned to get back in the car, "Oh and by the way, I have evidence of your infidelity so think on that you horror of a man." Maddy helped her back into the car and then spoke, first to Lucy then with Bear, "That was a bit mild Luce but well done. Bear, darling, we need to talk about this. I want to drive her to …" She very nearly let out where Lucy was heading and just stopped herself before John could hear. "Thought you might. OK. Want me to look after the animals for you. I've got a few days owing to me." "You're a darling. I'll ring you to tell you when I'm on the way back. We'll have a good talk then. Some stuff we need to sort. Yes?"

"Very definitely, yes!" Bear laughed, "Go, and drive carefully. I want you back in one piece." With that he kissed her soundly so there was no mistaking his affection and commitment to her well being. "Phew, you're a lovely man. See you Friday." Maddy whispered this last so that John could not even guess the length of journey about to take place. He was now some way off anyway and was dazedly walking back to his car like a man in a dream, or maybe a nightmare.

Bear watched as Maddy drove away with a rather shaken Lucy. He decided that he loved this very special woman. They had been friends for a couple of years. Their first meeting was a disaster as they were on opposite sides of the case in a trial. His colleague had been injured during an arrest and her firm were representing the defendant who stood accused of actual bodily harm against the policeman. They had crossed swords and afterwards at a chance meeting had agreed to differ. Drinks had followed then an occasional lunch or dinner. Gradually their meetings were regular and neither wanted their friendship to end. Bear knew all about Maddy's marriages. They had dissected each one to see where she had gone wrong. Generally they came to the light hearted conclusion that it was the men who were at fault and Maddy had nothing with which to reproach herself. Bear thought that she was an interesting and very bright lady who brought out the best in him. His past was not without baggage. He had been married to a very sweet woman who bore him one son. His lifestyle in the force had not been conducive to marital bliss and she had tired of neglect and found a very nice headmaster with whom she was now very happy. Bear had always made a point of seeing his son as often as possible but inevitably they had grown apart when his son became a teenager. Now Harry was safely at university and embarking on a career in law they had started to communicate again and were finding some mutual benefit. Bear's relationship with Maddy helped as she was able to give some good tips about career paths and had introduced him to her legal firm in the hope that he would be taken on by them in the fullness of time.

Maddy was eight years older than Bear. She valued their friendship and was rather scared of the next stage. She was getting no younger and she had failed marriages galore. They had been passionate but not yet intimate and she worried very much that she would not fulfil him sexually. Bear on the other hand was in love with her and thought that she was the most special person he had ever met. He had not told her this in case she ran scared. In this he was wise to wait. The moment had not yet come when Maddy was ready to commit. It would come, and soon, but the promise in his farewell kiss was enough for the time being. He instinctively knew that she had to get her friend away and his part in this was to ensure that the husband left them alone. He made some calls. An honest man he had occasionally strayed over the strict ethical line but mostly when he could roundly justify his actions, for the greater good. This time he called in some favours for his personal, or rather Maddy's friend's gain. He agonised but briefly and then acted. He had a thorough dislike of bullies and contented his conscience with rather general platitudes. There is nothing like a reformed character to uphold the opposite view from that which, in the past, had been his own.

Maddy and Lucy drove for about half an hour then Maddy pulled the car into a roadside pub and stopped. "OK Luce. Let's have some lunch. You could do with a decent meal and I think a stiff brandy. Let's indulge and have chips with something. Come on old thing. We've left

49

him behind. He won't follow. Bear will see to that." Lucy seemed content to let Maddy take control. This worried her friend but for the moment it was all she could manage. "That's fine Mad. Thanks. When we've eaten I need to phone Amy and let her know about her father. He may call her."

"Sure. Now let's eat outside it's a lovely day." The scampi and chips were good to average but for the hungry, emotionally wrung pair it was just what they needed. The alcohol helped Lucy unwind. Maddy drank lemonade as she was driving. Lucy relaxed even further when they set off on their journey and she slept. The sun shone in the car and warmed her right through. In her dream she was safe and cosy. Not for a long time had she had such a dream. It was restorative and when she awoke it was a much energised woman who sat up in the car and stretched.

Maddy had driven for about two hours and the southern downland had given way to the flatter counties that bordered the M1 motorway north of London. She had decided to avoid the inevitable congestion that threatened to gridlock Birmingham every day as cars and lorries thundered along the M6 and M5. She considered that the better route north to Scotland would be via the M1 and Scotch Corner and then to find the road to the M6. It would be fun and add to the adventure if they stayed overnight just south of the border and tackled the Scottish roads the next day. Crossing the border was always special and she wanted Lucy to savour the moment. After all this was the start of her new life, an independent life and she needed all the happy moments she could muster to help her through the difficult days ahead especially when John had to be faced. Driving over the border in the early morning light was magical for Maddy and she had found it to be like a homecoming. She was not Scottish but wondered if in a former life she had been part of that solid identity.

As they entered the routine part of the journey, the mesmerising experience that is motorway driving, Lucy sat upright in her seat. She had slept and felt so much better. Lunch had steadied her and she felt a warmth inside her that was the result of a full tummy and a feeling of safety. She looked around her and saw that they had passed Milton Keynes and were starting to see signs for the Midlands and Coventry. Suddenly she wanted some spiritual food as well as physical. "Maddy, will it be too much of a bother to go to Coventry?"

"Oh? Well of course not but …?" The question hung in the air as Lucy said in a determined voice, "I always wanted to visit the cathedral but we never got there. John didn't seem to think it important. I'd love to go there. Why have I been such a fool?" This last thought was almost shouted out and made Maddy jump. "Watch it, I'm driving and getting a bit tired you idiot." Silence was followed by a quiet, "OK we'll go." And so they did.

CHAPTER SEVEN
Liza Again

Liza awoke to the sounds of the family business moving the day along. Farm noises, machinery rumbling, people arriving and departing with shouts of greeting and inquiry, Edwin and Tom beneath her bedroom window, their muted voices rising to her level of consciousness gave her a feeling of home and safety. Lazily she stretched and rose, having taken a leisurely shower she went downstairs with a purposeful tread. Liza was sitting at the old oak kitchen table. Well worn, the table had seen many dramas enacted over its time worn surface, but it never revealed one secret. Edwin and Tom came in together for coffee and joined her at her breakfast. "You are doing nothing today, nothing at all. We want you to relax and get over yesterday." "No." The sharp reply was out of character and unexpected. Edwin had always looked after Liza and indeed felt his role with her was nothing if that was taken away. She said it again as if to reinforce its message, "No. My dearest Edwin. I've been mollycoddled for too long." She looked at her husband and son and thought, 'they're like two peas in a pod'.

She sat squarely at the table; head erect and with a straight back. Liza had gone from a prize pet to an Amazon with that one word. Actually that was how it seemed to Edwin but the reality was vastly different. Liza realised how shocked her beloved husband was and how the following might hurt him but for her survival, no, for their survival what was about to come was inevitable. "Ed, we are leaving the farm and going round the world, well South America actually." She paused for dramatic effect and drank her tea, ate a bite of toast and smiled triumphantly. "Close your mouths my darlings you look like you're catching flies. Tom is perfectly able to run the business for a while. We'll be away for about two months. Edwin we can afford it and if we don't go I can't guarantee what will happen to us as a couple." Tears came into her eyes as she saw the effect of this latest thought on her husband. "Tom, you will be pushed I know so if you want to think about getting some help while we're away you'd better start now. Go on, Dad and I need to talk." Tom looked hurt and got up and left the kitchen without a word. His tall slightly stooping back receded into the yard and she turned to Edwin, "Love we have become a stereotype. 'A comfy couple with no excitement.' What happened to our dreams? We had them you know. I still do but have only just remembered some of them. They were girlish dreams I know and impractical but we can have adventures and experiences, love, before it's too late. Please don't look like that."

Exasperated she stood up and walked round the table. She put a hand on his shoulder and shook him slightly with great tenderness and irritation as only a well married woman can. "Edwin," sharply she spoke again as nothing was forthcoming from him, "how often do you pour over the atlas in the long winter evenings wondering what Peru is like? And you're always longingly talking about 'one day we'll go to the Andes'." He looked aghast, "but darling just now we're expanding you know how hard Tom and me, well we're working our butts off." His Welsh accent grew ever stronger as his panic started to set in. "For God's sake Edwin, we're nearly sixty, just when is it going to be right for us to go away?" He looked cornered as he started to make more excuses, "Tom isn't ready yet. His divorce and … well everything"

"Damn his divorce and damn you too Edwin. If you won't make a decision then I will. I will go on a trip of a life time with or without you. We're drowning in our own success. We're complacent as two fat pigs in the mire. I've been as bad as you at procrastinating but no more. My dreams as a child were put away and I grew up but you know I never quite let go of them. They're buried deep within me. This last twenty four hours has taught me to dust them off. If only you knew and would try to understand what we went through yesterday? It was like several lifetimes of ... oh ... how do I explain it? Edwin my love we have to get away. I'll burst if we don't. Grown up dreams are just as important. Let's seize the day and plan our escape." He knew he had lost but it gave him no pleasure. The wife who had gone on a day trip to see some old friends had not come back to him. The safe cuddly woman had been replaced by a determined virago. Well perhaps that was a bit harsh but he wanted to cosset and plan and lead not be led by the nose. Surprises were his forte not hers. He had been supplanted and it felt uncomfortable. He would do as she wanted because he thought he always had. Clearly he had got this all wrong. These thoughts went through his head as he reeled from the latest shock. Where he had got it wrong was in thinking it was all about him. Now it was about Liza and her time had come. She truly had seized the day. Well cometh the hour then cometh the man, Edwin would shape up and seize it with her.

Tom, who was like most of the population and hated any kind of confrontation, decided humour was the way to break his parent's current crisis. He looked through the kitchen window and saw a bewildered father and an angry and exasperated mother so he put a plastic feed bucket on his head and marched up and down outside the window carrying a yard broom as a rifle. Each time he passed the window he bent his knees to create the impression that he was walking down a hill. He knew he had cracked it when on the third pass he saw Liza and Edwin collapsed with laughter as they stared out of the window. "Mission accomplished 'rifleman' Tom," he calmly put down the bucket and broom and waved a salute as he slowly walked away to carry on with the running of the business empire. The respite was to be but a brief one.

CHAPTER EIGHT
Beth's Homecoming

Beth's homeward journey was irritatingly two hours longer than that of the morning. Some stupid car transporter driver had, once again, gone too fast as he overtook in the middle lane of the south coast motorway and created mayhem for hundreds of others. As Beth sat in her little car, idling and cursing, she reflected on the day that had brought a new tragedic element into her sphere which was totally unexpected. The person she felt most for was Lucy. She knew that she was getting out but also she considered that it would take a long time for her to heal and regain the confidence that she had nearly had as a teenager. Growing up Beth had felt closer to Liza but she was so fond of them all, a feeling she considered mutual. Ronnie, she knew, would find a way to cope with the looming menace of George's illness. She had always coped. Coping was what Ronnie did best. She laughed and joked her way out of disaster. They had all marvelled at how she had risen again very quickly after the death of her son. Beth reflected, as she had not had time to before this day, that Ronnie unwisely buried those emotions that were too hard to lay bare. Had they given her enough support at the time? She found it hard to shake off the idea of impending doom when she thought about Ronnie. This motorway delay was certainly allowing her to consider as she had not before. Her mother's death and her own needs had been paramount although she had done little to fulfil the gulf that was her private life.

This latest thought was a step too near breakdown so Beth turned on the radio and found some soothing music. Beethoven was quickly followed by an advert for insurance. As Beth considered this to be sacrilege she re-tuned and found Radio Three. This could be a bit heavy at times for her taste but tonight she discovered that they were playing Verdi's Rigoletto live from 'The Met'. She settled down in her seat and waited, with Verdi, for the road to open. Her thoughts ranged between all her friends and how she was thrilled for Lucy but also just a little bit afraid for her. She considered that Liza was going to be all right in the end but had some growing up to do. Maddy was a dear and very capable so she didn't waste much thinking time on her predicament as Maddy had always made the right decision in the end. The opera had almost reached its desperate denouement before the traffic began to move. Although she was ready to get home she experienced a languid desire to stay put and feast on the music. She, for a brief moment, had been transported out of her lonely life and she raged against rejoining it. Re-join it she must, and anyway the police were moving people on in that irritated fashion they have with motorists. Frenetic waving of a uniformed arm does not always convey the precise meaning of the action required. She assumed, rightly, that they wanted her to drive on. Discretion being the greater part of valour she complied accompanied by Verdi's wonderful score turned up to the highest volume. The thrill of the music was almost orgasmic. She hoped in her small way that they were further irritated by this blast of music. Beth indulged in a wistful sighing smile to herself and drove home.

CHAPTER NINE
Ronnie's Regrets

A shocked Ronnie drove towards home with a very heavy heart. She loved George with a passion with which she had built her life. There were no half measures with Ronnie, she was either all enthusiasm or totally disinterested. This attitude applied to her love life, her work and her friends. She married later in her thirties as she had truly never felt that certain passion for her boyfriends which she required before she made a lifetime commitment. George had come into her life unexpectedly and with them both it was instant and all consuming passion. This not only applied to their physical passion, which had long since abated and become a glorious comfortable belonging, but also to their interests and attitude to their surroundings. 'Is anything ever that perfect?' She doubted it and losing their adopted son was the most bitter of blows. Neither had been able to articulate their grief and so the hidden canker had grown within them.

For George it had turned to cancer and now he was within months of what he considered a blessed relief. Ronnie railed against the injustice of losing both her son and her life long love. 'What had she done wrong? Where might she have made up for any misdemeanours?' Her Grandmother, a strong and austere woman, who was never a 'granny' always a grandmother, instilled into her that 'as you cast your bread on the water so it shall be returned to you ten fold'. That was how she remembered it but the actual quote from the bible was much more obscure in its meaning. Her family always did exaggerate and aimed higher and higher and were never content. This trait she too had inherited. Pushed from an early age she had willingly gone along with her parents' and grandparents' wishes. She was bright but most of all she loved the thought that by complying she was gaining their acceptance. Cruel, cruel world it is that leads poor mortals to expect what others just will not give. Her family all went to their graves wondering why she was so career minded when they would have loved what she never gave them, a grandson. They wondered what they had done to deserve such a selfish daughter who thought only of herself. As with many demanding people they had only to look inwards as the answer lay inside them wrapped deeply in their own self-centred world.

George had had a really good day. Ronnie always enjoyed her reunions and he liked it when she came home and parodied her friends' lives in amusing but kind exaggerations of their current crises. She was rather later than he anticipated but he rarely worried about her as she had never yet failed to come home. As the clock ticked away on the marble mantle, which was a jolly good find from a demolition site, he stood up with no little difficulty as the pains in his legs were increasing as the evening wore on. He crossed to the hearth where the grate was cold since the summer was advancing and no fires would be lit now until September at the earliest. He stroked the cold surface and found comfort in its smoothness and familiar touch. Ronnie made his life complete and he was letting her down by dying gradually before her eyes. She would perhaps have preferred a more spectacular exit or even to go first as he was more resilient and would cope. Alas, neither of them was used to just coping and needed to live each moment. He thought that was why she always drove so fast, as if testing the Fates to see how far she could push them before they broke her thread. The evening was turning into a nightmare of waiting. He wanted to clear the air and apologise for asking her to help him die. Even though she had agreed with a desperate resignation to help him, he knew she could never do it and he was deeply sorry that he had given in to a moment of weakness and asked her. He would endure and die when it was his time. He would make her see that the remaining days would be worth remembering. Where was she? The telephone rang and he slowly made his way to answer the call.

His daughter's voice echoed loudly through the seemingly empty house. "Hello Dad. Just wondered how you were? I'm back from hols now and was thinking of coming over tomorrow to see you both. Will you be in? 'Bout 11ish would suit me." Jane paused as she waited for the usual greeting and responses. George found himself unable to speak, instead he spluttered, "Oh God Jane she's late and I'm so worried." "Dad for goodness sake what's wrong? Do you mean Ronnie?" The pause was brief but Jane immediately took charge, "Right, I'm coming over now. It'll take about forty mins. Depending on traffic though should be ok at this time in the evening. I'm on my mobile in case of emergencies. See you shortly. Love you." With that she hung up and set about going to see her father. George stood with the 'phone in his hands, clasped as if everything would disintegrate if he let go.

Ronnie's world was turned upside down, literally. It had come out of nowhere and whooshed by her at an alarming speed. She had no idea what it was but it had momentarily blinded her and she had lost control. As the car spun around Ronnie's world seemed to slow down and she felt herself drifting. There was momentary pain and then nothing. She didn't even hear the awful sickening sound of crashing metal, she lost consciousness with her last known thought being of George, waiting for her to come home and his dear ravaged face floated into her failing senses.

CHAPTER TEN
A Spiritual Affirmation

As it basked in afternoon sunshine Coventry Cathedral opened its spiritual arms and welcomed in the lost souls. It was three thirty in the afternoon when they finally found the cathedral. Actually it was two cathedrals, side by side. One bombed in the early stages of World War Two and the other that had arisen, like a phoenix from the act of war, to represent the wonderful but difficult idea of reconciliation. They went, as many before them, first into the ruins of the old cathedral. The sun warmed brick stood magnificent in its destruction and held its glory with a defiant but welcoming aura. People sat around the edge on benches and chatted. People sat round the edge on benches and silently took in the spirit of the place. The burnt out remnants of two pieces of wood that were now in the shape of a cross bore stark testament to the resilience of man to aggression. The words, 'Forgive Them', boldly and superbly echoed the sentiment. Tears sprang to their eyes as they read the inscriptions around the walls. The most poignant for Lucy was the statue of two people on their knees hugging each other in the spirit of 'Reconciliation', the name of the piece.

Chastened and humble they walked out of the sunlight, under the portico and into a greater light. The unusual and thrilling 'new' cathedral was as magnificent as any old gothic construction and relevant to the modern world as only the most thoughtful architecture can be. Despite some publicity Lucy considered that this was a most modern and well kept secret, "How can this be so magnificent and not ... well ... not known so much? Maddy, its ...", she paused trying to find words to describe how she felt, "breathtaking, yes, breathtaking. Oh God it is so ... words fail me." Maddy turned her gaze from the baptistery window with all its ethereal splendour and colour and saw the silent tears of joy slowly wending their way down her friend's face. Realizing that words were just not adequate at times like this Maddy touched Lucy's arm with a gentle caress and searched in her pocket for a tissue to wipe away her own tears.

The cool interior welcomed them in and threw a cloak of peace around their beleaguered shoulders. Silent men and women wandered along with the same look of awe on their faces as they all gazed in wonder at such a revelation. With every step there seemed to be a different gift from another part of the world. Sculptures and works of art were thoughtfully placed to keep the idea of international unity at the forefront of the spectator. Lucy was overwhelmed and went to sit quietly in the main body of the church. She needed to sit, think and pray. This she did for some time while Maddy wandered on alone to admire the Graham Sutherland tapestry that filled the whole of one end. Lucy was lost in a kind of reverie when she felt Maddy touch her on the shoulder and whisper, "Luce we really ought to be getting on. I've booked us into a hotel I know near Carlisle. Ready?" Lucy nodded and rose. As she walked away from the cathedral she looked back and stopped, "Maddy, I know I've a long way to go but I feel somehow I'm not alone. Sort of renewed. I reckon I'm ready for the journey." Maddy knew that she meant not only the trip to Scotland but the journey that would bring her back to an adult world where she no longer need feel afraid. Maddy was so emotional herself that she decided to bring some ordinariness to the day, "Look at that traffic warden, she's positively relishing giving that chap a ticket. Do you think there's a college for traffic wardens and doctors' receptionists where they take away their humanity and sense of humour?" Lucy was in no mood for levity so made a grunting non committal reply. She couldn't quite switch off as quickly as her friend seemed to do. "Thanks for stopping Mad. I know you want to get on and I'm being a bloody nuisance and a bit of a fool but ..."

"No not at all, hmm, well just a bit. Come on lets get going." The two of them walked away with renewed spirit determined never to forget Coventry and its surprising indomitable spirit. With one last look back they saw the sun shining through the broken façade of the old cathedral with such beauty that it gave a permanence to their belief that all would be well.

CHAPTER ELEVEN
Beth's Next Step

As Beth drew up into the drive of her modest semi detached house her heart fell at the sight of the darkness that surrounded the building. The whole atmosphere was one of bleak emptiness. It had never occurred to her before that she could make changes. The last few years had been spent in coping and 'making do'. Today had brought home to her just what she might do with her life. Her job at the bank was static. Long ago they had given up, passing her by for any promotion. She didn't know whether this was because she had stopped applying for the jobs or whether she had felt that it was a fruitless exercise. Whatever the cause, the outcome was the same. She was very good at what she did but it had long ceased to exercise her brain in any way. She switched off the engine and got out of the car. She stood for a moment drinking in the quiet of the evening. It was a good neighbourhood and her immediate neighbours had been lovely to her throughout her mother's illness and final demise. She asked herself just what did she want. Her answer in her mind was 'not this'. Wearily she opened the front door and busied herself emptying the car and shutting things up to repel all boarders. As she was making things secure she had a wild idea that security was not what she wanted now.

Beth remembered that Ben had said he would call and so she pressed the button on her answering machine. There was only one message and that was not from Ben. It was the local dry cleaning firm telling her that her curtains were ready to be picked up. Well what excitement!

An hour later Beth had had a long soak in the bath and was dressed in her nightclothes. As she sat down in her welcoming all enveloping arm chair she hugged a mug of tea to her and stared into the distance. She was looking at her life and all the decisions she had made that had brought her to this moment. She was alone, with no companion, not even a budgerigar, to talk to when the curtains were drawn and she stared into an abyss. The day had been eventful and frightening and wonderful and exhausting. She loved her friends and the realisation came to her that apart from them she had few close friends to call her own. Beth was much admired in the local town for her devotion and quite a few people would have called her friend but none had come to be a close companion. She had kept them away, held them at arm's length, for what purpose she had no idea. Now she needed to get out and find a new life. She was surprisingly philosophical about Ben. He had been fun and the sex had been good but he was just a stepping stone to the next stage, whatever that was going to be. She was pretty certain anyway that she was not his only conquest at the art class. He was very well endowed and obviously liked to share it. Thank god they had used a condom. How awful to get to her late fifties and then get a sexually transmitted disease. She shuddered at the thought and decided he would be her only sexual encounter without being emotionally tied in to someone. It was not particularly satisfying anyway, a moment of sexual pleasure and then no comforting cuddle. Beth watched the late news on the television and then went to bed. Tomorrow would be a new day and with each new dawn comes hope.

Unusually for Beth she slept in and woke up, not to Terry Wogan who usually got her going in the mornings and always in a good humour, but to the other chap that follows him. She didn't know his name as she rarely listened to this station after half past eight. Even on her days when she wasn't working she preferred to listen to Radio Three and their more gentle classics. The more raucous music ensured that she leapt out of bed so that she could turn off the radio. Peace returned and she decided that a cup of strong tea and a digestive biscuit would be a good way to start the day. What this day had in store for her she knew not but she did know that it was the day to make some changes. She had the rest of the week off from work as part of her annual holiday and she was not going to waste a second. Because of her late start it was nearly midday before she was bathed and dressed and ready to go out. She had written a letter to Ben to explain that their brief liaison was at an end. Beth decided to walk round to his house and post it through his letter box. This would enable her to relax about it knowing that he had received the letter. She had been very nice to him and about him so she guessed that he wouldn't be too upset.

As the time was nearly one o'clock by the time she had delivered her 'Dear John' letter she continued walking towards the centre of the market town where she found her favourite Italian bistro and had lunch. Beth tucked herself away in a corner so that she could watch the comings and goings without bringing any attention to her lonely repast. She felt a little self conscious as she seemed to be the only diner lunching alone. As the waiter brought her wine and olive bread she was spotted by a colleague from the bank who had just entered, also alone. This colleague had always been pleasant and as she was also without company they lunched together. Companionship at a crisis in one's life is very important and as this kind of meeting happened so little to Beth she decided that the coincidence was a sign that she was on track to the new 'her'. To those for whom such lunches are typical of their day it would seem like a very minor and unimportant happening but to Beth it was so unusual that she felt alive. She and her colleague parted company in good spirits and they both walked with a little more spring in their steps. Beth was not the only lonely person in the world and perversely that made her feel better.

Beth considered that her usual wardrobe of tailored suits for work or staid leisure clothes made her a 'type' to which she no longer wished to belong. Today was turning into a real watershed and so she went shopping. She had some money saved and had been careful in the past so she indulged herself. Bright colours, gypsy skirts and flowing tops all tumbled into her possession. The sales assistants were pleased to be able to help as she actually had no idea what suited her and what didn't. It would be a day of mixed fortune as far as clothes were concerned as not all the shop assistants had impeccable taste but Beth had stopped the rot of approaching sixty dressed like her grandmother. Several hundred pounds lighter she returned home and collapsed into her armchair with a very welcome cup of tea. She had arranged her purchases all along the sofa and chairs and hung some on the door jamb so that she could survey her day of madness while she ruminated and relaxed. As she looked at the motley assemblage of clothes she laughed and laughed and laughed. Just imagining her self in most of them gave her a renewed sense of adventure. She was very tired today after yesterday's fraught tensions and looked forward to curling up on the sofa with a bowl of pasta and a glass of wine. She had done enough today to break the cycle but she would pace herself. This evening she would make the necessary 'phone calls to her friends to establish that all was well with them and then as her niece would say 'she would chill'. Robbie Burns wrote about the best laid plans of mice and men going wrong, well Beth would have done well to remember that poem this night. Ben's ego would not let her go without a struggle. Besides his ego, he rather liked her.

CHAPTER TWELVE
The End For Ronnie?

For some reason it had been a busy evening on the motorway. Mid week days could be deadly dull or so busy that the police and ambulance crews were stretched to the point of meltdown. At times they almost failed to meet the government target response times. The night of the picnic was one such night when every idiot was out and about on the roads. There seemed to be an unholy rush for everyone to get everywhere in record time. The police had seen it all before and cleared up wreckage so many times they almost got used to it. Only their gallows humour kept them from going into deep depressions as they helped other emergency services scrape bodies off the road surface and pick up the ephemera of lives that lay strewn about the mangled bodies of vehicles. Rarely did the protection offered in glossy brochures live up to the car salesman's hype. Some motorists drove as though they had magical protection from a greater being and that whatever speed or dangerous manoeuvre they executed nothing would harm them. Inevitably the involvement of children in an accident pulled at the hardened hearts rather more than most. A bloody teddy bear was guaranteed to bring a tear to the most dried up cynic.

After her brush with the two reluctant constables Ronnie drove much more carefully than usual. She knew she had risked both herself and others. She felt ashamed and became desperate to see George and tell him all about the day and more importantly about how she felt about him. He should not have asked her to help him, she shuddered at the thought, die. He knew he was in the wrong and so did she. What was her fault though was the way she had handled it. She had temporarily cut him out of her affectionate embrace. She wanted him to suffer as he was making her suffer. Why did he have to have cancer? Why did she have to watch this robust and hearty man disappear before her eyes? She had loved him from the moment they met. For her the people she most admired when at school were the achievers. It was not for her to be besotted with fainting, dainty heroines. Not for her the little woman waiting to be rescued by a strong man who would whisk her away and never let her lift a finger to help. No, it was the joint companionship and shared passion in equal measure that made Ronnie's life sing. The jolly hockey stick kind of girl, the kind that gets things done and so she had emulated those girls from 'Mallory Towers' and other stories that encouraged the feminine to fulfil their potential. She got on with living. As her business grew she forgot the quieter side of her childhood when she had taken time to enjoy reading. She had not read a good novel for years. There never seemed to be time enough for such pleasures.

As Ronnie drove home that evening she was still suffering from shock at the way she had carelessly taken two of her friends' lives in her hands and put them in mortal danger. Driving more slowly gave her time to reflect on how close she had been to disaster. Since the death of her adopted son she had embraced a new degree of recklessness that had hitherto been buried deeply within her. Needing to be under control and make a success of her business she kept a tight rein on her wilder character traits. George knew and loved her for her wilder side and together they harnessed such energy in sailing and skiing regularly throughout the year. His wealth was assured through his earlier business life and hers was achieved through extremely hard work and dedication to financial success. It was only in the last year that she had found a trustworthy deputy with whom she could reliably leave the company for regular breaks. It wasn't that there were no good people to whom she could have entrusted the business but she had not been ready to relinquish control. Ronnie still occasionally felt uncomfortable in going away but it came more easily now. George's illness had shocked her into caring less about commerce and much more about life. In the past few weeks she had even been seen reading a poetry book. For the sake of her emotional wellbeing this was a good thing but the circumstances that occasioned such a return to wordy pleasures were obviously not. Reading Yeats and Shelley, Keats and Wordsworth brought back much nostalgia and helped Ronnie to cry, silently and secretly so that George would not have the added distress of seeing her disintegrate. Actually George would have liked to see this emotional side coming back as he worried about her ability to cope when he had gone.

Over and over again Ronnie recited the lines from one of her favourite poems, it had struck a chord when she re-read it thirty years after first revelling in the sympathy of the meaning, "To her fair works did Nature link the human soul that through me ran; and much it grieved my heart to think what Man has made of Man." Even more so did her heart break when she thought of the flowers described by Wordsworth in the next verse and the idea that the little periwinkle enjoyed a breath of air touched a long hidden sentimental chord inside her. It was in this state of emotional distress that she drove on through the evening and as the light faded all together she briefly made a mental note of the gathering gloom and thought how well it suited her mood. She glanced at the clock on the dashboard of her car and calculated that she would be with George in about twenty minutes when she would make it up to him. She would devote all her energies to making his last months as happy and carefree as she could. She drove on with a gladdened heart and her spirits lifted. How marvellous to come to the realisation that it isn't quantity but the quality of a life that gifts the memory with sustaining moments of joys remembered.

The two fourteen year old twin boys had always been 'in trouble' with both the law and their school. Their parents had long since abandoned them to their fate whatever that may be. They were uncontrollable and that was that. It wasn't their fault, they were just naughty boys. Their parents did not believe half of the stories about them. Even the police were at a loss as to know how to get through to the parents that these boys were heading for trouble in a big way. The parents were both hard working and hard drinking people who deserved a pint at the end of a long day. There was always food on the table and the boys had bedrooms to die for. Every kind of computer game, television and music centre and posters of rap artists whose popular lyrics encouraged violence, racism and homophobia surrounded them with foul imagery that imprinted darkness on their sponge like brains from the time they awoke to the time they eventually went to bed. It was a phase wasn't it? They would grow out of it soon enough, why they were good to their Granny and often went round to help her. Granny lived in the next street and daily feared the visits of her grandsons. Granny was frail and scared. Regularly they extorted money from her and had on one occasion given her a bruised arm when she tried to tell them off. The pain remained with her still. Pain that went deeper than a sore arm but to the very core of her heart when she realised that her own flesh and blood could treat her in such a way. She had tried to tell her daughter about it but her daughter didn't want to believe it and so put it down to senility on behalf of the old woman.

The evening of the picnic the boys decided to up the ante and take a car and go for a drive. They had been in a car with their pals before but up to this point in time neither had actually driven. It would be fun and they would give the police a run for their money. Local police officers had had their fill of the twins and were anxious to get them sorted before they hurt more people. New BMWs were not exactly commonplace in the twins' neighbourhood but they had only to travel to the far side of town where there was more genuine affluence. They had set their minds on a BMW and that is what they would drive. It took them very little time to find a target. Black and new the car had long been a desire of the young couple. Fate had dealt them a cruel blow and they had recently been told that they would never have children of their own and the only way was to adopt a child. The process for this was long and arduous and neither yet had the emotional stamina to start going through hoops for social services. This very day the man had picked up their new car and was planning to surprise his wife. Unfortunately he had been delayed at work and so it was later in the evening when he finally drew up in their driveway. He leapt out of the car, leaving the keys in the ignition, and went inside for a moment to get his wife. In a trice the teenagers had jumped in and driven away down the short driveway and out into the road. Looking neither left nor right they had narrowly missed another car, luckily going quite slowly, and they sped away. The motorway was their aim. So arrogant were these youths that they were taking the fight against authority and the police in particular to their own well patrolled patch.

The local police were alerted within minutes of the theft and were giving chase both on the ground and with the help of the police helicopter which had just got airborne. Power and speed can give a thrill beyond verbal expression; at least this is how the twins felt. The faster and more reckless their journey both excited and frightened them. Twin number two was the boy with the least conscience. Twin number one, the elder by five minutes, began to be more frightened than exhilarated by this experience and started to suggest they abandoned the escapade and ditch the car. His brother took no notice as he was in his element and as he swung on to the slip road he felt that he had never been so free. The BMW topped a hundred miles an hour as they almost flew past other cars. Ronnie was in a heightened state of awareness about her personal dilemma and, although driving with more caution than usual, was unaware of the impending disaster. As the BMW came up beside her something made her look at the car, the driver looked back and for a moment she saw a young boy, grinning. She faltered; he swerved and took her wing away. As both cars climbed the bank locked together the motorway became a seething mass of vehicles stopping to help or stare. The police were quickly on the scene. The helicopter had tracked the boys and so the pilot was able to inform the emergency services who were even now on their way. The ambulance and fire crews were on site within minutes of the disaster. What they saw when they arrived was carnage.

71

Two cars were wrecked. They were destroyed and there was one body lying prone and unmoving near the tangled mess. Other people were obviously involved and so started the task, the dreadful nightmarish task of seeing who was still alive, if any, and how they could be freed.

CHAPTER THIRTEEN
Liza Flexes Her Muscles

Liza was not perfect. None are. One particular imperfection now came to the fore with great force. She had been a dreamer as a child and she had put away much for a stable life and a comfortable life. Edwin had treated her well and with great affection. He had rarely really known what was in her mind but then she had kept much hidden, buried, and even she had little idea that these desires were still lying dormant not extinct. The picnic day had been a watershed, was it only yesterday that they had experienced all that drama? It seemed to Liza that she had been back at the farm for days not hours. Tom and Edwin were out discussing the business, or so she thought. They were actually discussing Liza and how she was and how she seemed and what was it she wanted. Edwin was a bit lost and Tom, being his father's son was also lost. Tom's lost state had added complications as it made him consider his own situation. He was close to getting reasonable access to his children but was still very confused as to how a marriage can go so quickly down hill with no hope of ever getting up the other side of what turns out to be an abyss of misery. Father and son discussed the situation and after half an hour, a lot of talking for them, had proceeded no further than, "Mum needs to get away Dad." A pause followed that was long enough for several cows to pass through the gate by which they were standing. "Yes, but South America? That's what she said, South America! I know I've always longed to go but it was a dream. I…"

"Dad for God's sake stop and think. It will only be for a few weeks. I can get someone to help. The boys will have to come here and help or just do ..." Tom's words tailed off as he realised his father had wandered away and was no longer listening. Furious he shouted, "Don't muck this up." With that parting shot he too walked away to get on with the myriad jobs that needed his attention.

Liza had cooked a substantial shepherd's pie for Edwin and Tom. It was bubbling in the range oven. She had felt desperately frustrated both yesterday and today. Only she knew half of the reason, the rest she was having to work out for herself. Edwin and Tom knew a mere fraction of what was going on in her head and so remained at sea, bobbing along in a tiny dinghy of confusion and remorse. As yet it was remorse for what they knew not but were both equally sure they would be told in the fullness of time. Edwin had an idea that actually Liza was not so sure herself. Although a practical man he had flashes of insight into his wife's emotions and this time he was spot on. When Liza was upset she baked. The array of cakes, scones, casseroles and biscuits were a testament to her state as the production line was always in proportion to the anguish. After a huge day on the farm and minding the gallery both men were ravenous and so partook of the feast, temporarily unconcerned as to the reason for such a spread. The plates were scraped empty and the three sat, sort of contentedly, in the sitting room. "I'm sorry my loves that I've been difficult today. I .."

"Don't worry ..." Tom was interrupted by his father,

"I'll say diffi..."

"Shut up both of you, I'm trying to explain." Her conciliatory tone had been a blind, a ruse, a stratagem to make them listen but even so she had to resort to a command rather than appeasement, "For god's sake I've been thinking all day, don't smile like that I'm close to bursting with frustration." This last was directed at Tom who had been about to make an inane comment reference his mother's thinking powers. She knew this and felt so close to exploding that she got up and left the room, tears of anger and frustration coursing silently down her face which was still pink from the heat of the kitchen.

Edwin and Tom looked at each other and shamefacedly grinned in that embarrassed way that heralds a feeling of guilt at not being receptive to a loved one's confession. They heard the 'phone ring as Edwin was about to follow Liza and when they also heard Liza answer it with, "Oh Beth, how lovely." Edwin thankfully sank back down into his capacious armchair and reached for the paper. He put on his reading glasses and turned to the crossword page. Tom was nonplussed at this display of relief so he took himself off to the local pub for a pint of Devon's Best. He walked by way of the home field and the small copse that lay on the outskirts of their farm. This way he cut off a mile from the way by road and so it was that within half an hour he was established in The Plough enjoying his beer and considering his future through the bottom of a glass.

"Beth, how are you today? What a day yesterday." Liza began the conversation with the usual introduction and waited for Beth to come clean about her feelings about the picnic and all that had happened. She was a good listener and usually was content to give her news last. "Oh Liza what ever is going on with us all? I'll tell you about my day but you go first."

"Well Beth its been horrid. I don't know how I feel about anything. All this has come out of the blue. I've given Ed a really hard time and Tom is driving me mad. I've told Ed we have to go away to save our marriage. I didn't mean it but it just came out." "Oh Liza! What? You're so solid. You've always been solid. Sorry to keep using that word but it sort of fits somehow. What did he say?"

"Not much actually. He was upset and just didn't understand. I'm not surprised as I don't either." Before Beth could say anything in reply Liza continued, "I told him we had to go to South America for two months. Where the hell did that come from?" "Oh Liza you fool," Beth laughed, "it sounds fun though, you should follow it through, see where it takes you. Heaven knows I'm the last to give relationship advice but it seems to me yesterday was a watershed in more ways than one. The stars must have been lined up just right to give us all a shake up. What next Li?"

"Well I've just tried to talk to them but they wouldn't listen without mucking about so I think I'll make it my plan to go ahead with the threat."

"Good on you. Do you need some time away, you could come here, plenty of room now Mum's gone." She paused and then said, "Li that's the first time I've said that without crying. Do come, just for a few days and we can talk about everything, we haven't done that for ages." Liza quickly took up the invitation and so it was arranged that the next week she would stay with Beth from the Monday to Thursday. They finished with, "OK see you then, heard from any of the others?"

"No," Liza said thoughtfully, "but I haven't checked my emails today. I'll go and have a look and let you know if there's any developments." Liza walked back into the sitting room to find Tom had disappeared and Edwin halfway through the crossword. "Budge up, let's have a look to see if there's any I can do. You need me, you know!"

"That I do." After they had finished the crossword, tidied up the kitchen and gone to bed, Liza snuggled up to Edwin and said, "Night love, we are going to South America you know." With that she kissed him and fell asleep.

Tom walked back to the sleepy farmhouse, he had much to be thankful for and was full of confidence that he would soon see his children regularly and what a time they would have. His mum and dad and brothers had been brilliant support, well nearly all of them. One brother was a rector and instead of being filled with the milk of human kindness he seemed to be filled with the sour milk of judgement. Oh well Tom was not thinking about him this night, just nice things. Three pints of beer can have a pleasing effect on a person, four though, that was another matter. He had not been a drinker when he was married but since his separation he had regularly enjoyed a pint or three at The Plough. The camaraderie at the bar was something he relished and whatever came along he knew that the social side of the British pub would always be a comfort. He was not a toper and knew that anymore than three pints and he was an idiot. Hence the three pint limit. Tom was a strong man and, like his father, knew his own limitations.

CHAPTER FOURTEEN
Next Stop Carlisle

They had been back on the road for an hour when Lucy spoke for the first time. Maddy had been concentrating on the motorway and all its frustrations. Another hour and they would be off the motorway and onto the 'A' class road that would take them to their hotel near Carlisle. As the Midlands gave way to the northern landscape Lucy felt able to talk without stumbling over her words. It was the Coventry effect that had her tongue tied and in awe. She could not remember feeling so at peace for a long time. This much benighted woman also felt strong and just a little bit feisty. It was good to feel this way and a self-absorbed cloud of defence and insecurity had melted away. Now she was able to think of others, which she had not done for a while. Lucy was typical of the recipient of violence in that she became obsessed with survival and had little constructive emotional time to consider others in too much depth. Now a window was clearing and she focussed on the picnic yesterday and all the revelations that had come pouring forth so suddenly. "Mad, how do you think Ronnie will cope with losing George? Do you think Beth was right about her as she drove away? I've been so self…"

"Stop right there Lucy. No more guilt and no more 'if only's'. I dare say Ronnie will cope." Then feeling she had been harsh added, "Although coping is no life, not for our Ronnie. Living 100% that's living for Ron. She will be devastated as she was when their son died. Part of her died too and now more of her great heart will go." Lucy thought for a while and then offered, "As long as she doesn't become bitter. That's awful, I've seen it in my family. Its as though they can't forgive God for letting their loved one die. Well, we must be there for her. You've all been brilliant for me. I know I can cope now as you've helped give me a push. Thanks Mad."

"I was due an adventure. Anyway wanted to get away from Bear for a while. I'm getting too close and feel he is too. God Luce I've made so many buggering mistakes that I've bloody well nearly jumped off Beachy Head." She laughed, "Can't stand heights though so ..." She didn't need to finish.

"You are an idiot Madeleine. You, who had everything, or so it seemed. Anyway, you didn't and that's good 'cause otherwise I'd be on a smelly train now and quite lonely. How's that for selfish?"

"I think Liza can be selfish. Edwin puts up with a lot from her you know. I stayed overnight once enroute somewhere and she was very bossy. Good hostess though." Maddy made this observation then added, "What's with Madeleine? Only mum called me that when I was in trouble."

"I thought you needed reminding that you are not always right and always in charge. The old Lucy is coming back. I can feel her nudging." Lucy smiled and snuggled more comfortably in the seat and started, for almost the first time since leaving home, to notice the countryside and the different look to the houses and villages that slowly but inevitably came into view and as quickly were left behind. "C'mon let's have a quick coffee break then bash on to our hotel. We deserve a nice glass of wine and a lovely home cooked meal."

"Mm, nice." Was the only reply and they settled once more into companionable silence.

Luck was on their side this early evening. They were held up but briefly and then flew across the northern counties on good roads that seemed, however busy, to be always flowing at a steady pace. Traffic was lighter and less aggressive than in the home counties. This may have been true or a reflection of the lessening tension of both the women as they drew further away from both their individual domestic difficulties.

At the last stop Maddy had telephoned Bear to make sure all was well. All the animals were fine but of course missing their mistress. Bear was careful to keep the line between making her feel wanted but not needed at this moment. Maddy felt better about the sudden departure and foisting the domestic duties on Bear. He didn't seem to mind at all. He had decided that he wanted this woman and would go to great lengths and be very patient to get her. He knew she was running scared and so as they were saying goodbye on the 'phone he said, "By the way Madeleine Mine, be prepared for a surprise when you get back. Take care Love. Ring me again when you have a chance. Bye." He firmly cut off the call and hoped that he had done just enough to make her want to come back to him.

Maddy had stared into the distance for so long that Lucy had to jolt her out of her reverie. She had not divulged the conversation's end to Lucy but just reassured her that all was well at home. "He said he left John in no doubt that he must leave you alone. Let's hope he takes the hint." This last had left Lucy worried again in case, when she got to Amy's she found John had got there first. She went quiet and sat there more shrunken into herself than since before Coventry. As the awful scenario played out in her mind she felt increasingly scared. She asked her self time and time again why had she told Madeleine about all her arrangements. Why had she acquiesced so readily to being driven instead of taking charge of her own life? Why was she still so frightened when she knew that both her daughter and her son-in-law were with her one hundred percent? Of course she knew the answers to all these and many more questions. It boiled down to the same thing and that was she was a weak and insipid loser who needed the kindness of others to keep her from falling apart. In lucid moments she knew that John was a bully and had taken pleasure in undermining her, as had his mother. Her mother-in-law had certainly done a good job on him. She would be proud that her offspring was formed in the matriarchal likeness par excellence. Lucy thanked God her children were all aware of their father's nature and had determined never to be like him. They had survived and were now spread far and wide across the world and rarely set foot in their father's house. Unfortunately this had also meant they rarely came to see her. Through the years she had managed to get away. John's affair with Cynthia had made this increasingly easy. Occasionally she felt that Cynthia had brought her good luck. Without her John would have concentrated more on his wife, and this she knew she did not want.

The gloom that settled over her mind gave Lucy a desperately dependent air of which she was unaware. Maddy looked at her companion out of the corner of her eye as she drove on through the early evening towards what she hoped would be a temporary sanctuary. After about an hour Lucy smiled and sat up in the seat. "I was having a moment of great doubt Mad, but suddenly I remembered the sun shining through the ruins of the old cathedral. It seems such a symbol of hope doesn't it?" Maddy secretly thought that her friend needed more help than she could give her but agreed with the observation, "Yes, it was wonderful. We all need to know that there's hope I s'pose." Maddy was very tired by now and was feeling a little lost herself. She had acted on impulse and out of a sense of compassion. But if she was honest she also was running away and probably with less cause that Lucy. Bear was a lovely man and clearly fond of her but was that what she wanted? Her failed relationships were a torment to her and she had begun to feel she would never give or receive that trust which she felt was a key component in a relationship. Bear was the closest she had ever come to finding it and here she was, running scared. "Oh well," she thought, "we'll be at the hotel in about half an hour and then we can relax. We can analyse the day then." She drove on and finally saw the turning she was looking for and she parked in the hotel car park and switched off the engine. The quiet and solitude of the moment was wonderful. They had made it. With an enormous sigh of relief they both got out of the car and went to check in. As they walked towards reception Lucy, very simply and with great sincerity, said, "Thanks."

'The Bridge Hotel' was built of local stone and sat high up on the shoulders of the hillside looking down over the mature river with its old stone bridge. Two miles from Carlisle the hotel enjoyed a rich variety of guests over the year ranging from walkers, business types (whose main interests lay in the bar), families who in school holidays came to enjoy the breathtaking scenery and border pursuits, grey haired couples who came because they had time to come and loved to walk and odd people like Maddy who had discovered the delights of this superb hotel by accident and had added it to her list of 'nice places to be'. The hotel had a small spa complex and thus catered for those who just came away for a pampering weekend. Luckily for Sam and Sandy Sidebottom, the energetic and successful young owners, their hotel had yet to be discovered by those seeking new places for 'hen' or 'stag' weekends. Those particular motley groups currently favoured sunnier climes and the Mediterranean resorts did very well out of them. Sam and Sandy had acquired the hotel with money won on the national lottery. They were local people and had decided that this was their dream long before they actually had the financial means to achieve their goal. Sandy was a beauty therapist and knew enough about that side of the business to ensure success. Sam had been a farm labourer with great potential. They didn't actually remember Maddy from her three previous visits but their computer knew that she was a 'returner' and so it was marked on her reservation. This meant that she was entitled to a free bottle of wine with dinner. Details such as this added to the success of The Bridge.

Maddy and Lucy were welcomed by the receptionist, who happened to be Sandy's niece, and were given first rate and first floor rooms. As the evening was progressing rapidly they decided to have dinner immediately. Truth to tell Maddy was shattered with all the driving and wanted an early night. She also wanted a long uninterrupted conversation with Bear, she was missing him rather more than she had imagined she would. Lucy wanted to curl up in the anonymous bed and sleep the sleep of the just. It would be the second night in a row that she could sleep and not be afraid. Tomorrow would bring more trials and tribulations, she was sure, but tonight she would enjoy the wine, eat her delicious fish (locally caught and not over sauced) and let her friend have some time to herself.

She wanted to be able to think that at some time in the future she would be able to repay Maddy for her kindness but just for now that was a bridge too far. All was going well when two inebriated business men, let loose from the burden of being at home and having to behave themselves, started to make comments about the two women dining alone. Lucy was certainly not in any state to receive ribald comments without retreating into her shell. "Mine's all right but I don't fancy yours." "Mm, skinn-ey. Bit of flesh that's what I..." "Yes a nice arse and..." "No, not arse nice big breasts you can..." A third man who was also with them and had only just made business contact with the two that night was appalled. Their voices were loud and offensive even without the awful content and implications. He had never considered women as objects. Yes, he desired them but had been brought up to respect and admire from afar. Perhaps he was repressed but, so ashamed was he of his companions, he felt drawn to offer apologies to the two women, one of whom was clearly distressed by the sudden intrusion into their dinner. It did not take a sensitive man like him to realise that one of the women was over reacting to the comments. She looked ill and frightened. She was slim and somehow had withdrawn into her own body as if to make her invisible. As he approached the table she looked up at him and stared, unblinking into his eyes, pleading with him as though in silent prayer. His heart melted. He stood by their table and stammered, "I ... I'm ... so sorry about those two. I have only just met them. They're drunk and I must apologise for them. Pl..." Maddy cut him off with an icy, "Thanks but leave us alone. My friend is very tired and needs to be left alone." With that she turned away and left him standing, unsure of his next step. "I just wanted to tell you I am not, one of them." Lucy looked away and then slowly turned back to say in a shaky voice, "Appreciate you coming over." At that moment the strain got the better of her and she flung down her napkin and fled from the room.

Temporarily the dining room came to a silent understanding of the situation. All was quiet and then, as happens when something untoward occurs a swelling babble of comment filled the space then settled down

83

once more to a general level of conversation. Maddy stood up and faced the man. She was tallish but he was taller. He had a nice face and although she was tired she felt compassion for him and tried to make amends for her earlier rebuttal. As she held out her hand she said, "Yes, we do appreciate what you've done but your companions are hideous."

"Yes I've realised that and believe me they will be sorry in the morning." He turned to go then threw back at Maddy, "Very sorry." He took one step away then added, "Here's my card. Please tell your friend we are not all bad. She seemed ill." He left then and passed the table with the stunned drunks, who were being ushered out by Sam and Sandy, without another glance at them.

Maddy slowly looked at the card and read, 'Robert McHeath Ltd, Engineering Contractor, Dundee.' His soft Scottish voice had hardly registered with her until that moment. She smiled and purposefully put his card in her handbag and went to leave the dining room. On her way out Sam offered her his apologies and said that the two men would be barred in future and that she was to consider the dinner 'on the house' to make up for any unpleasantness. She gratefully and graciously accepted then went to make sure Lucy was all right. She gently knocked at Lucy's door and pushed it but it was firmly closed. "Luce, it's me, Maddy. Let me in." After a few moments the door opened and Lucy's drawn face peeped out. "Mad, I'm all in. Sorry for running out on you. I'm fine really, just took me by surprise."

"Ok, look you'll take time to heal you know."

"I know. It's just, well, you know. 'Night Mad. Thanks." She shut the door and went back to her bed where she felt safe. She slept well and by the morning had recovered some of her spirit. She knew she had dreamt but couldn't remember what she had dreamt. A pleasant faced Scot featured in one of her dreams but it was very hazy and so she shut it out of her mind. She had to concentrate on getting through the next day.

Maddy crawled into her own bed and sank gratefully down into the clean sheets. She stretched, yawned and fell instantly into a dreamless deep refreshing sleep. What a day. Her last thought before she drifted off into sleep was that she hadn't had the chance to 'phone Bear. She felt a nice warm feeling inside then she fell into the arms of Morpheus. He kept her safe until morning.

Freshly showered and revitalised the two friends met in the breakfast room. The view was breathtaking from the window. They had both been far too wound up and tired to take any notice of the surrounding countryside when they arrived the previous evening. Maddy of course knew the area but briefly and so was also enamoured of the beauty and spare open feeling of the landscape. It was a clear, clean morning and with an early mist that would soon burn off leaving the promise of a sunny early summer day to be fulfilled. "Morning. Sleep well? You look better. Orange juice I think followed by something nicely sustaining." Lucy accepted the greeting and they both set about the serious business of breakfast. Sandy was the morning chef that day and went all out to make the women the best they had ever had. She felt any slight on their hospitality very keenly and wanted to make amends. Maddy and Lucy partook fully of the offering and felt suitably replete. "Come on Luce, next stop Scotland. Today's gonna be a bright glorious day." The last part of this was accompanied by a lilting singing to a half remembered show tune. They went towards the stairs to get their bags and stumbled, literally across the pleasant Scot from the night before. "Good morning ladies. Did you sleep well?" Lucy replied in the affirmative and blushed slightly. The two turned as if to go on their way when he added, "Please don't judge everyone by last night. I hope we meet again. You have my card?" He held out another to Lucy this time. She took it, blushed some more and said, "Thanks. Bye." He sighed and realised there was no more conversation in the two of them for the moment and so he went to check out.

Maddy and Lucy set off for the adventure that lay ahead of them.

CHAPTER FIFTEEN
More Changes for Beth

As Beth put the 'phone back on its stand she felt a little cheated. Liza had clearly had a momentous day since the picnic. "Was it really only yesterday that they had met and said so much?" She desperately wanted to talk to someone about EVERYTHING in her head but she was tired and now not dressed appropriately to go out so she contented herself with finishing a good book that had been recommended to her by a colleague at work. The modern thriller was by a well known personality who had taken up novel writing as a new career. The book was gentle and well written and quite sentimental. Always Beth needed a happy ending. Books that left one crying or wishing the hero or heroine had not died or left or got terminally ill were no good for her. She brooded for days on the unhappiness. When she was really low she would re-read some of her favourites, the top of that list was Jane Eyre. Jane comes through terrible adversity to triumph and happiness.

Beth never lost sight of her ultimate goal, happiness with 'someone special'. Perhaps she was too fussy. Her expectations were high. All she wanted was to love and be loved for who she was, it seemed an impossible goal at times. Her mother had squashed many a likely romance, some times just by being 'around'. Baggage, it seemed in any form, was a big turn off for many. Well now she was financially 'comfortable' although not really wealthy. She had kept herself in good shape physically by exercising and eating healthily. On the downside she was in her late fifties and starting to notice signs of wear and tear. She was at an age when she required soft focus lighting to make her look good. What she failed to enter into this mental bookkeeping of her pros and cons was her wonderful smile, warm nature and loyalty. As she was drifting in and out of her reverie and reading the novel at the same time she was startled by her doorbell. She jumped out of her skin and muttered to herself, "Who on earth is ringing the bell at this time of night?" This was said at the same time as she looked at the clock and was very surprised to find it was only half past eight.

Beth looked through the spyhole in her front door and was astonished to see Ben standing there on her doorstep with an enormous bunch of flowers in his hand. She opened the door and rather guardedly asked what he wanted. "Beth, I've read and re-read your note and wanted to ask you to re-consider. Can I come in?" As she continued to look at him he added, "Please?" Not at all sure she wanted to let him come in she felt that the only way to get rid of him was to say again what had been in her letter. She stepped back and waved him in. He handed her the flowers as he crossed the threshold which she declined to take. Once they were sitting, not so comfortably, in the sitting room Beth asked, "Why now? Just because I've broken the bond. Not that it was very strong anyway. I understand that I was one of two or three. Possibly more. Who knows?"

Ben sat open mouthed, "I ... I ... I..."

Beth jumped in with, "Yes. That's a word you use, all the time, I."

"No, no, I ..."

"Well, what is it? We've known each other for a few months and not once have you given me flowers. Now, I don't want them. Please go."

"But Beth, darling girl I don't want to lose you. I thought we were OK."

"Did you? Well it just goes to show how perceptive you're not doesn't it? I was vulnerable and you spotted it a mile off. Well now I'm not so vulnerable you can go off and find someone else." With that she stood up, unfortunately he didn't. He held out a hand to stop her as she passed by his chair, "Beth, we could..."

"No. Let go and just go." Slowly he stood and turned a sneering face to her, "You'll not get anyone else. Your too old and, well let's face it, none too pretty." He dumped the flowers on the floor and swept out without another word.

Shaken by the whole experience Beth locked the house up and put the chain on the door. She knew she had been right to end the affair which had been little more than a physical one. What she hadn't expected was his ego. What a cruel man he had turned out to be. She supposed he might be right about her being too old and ugly but then being with him would have been a disaster. Better loneliness than being hurt daily by someone who didn't really care for her. She decided to 'phone her cousin who was always a good source of comfort. He and his wife lived in the next town and had a soft spot for Beth seeing her while away much of her time on others. Over the years they had visited her regularly and had sympathised when his mother too had fallen ill and died several years before Beth's own mother. Her cousin was able to offer a shoulder to cry on over the telephone and after twenty minutes Beth was back in her comfy chair feeling a little better. This improved feeling may have been due, in part, to the rather large brandy she had poured out, medicinal purposes only, of course. Thinking this made her smile to herself as, during the nicer times with Mum they had always said that when they had a drink. "Hey ho," she thought, "back to the drawing board." She lifted her glass to the light and watched the brown liquid swirl round, "Here's to me." She stared into the distance and thought of oilskins, choppy seas and a rather nice, slightly grizzled coxswain with a crooked smile. Out loud she said, "Well, a girl can dream." Shrugged her shoulders and switched on the late news on the television. Tomorrow is another day.

The next day, the second after the picnic, Beth woke up with a lassitude which took her by surprise. She had always been disciplined in her daily habits. She rarely spent time in bed except for sleep after exhausting days at the bank, caring for her mother or domestic chores that seemed to fill an increasing amount of time. Beth got up and made a cup of tea and took it back to bed. She snuggled into her duvet, drank her tea and listened to the radio. Terry Wogan was his cheerful self reading witty emails from the general public who were a source of much untapped talent. Strangely this dogged cheerfulness grated on her senses and she didn't want to listen any more so she re-tuned to the news station and concentrated on the more serious items of the hour. Perversely this change in habit sent Beth straight back to sleep. Her dreams were disturbed and full of people pointing and staring and leading her up blind alleys until she was running away from everyone. The fear of the close walled entrapment seemed to permeate her very soul. She woke up sweating and shivering. Feeling very heavy headed Beth sat up and shook her head when she saw the time. It was nearly 11 am and she had never, never slept in that late since her teenage years. Even then it was rare. The ringing continued to bang into her newly awakened consciousness until she realised that someone was trying to 'phone. She quickly got up and ran to get the 'phone which, of course, stopped when she was inches away from answering. Her answering machine didn't cut in so she assumed it was a marketing call and sighed a sigh of relief. She pulled her robe around her as she felt chilly. Early summer was still offering the promise of good weather and no heat wave was yet in view. Beth went into the kitchen to make breakfast. After a refreshing shower she thought she'd check the 'phone to see who had tried to call.

As she dialled Liza's number she wondered why her friend had not left a message. She hoped there was not more drama from Devon as she wanted a day to sort out some major life changing decisions. Selling her house and moving away was one of them. Liza picked up the call and immediately said, "Oh Beth, thank god. It's Ronnie, there's been an accident. You're closest. I'll tell you what I know and then you take it from there."

So it was that by 4pm that afternoon Beth was at the intensive care unit of Ronnie's private hospital waiting to be allowed in to see the mangled and desperate body of her friend. George was there and had greeted Beth with great warmth. He was stunned and disbelieving. His marvellous Ronnie was lying in a coma and clinging to life with a barely visible thread. Machines all around her monitored her progress, or lack of it, and made comforting beeps which matched the visual displays. These presented a confusion of information the nurses seemed to find reassuring. Ronnie was now into her second twenty four hours of intensive care and the doctors were guardedly non-committal. George had been back and forth to their home only once in that time. His daughter had been at his side but she needed to make arrangements for her family and was temporarily absent. He was very pleased to see one of Ronnie's old friends. Their social circle was quite wide but just at this moment he wanted none of them to see her in this state. It wasn't a rational decision but he was running on instinct and cared not whether his decisions on irrelevant matters caused any social rifts. Their close friends understood and respected his wishes. They would be there when he needed them. He knew that Beth and the others were very important to Ronnie and so he welcomed her and briefly filled her in on the accident.

Despite his daughter being very understanding, George had felt rather isolated. Ronnie's sister was abroad and they had not yet managed to get hold of her. She was travelling with her husband and was currently on a small yacht adventure in the seas off China. The holiday opportunities that were opening up in the former hotbed of revolution were legion and Ronnie's sister had always been first in the queue for ground breaking adventure. He couldn't think about his sister-in-law for the moment but he wished she had been close by. She and Ronnie were very close and fought and loved with great passion because ultimately they loved each other. There were no half way measures with the sisters, everything was done with absolute commitment or they considered it just not worth their precious time. Beth had known Ronnie since they were children and so George thought she was the next best thing to family. He wanted a prop and he knew Beth was a compassionate and caring friend, even if she was generally thought to be understated. He reflected on the mousey woman who sat beside him in the hospital corridor. They had previously been in the family room but had wanted to be near to Ronnie so they chose the uncomfortable steel and plastic pristine chairs outside her room.

In contrast to Ronnie, Beth was small, neat and quiet. Her still presence was a balm to him at this time of crisis. He prayed as he had never prayed before that Ronnie would come back to him. Selfishly he was desperate to make amends for their last few weeks of heartache. At the same time he couldn't bear the thought of her suffering great torment. He was unsure which of the emotions was stronger. They ebbed and flowed as the tide with the vagaries of the moon. Beth touched his arm and asked, "Would you like a coffee, or tea?" Even this gentle intrusion seemed too much and he turned a haunted face towards her, "No, not now." Beth got up and went to find some refreshment for herself. She had rushed out with barely a thought of lunch and suddenly felt in need of sustenance. Liza had said she would come up as soon as she could, bringing forward their planned time together. Beth was hungry for her good friend's company and went outside to check her 'phone for messages. Liza had left a text informing Beth that she would be at the hospital by early evening. This information brought a new composure to Beth and she felt she could cope with George and his formidable daughter for a few more hours. Jane was very much like Ronnie in her dynamism and energy. This was quite possibly a factor in their apparently cool relationship; they were just too alike to really bond. They both needed to be top dog.

When tragedy strikes one's thoughts often turn to the truth. Beth's thoughts at this moment whilst she was back in the corridor, sipping a very hot, awful tasting, coffee turned to Ronnie and Maddy. She was very fond of both of them. Both very strong characters she pondered on why Maddy had made so few reunions compared to the rest of them. In a moment of clarity she thought it was because of Ronnie. Always bossy Ronnie 'took over' and Maddy, not wanting to spoil those rare days, decided not to rock the boat, and so stayed away. Beth was convinced that she was right and her thoughts ranged back to all the reunions they had over the years and their school days when their friendship was cemented.

91

CHAPTER SIXTEEN
Flashback

As Beth sat in the rather plush discomfort of the waiting area for some sign from the nursing staff that they could go in and see Ronnie she reflected on their schooldays. She had often wondered at the unlikely group that they became with all their different personalities and outlooks and backgrounds. Maddy and Lucy had been the first to acknowledge a deep friendship. They lived within a street of each other and Maddy's home was always welcome to her friends. Her mum had been a housewife and had no formal qualifications from her schooldays. Her parents, back in the 1950s had not believed in encouraging their daughter to achieve at her lessons. Maddy's uncles had all been bright scholars and two had even gone on to university when they left school in the 1960s. People from less affluent backgrounds just did not do that sort of thing. They went into trade and got by as best they may. Maddy's grandparents had been so proud of their sons and equally glad that they had a daughter who could stay at home and look after them when they got old. Unluckily for them she had met and married a man who also wanted to be looked after. Maddy's mum was caught nicely in the web of expectation and emotional manipulation. She had two children, Maddy and her brother. Her whole life was taken up with cooking and cleaning and, when she had time, reading. She devoured all books with a passion that had gone so long unchecked that she knew so much about so many things. It was unfortunate that she treated her children much as she herself had been treated. Maddy's brother was encouraged and cosseted whilst Maddy seethed and achieved all by her own endeavours. This inequality did not drive a rift between the siblings that took an aggressive turn; rather it was resentment buoyed up by seeming indifference. It took them until they were well into their early twenties before they fully reconciled their love and support for each other. Her brother had emigrated to New Zealand in his thirties and there had been rare but emotional holidays of filial affection.

Beth had been an only child. Her parents had been considered older than her friends' and so she had been brought up in a fairly conservative and 'old fashioned' way. Not for her the new delights of going to discos. Not for her the new fangled denim jeans that everyone but everyone had to wear. No, what was good enough for her parents and grandparents was good enough for her. Besides there was little money about and surviving and paying the rent was a hard enough struggle. Council housing in those far off days had not the stigma that it had acquired in recent times, now being, perhaps unfairly, associated with run down crime ridden estates where there were 'no go areas' and the police went around in pairs or not at all. These thoughts flitted through her mind and she mentally made no judgement except that she was glad she had been able to buy her own home and give her mother a comfortable end to her days. The image of death brought her sharply back to the present and her friend, lying in a state that was half way between life and death and no one could second guess the outcome.

George sensed that Beth had come back from her day dream and offered her, for the millionth time, another cup of coffee. This time she accepted. Getting ordinary everyday things was a welcome distraction from the waiting. Minutes seemed like days when the thing you are waiting for is so important and potentially devastating. As George went to collect the drinks his daughter, Jane, arrived and filled the area with her presence. "Where's Dad?" She almost barked the question at Beth. Realising that this was rather rude she added, "Thanks for coming, nice to see you. You're Beth aren't you? Dad told me he was going to call. Sorry if I sounded rude. I'm Jane." She held out her hand and Beth took it. "Hello. Yes, a bit abrupt but under the circumstances, may be understandable." Beth found that she did not warm instantly to George's daughter, but then there had always been a slight hesitation over the years when she met George. There was a command and an expectation of control in all circumstances that made her uncomfortable. She knew that Ronnie had many spats over the years with her step daughter. They were all too alike and used to getting their own way to ever be real friends. Beth decided to probe, "Do you know what happened, Jane?" Beth's voice was low and took some time to register with the young woman, "We were all at our reunion and had a brilliant if eventful day." Jane answered somewhat distractedly, "No, not really. I rang Dad, I'd been away and was … and anyway he seemed worried so I went round and the police weren't far behind." She paused as if wondering how much to tell this virtual stranger, "It seems that some yob decided to steal a car and never gave a thought to the consequences." She spat out the words and walked away to find her father.

Beth asked the nurse attending Ronnie if she could sit in with her and she agreed. As she quietly entered the room she was astounded to see her friend lying so still with all the equipment hooked in to monitor her and keep her going. She thought as she watched Ronnie that it seemed as though the machinery was nothing to do with her and that she was just lying there trying to get some rest despite the beeps and hums. Tears came to Beth's eyes and she sat down at the same time reaching out to stroke her friend's hand. Very softly she spoke, "Hello Ronnie. It's Beth. You're in a bit of a pickle. I'm just sitting in for a while until George gets back with some coffee." Beth drew breath. She knew that the hearing is the last sense to go so she rambled on in hushed tones about the reunion and Lulworth Cove and the boat trip. There was no response from Ronnie so she sat back and watched for a short while. The relative peace was shattered by Jane who bustled in and said, "Dad wants to be alone with her." George's voice cut across his daughter's, "That's true Jane but Beth is a dear friend she deserves some kindness you know. Ronnie would want her to be here too." Jane coloured and once again apologised.

Beth sent up a silent prayer for Ronnie. She also snuck in a request to God to send her Liza as soon as possible. She considered that being the only one, 'non family', in such circumstances left one open to family hostility. This can be just misplaced anxiety which in this case Beth thought was generous. Jane, she felt, needed to be in control of her father. Of course she was losing him to cancer and that was unbearable for her so her natural instinct was to 'close ranks' and cope behind a veneer of efficiency. 'Liza, Liza, where are you?' Beth's thoughts sounded so loud to her that she thought for one awful moment she had exclaimed out loud. The time passed and she had no idea what the actual time was. She had come out of Ronnie's room and had wandered through the hospital in a daze. She glanced at her watch and saw that it was ten o'clock. She decided to take her leave of George and come back in the morning, when hopefully Liza would be with her.

As she drove away from the harrowing sight of her friend's life in ruins she reflected once more on their teenage years and their dreams and early promise. Well, at least they had lived their lives to the best of their ability and circumstance. They had all made choices and now, in the late summer, or early autumn of their days they were all coping with the consequences. Beth considered much as she drove home and came to the conclusion that there was still much to live for and she was going to make those changes she had begun and to hell with conventional expectations. She would confide in Liza and bounce her ideas off her. Whilst parking the car she noticed that the curtains were drawn and there was a light shining through the downstairs windows. Her front door swung open as she walked up the path and she was enveloped in a hug of gigantic proportions and overwhelmed by Liza's perfume, knowing Liza it was expensive and liberally applied. "Oh Liza its so good to see you. What a tragedy! Poor Ronnie. Let me get in and we'll have a drink and I'll fill you in."

"It's all ready I was waiting for you and I've done some supper. It'll be done in an instant. You OK old thing?"

95

"Mm. Not so bad. Good journey?"

"Yes surprisingly trouble free. You sit down in your own sitting room and I'll bring it through. You must be whacked"

Liza and Beth shared a very busy hour or so consuming their pasta and tea and then wine and cheese all the time managing to tell each other all about everything from Ronnie's accident to Liza's confusion and Beth's plans. The conversation bubbled and they interrupted each other and surprisingly laughed and chatted well into the night. "I found the bedroom you made up for me, thanks. Look, we've both had a huge day so let's get to bed and carry on with this in the morning. That's one big bombshell you've just hit me with." Beth laughed at Liza's reception of her ideas for life changes. "I want encouragement not drawbacks so sleep on it then tell me I'm not daft."

"Sleep well. Help yourself to anything you need."

"Thanks, 'night" two sleepy middle-aged women went wearily to bed and slept soundly. The best night's sleep either had had for a long time.

CHAPTER SEVENTEEN
Scottish Welcome

Maddy and Lucy, blissfully unaware of the trauma in the south continued on their journey of discovery in the soft warm light of an early summer Scottish morning. As they passed the border, an imaginary line drawn in the sand but with huge emotional emphasis, they drove in quiet, relaxed peace. The peace too was an illusion like the border. It was a peace that exuded excitement of the most thrilling kind, the excitement of the unknown. Maddy's unknown was her relationship with Bear and all the uncertainty of her intended move to the West Country. Lucy's unknown was more profound in that she had no idea how she would cope in her liberation. Indeed it was still unclear to her how she had got this far. Years of wanting had suddenly become reality and she was not a little scared. She was sure of her daughter's welcome and that of her son-in-law who had not been backwards in his condemnation of his father-in-law. Her grandchildren were little strangers as they had rarely come south and spoke with strong Scottish accents. It was this Lucy felt that set them apart. She would do something about that, with time.

The morning unfolded and embraced the travellers as they entered the strange world that is the border country. Seemingly empty the expanse of heathland on either side of the road brought with it a colourful 'otherworldly' hue to the still damp day. Maddy, as always was entranced with anything Scottish. Even the very heather seemed to say, "We know you're English but you're all right, come on in." This is how she thought of it. She briefly wondered if being Scots was like being English, a state of mind, or did one have to be born of the good stock and then, and only then could one claim any kind of Scottishness. The Scottish psyche was probably as complicated as any and her mind wandered round the issue of the 'fighting Celt'. Why was it that they all had such strong and bitter memories of 'old foes'? "Welsh and Irish all seemed to hate the 'Bastard English.' Historically this hatred may have some foundation but what was really true? History is notoriously written by victorious sides and often for political gain, so who does one believe?" Maddy gave herself a mental shake and decided such mighty questions were not for this morning and that she wanted to get Lucy to safety as soon as she could, without mishap and then she could revel in the luxury of mental debate with her own brand of argument.

Driving along through the southern part of the Scottish borders with a good feeling one gets from a substantial breakfast and a good night's sleep gave both the women a sense of well being such that when disaster struck they were totally unprepared for it. Their demeanour had been tense and suspicious whilst in England but now the change of country had given them a false sense of safety. Lucy's daughter was expecting them to arrive in the mid afternoon as the night previously Lucy had telephoned to say they would lunch on the way and arrive in time for a cup of tea.

The truck had pulled up by the side of the road so that its wheels were on the grass verge but the body protruded into the single carriageway causing any who wished to get past to pull out. It was unfortunate that as Maddy drove up to the offending vehicle prepared to overtake the man stepped out and waved his arms as if in distress. Later, when looking back, she was to think over and over again why she had stopped and not just kept going. He pulled a gun on the women and swiftly got into the back of the car and ordered them to drive on. He directed them to a dirt track that seemed to lead to nowhere. He was sweating and was unkempt, probably about twenty years old with long greasy hair pulled back into a ponytail. His accent was strong but educated Scot and he instructed the women in sharp brief sentences. Lucy had become like stone. Cold and unmoving she never once took her eyes off the young man and his offensive weapon. Maddy shook as she drove the car but kept an outwardly cool exterior. Only those who knew her well would know that she was frightened and becoming desperate. The dirt track ran out and he told Maddy to stop the car just inside the neighbouring field tucked into the hedge.

The silence when the engine of the car was turned off was overwhelming. The early morning was still beautiful, people still went about their daily routines and the world didn't stop. Maddy and Lucy looked at each other and then at their captor. He had started to shake almost uncontrollably, Lucy recognised desperation in his eyes and there was something else, was it pain? Perhaps it was but she was in no position to feel sorry for him, first they must get the upper hand. But how? Maddy was slightly slumped in her seat and was in as much shock as Lucy but somehow Lucy's stillness gave her time to observe and make a plan. Her own state of desperation, so long a shackle, had inured her to pain. Now she was so close to getting a life back she was damned if she was going to let a little thug ruin it for her. There must be a way out of this. Seconds had passed, not minutes or hours, just seconds. Their captive state was only temporary as some one who is as reckless as this man would probably not allow much time to pass before deciding on his next course.

The seconds ticked away when suddenly, into the silence that had befallen them came two distinct noises. Both of which made all the occupants of the car jump and react in distinctive ways. Maddy's mobile phone rang at the same time as the local farmer's dog ran up to the car and barked at the intrusion on his territory. This well trained border collie was walking with his master, as usual, round the fields and was intending to accompany him to the sheep and perform his usual tasks as and when he was told. Today they were taking the new young dog out as part of his training. The farmer was really looking forward to the day as he had got the dog from a neighbour and had high hopes of the youngster being a champion sheep worker. His pedigree was certainly a good one. The old dog was tired and his bones creaked a little on soft Scottish mornings when the mist melted into his old body. This young replacement would do a good job, he just needed some guidance. "What the bloody hell the car was doing on his land?" The farmer's thoughts almost shouted in his head as he went towards the car. "Bloody tourists. He'd soon have them off his land."

The crack of the gun shot through the senses of all the people who were involved, wittingly or unwittingly, in this increasingly dangerous and bloody scenario. The young man stared at the body that lay dying on the ground. The farmer raised his shotgun and fired at the car then flung himself to the ground to avoid any more shots that might come from the alien vehicle. The younger dog went to the now lifeless body of his proposed mentor and sat by him, sniffing him and occasionally licking him as if to bring him back. The death of the dog made Maddy so mad she turned and attacked the young man, picking up her mobile phone and hitting him on the head with it. Lucy joined in and wrested the gun away from his limp hand then threw the gun down on the floor of the car as she couldn't bear to feel the weight and coldness of the weapon. As Maddy turned to fight the young man the farmer's shot entered her side of the car and blood appeared all over the inside of the car and Maddy stopped fighting and slowly crumpled. As she lost consciousness her thoughts turned to Bear and her beloved animals. "Please God get me through this. I love him and there's so much to do."

Lucy heard someone screaming, realised it was her and abruptly stopped. In the quiet that ensued she thought she heard a man sobbing and swearing at the same time. She did. It was the farmer and he was immediately grieving for his faithful old dog, shouting vengeance at the group who had stolen his tranquillity and cursing the person who shot from the car. The young man was in shock in the back of the car, his weapon had been taken from him and he realised that for the first time in his life that he had taken a life. Temporarily he remembered his Granny telling him about the Bible and all those old fashioned rules she lived by.

"Well Granny, you'd be proud of me now. I'm a junkie, up to my neck in drugs. Supplying and the heavy. Once you're in, you're in. They'll not let me go now." He would have been surprised to know that his thoughts were spoken out loud. His self important ramblings were over heard by the two still conscious people, Lucy and the farmer.

Lucy made to get out of the car when she was aware of someone else on the scene. He seemed familiar but she couldn't place him. He was admonishing the farmer and whatever he said had some effect because he put down his gun and rushed to the car. Lucy hurried round to the side where Maddy was lying in her own bloody state and tried to find the source of the bleeding so she could try to stem the flow. A little blood goes a long way and initially it seemed as though no one could have survived the carnage. That word popped into Lucy's mind and refused to leave. It wasn't carnage but she was in a state of shock and would hold onto her own thoughts for the moment. Gentle but firm hands pulled her away from her friend's prone body and quietly took over her care. She sat down on the slightly damp ground and stared at the lifeless body of the sheepdog and wept. The farmer had the young man in his grip and was restraining him in a rough fashion, intent on causing him the same hurt as he had inflicted. Somewhere inside the farmer his own decency and sense of right and wrong surfaced and had a struggle with his innate desire to floor the perpetrator of such a senseless action. He was still deciding what to do when another person arrived on the scene and took control. This latest arrival was the local constable who had received a call about a disturbance up on Downie's farm. He was a friend of Ian Downie and immediately took the young man away from his friend. He could not bear to see him charged with assault on top of everything else. Soon he would be handcuffed and in the patrol car. This was way out of his league but he would have to cope until the detectives arrived.

The early summer sun continued to shine, young Gil continued to sit by his old friend and whimper, Lucy continued to weep and Maddy continued to bleed.

101

CHAPTER EIGHTEEN
Beth and Liza Make a Pact

They had breakfasted well and were on their third coffee. Both knew what the day would bring, or thought they did. There would be the seemingly endless wait while nurses and doctors 'did their stuff'. Ronnie would lie as she had for the last two days joined up to the living world completely unaware of the fuss going on around her. People would be speaking in hushed tones as if she were already dead and Beth and Liza would want to scream with the frustration. Guiltily they considered how George would be feeling and how his life had done a complete about turn. He had been the one to stare death in the face and prepare for that final step, always with Ronnie by his side. Her not being there had never occurred to him. Sudden incapacity or death brings with it its own secondary shock factor and George had reached the point where he was still in some disbelief that the positions were not reversed.

Beth and Liza packed their copious handbags full of 'things likely to be of use whilst waiting around all day in hospital'. Some of these essentials included bottled water, light novel, crosswords, paper tissues, roll of mint sweets, tweezers and small scissors. Into the car went a small picnic of sandwiches and coffee and cherry cake. The pair were quite light-hearted as if going on a spree instead of watching their friend battle with life and death. Slightly guilty they spoke in reverential tones as they entered the hospital and took the lift to Ronnie's floor. As they came out of the lift Beth was aware of more commotion than last night in the corridor waiting area. George was standing as though pushed to one side, Jane was hanging onto his arm and trying to pull him gently away from Ronnie's doorway and the doctors and nurses were there in abundance wafting in and out with their measured professional way they all had when the chips are down. Beth feared the worst and Liza caught the mood very quickly. They walked quietly up to George and his daughter, "What's going on George? Jane?" Beth spoke to both of them in turn as she realised she was breaking into a tight circle of shock. As there was no immediate answer to the question she added, "You remember Liza, George, don't you? Jane I don't know if you've met before. She's here to see Ronnie." George, grasped his daughter's hand and started to walk away saying, "Come to the visitor's room Beth and we can talk." He smiled weakly at Liza and clung to his daughter as if to prevent her leaving. When, a few minutes later they were all sitting in the waiting room George spoke again, "She's taken a turn for the worse Beth. It's only just happened. As you can see they are all working hard to stabilise her." He shuddered to a halt and Jane spoke for the first time, rather rudely she ignored Beth and Liza and just said, "Dad, what do you want, do you want company or to be quiet?" As this was clearly a jibe at Beth and Liza the two friends looked at each other with surprise and rose from their seats. George stopped them with a wave of his hand while he admonished his daughter yet again, "Jane for goodness sake, these are Ronnie's very dear friends as you well know." Feeling this was harsh he added, "No need to protect me so much my dear, relax a bit will you and we'll get through this." He planted a kiss on her cheek and she sat back. George continued, "Anyway, Ronnie would want them to be here, I'm sure of it." Jane was only temporarily silent but she knew when to stop and regroup. She would always look after her very precious father.

Liza spoke for the first time since they entered the corridor, "Jane, we haven't met but please be assured that we have your father's best interests at heart. We won't get in the way and it might help if we're here to give him a break. I expect you're busy yourself, aren't you?" Liza could be very persuasive and intuitive. She had summed Jane up in a matter of moments and had decided that given a way out of the situation she would be loathe to take it as there was a little of the martyr about her. A polite but frosty reply from Jane came out in a staccato voice, "Thank you. We're grateful for your concern. I'll stay with my father for the time being." As an after thought she added, "I've made arrangements at home so I can stay until late afternoon." Secretly Beth thought, "Damn, we'll have a long wait and we'll have to try to cope with her anxiety as well." She was feeling rather low in emotional energy. What she said was, "How nice, we can all help each other then." Liza rose and offered to get everyone some coffee. This was generally accepted and off she went.

It was while Liza was gone that the doctor came in to talk with George, "We have made her comfortable for now. I'm afraid your wife has had a seizure and we are yet unable to evaluate the extent of the damage. She's now under constant monitoring. A nurse will be in the room at all times." George nodded his understanding of this news and the doctor patted his arm. He looked around at Jane and Beth and said, "Try to keep the number of visitors in the room to two at the most will you. It will help. Keep talking to her though. You never know."

"Is there hope then?" George made a desperate plea. The doctor shook his head at the same time as saying, "We just don't know, sorry." He left the room and the three of them sat and said nothing for a long time. There was no need; they all knew what he meant. Liza returned with a tray of drinks and biscuits, dispensed them and then sat down. She had picked up the mood but George explained what was going on to her anyway, it seemed to help him. As he spoke the awful words they took on a clearer reality that they all found shocking.

Beth and Liza had arrived at the hospital at about eleven o'clock in the morning. By the time two o'clock had come round they had all spent short spells in the room with Ronnie. They had all cried and hugged and helped each other, even Jane who seemed more accepting of the friends' intrusion as she saw it on her father's time with his wife. On the other hand she watched as he responded to their friendship and warmth and took comfort in their presence. Beth decided to offer to take George out to lunch with Liza and leave Jane on her own for a while. George declined and asked then to bring him back a sandwich and insisted that they went out for a break. As they drove away to find a nice pub for lunch they both felt a little guilty about leaving father and daughter alone in their individual misery. They found a nice hostelry and ordered the local speciality of fish platter and salad. They also asked the landlord to put them up some sandwiches and told him why. He was very obliging, well all trade was good trade was his maxim, and they sat overlooking a lake and trees and both sighed and settled into the plush chairs. They were emotionally drained and for a while said nothing, just sipped their drinks and gazed for inner balm on the world outside.

Liza broke the silence, "She's in a mess Beth."

"Mm. I know. She looks so different. I hardly recognised her when I first saw her yesterday. Dear God, was it only yesterday? It seems a lifetime." Liza looked at Beth in a strange way and asked, "Do you remember what you said when she drove out of the car park at Lulworth?"

"Yes, it's been plaguing me."

"Perhaps you've got second sight." Liza warmed to her theme, "Was your grandmother a witch or anything like that? How about that aunt of yours that no one ever speaks of? Didn't she die in mysterious circumstances?" Beth decided to humour her friend and replied, "My grandfather was a warlock and my aunt was burnt at the stake having first been subjected to a ducking stool. Honestly Liza, it was just one of those moments when somehow we humans seem to have more clarity than normal." Their meals arrived and they tucked in. With a break in eating her fish Beth continued, "Don't you think that we have use of only a small amount of our brain and that we've lost the ability to be as intuitive as our forbears? I sometimes think we are like computers. They say we only use them to 5 percent of capacity or something like that."

"Is it five percent, I thought it was fifteen."

"Oh it doesn't matter anyway. Ronnie's dying and whether I saw it or imagined it doesn't alter the fact of it."

"Come on, let's get back, time's running out I think." Then Liza added, "I'll sort out the bill, we'll discuss it later. No time to argue now. Come on." Her look brooked no argument so Beth went to open the car ready for a hasty departure.

As they neared the hospital the two of them felt anxious. As they walked along the seemingly endless corridors towards Ronnie's room their footsteps became more hurried. They didn't talk, they just walked with a purpose, unspoken but so plainly understood, their friend was dying and they must get to say goodbye. George was sitting with his head in his hands when they entered Ronnie's room. He had shrunk into his clothes and seemed to have lost weight. They'd only been gone an hour and a half. "George?" Beth broke into his misery with her soft voice and touch, "Is she ...?"

"No, not yet, but it won't be long, the doctor's hovering, he's in and out, oh my god Beth, she's going, she's leaving me, that sounds selfish, ..." How long he would have gone on in this way is debatable but Beth interrupted him, "George, hush. She may still be able to hear you. Let's tell her we love her shall we?" As Beth turned to look at Ronnie she saw Liza had taken Ronnie's hand and was soothing her with words of deep friendship and love, "Ron, old thing, you've been such a friend you know. There were times at school when I would have crumbled without you. We all love you. Do you remember Miss Inkpen? What a stinker she was! Stinky Inky! Always at me but she liked you and you stood up for me. What did she used to say, 'Girls, if you can't climb a rope you are fit for nothing in this life.' I can honestly say I have never felt the need to climb a rope in my entire life. Wherever you're going Ron, be happy." As Liza spoke these words Beth marvelled at how her non-believing friend had implied that there may be some kind of afterlife. What strange thoughts come in times of great emotional crisis.

Beth stood behind Liza and also took Ronnie's hand, "Ronnie, Its Beth, I'm here too. Liza's right, we do love you and I'm so sorry you've had this accident." Beth tailed off and wondered what to say then added, "Stinky Inky ignored me, I just faded into the background I suppose, but you were magnificent on the horses. Tall and athletic and I never saw anyone with so much spring at the vault." All three were silently weeping and were unaware of the doctor who had come in to check his dying patient. The vital signs were fading fast and he knew it was a matter of minutes not hours. He turned to George and said quietly, "Your daughter is back, do you want her in here as well?" He then added, "She asked me because she saw how engrossed you all were." At these words they all looked up to see a different Jane, a sad and lonely Jane who was scared. As she lost her step-mother she knew that soon she would also lose her father to the cancer that had taken hold. Tears were falling down her face as she went to her father and held him. "Oh Dad, Dad, Dad."

Ronnie died at four o'clock in the afternoon when the sun was shining and her beloved husband, step-daughter and close friends were with her. She liked that. She was sorry to go but she could hang on no longer. Her time had come.

Beth and Liza drove back to Beth's home having left George and Jane to deal with all the formalities. Their abiding memory of that final time with Ronnie would be of a lifeless body that seemed to bear little evidence of their vibrant friend and the stricken couple they had left behind in that futuristic room. Jane had crumpled into her father's frail arms and held him as if she thought he would fall over without her. In truth she had lost a friend and sparring partner in her step-mother. They had worked out a way of loving and coping with their own egos and fiery characters which made a bond as strong as any biological mother-daughter could have had.

Liza broke the profound silence, as they neared Beth's house, "We must not let the group fade away. Our number may be depleted but we must always try to make an extra special effort to meet up." Beth concentrated on driving and then concurred, "Yes. You're right; we owe it to ourselves as well as Ronnie you know. I just was so absent when she went through her tragedy. I commiserated but never offered to go and see her. I was so wrapped up with Mum at the time but, no, that's an excuse. I didn't want to face her. Seeing Ronnie bereft would have shattered our preconceptions." There was a pause then she added, "God how we've all changed!" Liza disagreed, "No I think you're wrong, we've grown up but fundamentally we haven't changed. Perhaps we have to find ourselves again. That's why I've been horrid to Edwin. How I wish he were here now." As they settled comfortably back into Beth's living room with a glass of wine in their hands Liza continued, "I'm going home tomorrow, Beth. I'll come up again for the funeral but I really need Ed now. I've got some serious apologising to do." "Well don't do too much; the issues are still there Liza." Beth was a bit peeved that she was going to lose her companion so quickly. "I had so much to tell you. It'll have to wait now but I've made some decisions. But first we must tell Maddy and Lucy. I'll call Maddy's mobile."

CHAPTER NINETEEN
Scotland Again

It would always be a source of confusion to Lucy, as she looked back over the events of that life changing morning, as to how quickly the emergency services were on the scene and dealing with the casualties. The main casualty was, of course, Maddy, who was deathly pale and had fainted. One of the paramedics who attended the incident was dealing with the farmer who was not only in shock from losing his dog but also from shooting someone, something he had never done before. His condition was not helped by his attack from Lucy who had sat shaking for a while then had been taken by an urge, so strong to avenge her friend's shooting that she ran at the perpetrator and beat him soundly until she was pulled off by the one person who had arrived at the scene and was not wearing any kind of uniform. He held her in a vice like grip but spoke words of such softness that she calmed down and ceased to struggle. He then continued to hold her as he put a car rug round her shaking and rather thin shoulders. She allowed herself to be led to an ambulance and was immediately taken over by a paramedic. She remembered nothing of the journey to hospital.

Maddy's condition was at first thought to be serious but not life threatening. She had been shot in the lower arm by the distraught farmer. Once the blood and mess had been cleaned the doctors discovered that she had a minor fracture below the torn skin and muscle. She would heal well but probably with some ugly scarring. There may be a need for skin grafts in the future but that would depend on how she felt about the wound and the necessary further pain that that would induce.

The farmer, Ian Downie, was treated for shock by the local doctor who was called in by the constable. As Downie refused to go anywhere for treatment the doctor made a visit and prescribed a sedative which he knew the man would not take. More likely he would drink himself into a stupor and try to bear the brunt of yet another blow to his quiet and difficult life. All the locals knew that his wife had upped and left him two years previously. She had tired of the loneliness. She had wearied of the endless moods of her husband brought on by the alternating drinking bouts and hard fruitless work. She had wept with frustration at the lack of money to go anywhere and do anything. She was a townie and all the surrounding farmers and their wives, shook their heads and tut – tutted at bringing in so feckless a woman to their world. They all said it would never last, and it hadn't. Mrs Downie had left with a tearful backward glance at the man she had fallen in love with, at the dogs she loved, at the lonely house and the beautiful but cruel land. Ian Downie always hoped she'd come back when she'd 'got it out' of her system'. It had been right to dream, it was his right to dream, because sometimes that is all the hope the lonely farmer had to sustain him in the heat and the cold. So it was that on this summer's day he was left with a young untrained puppy, a possible action against him for actual bodily harm and a bottle of whisky.

Robert McHeath was the engineer who had been at The Bridge Hotel the night before. He had given both the women his card and had set off just before them that morning to indulge in his hobby before proceeding home to Dundee where he was going to take a well earned rest. It was the first break from work that he'd had in a year. The engineering contract in the south was lucrative but involved and costly in terms of his personal life. He had parted from his long term partner in the summer when she tired of waiting for him to propose marriage to her. She was divorced and had so much emotional baggage that he wondered how he ever thought they could make a go of it. Ha had married in his thirties and then quickly lost his wife when she drowned in a swimming pool on holiday in Spain. He had not been back to Spain since and closed his life down to work and painting. His disastrous liaison with his last partner was the result of a blind date set up by well meaning friends. He was content now to go back to his engineering and his watercolours. It was in an attempt to catch the morning mood of the beautiful countryside that had drawn him to set up his easel and as he sat and started to paint he noticed the van half on the road and half off on the verge. It was a lonely piece of road and he considered it an intrusion into his chosen view. He waited to see if it would drive away and as he contemplated the rest of the scene planning which brush to use for each element of his painting his eye was caught by the approaching vehicle. Was it fate that made him stop at that lonely spot? Many eminent minds have debated fate versus coincidence ad nauseam but he was an engineer and so considered it a happenstance, a coincidence and a lucky one at that. He saw the hijacking of the two women and abandoned his easel as he rushed to his car and followed them. He called the police as he sped after the Lexus.

So it was that Robert McHeath was following the ambulance that carried the two friends to the local hospital. He had given his name to the police constable and agreed to go into the police station and make a statement when he had seen that the two women were all right. Why he felt obliged to do so he was unsure. He certainly didn't want any more complications in his life. He had had a lucky escape earlier that year so why did a pale faced and undersized mature woman touch him so. Obviously she was not well as her friend had been very protective the night before. A competent woman her friend seemed. He would consider why he was intrigued later but for now he had to see that they were well cared for, make a statement to the police and then go back and retrieve his painting equipment. What a start to his holiday! He was tired and longed to get to his home but he felt he could not walk away just yet. The two drunken business men from the hotel had wanted him to contract for a new job in Dubai. He had decided that they were not the kind of people he wished to work with and so had left them high and dry

111

the night before. There would be other jobs but he didn't know if that was what he really wanted. He was now in his mid fifties and wondered at retiring and travelling the world to indulge his love of painting. His sister and brother had been on at him for a while to stop working so hard and enjoy his life. They felt he was too buttoned up. They were both married with grown families and were worried about their younger brother and his rather nomad existence. They were pleased he was coming back to Dundee for his break as they could spend some time talking with him.

The small hospital was unused to gunshot wounds but they coped well and by mid afternoon Maddy was back in the recovery ward stitched up and beginning to come round from the operation. Lucy was in another ward for observation and was being treated for severe shock. She was sedated and was unaware of any visitor by her bedside. Robert didn't stay long as he just needed to know they were safe, he kept asking himself why he was concerned but came up with no answer. As he was no relation to either of the women he had difficulty explaining his interest. The police had informed the staff at the hospital about the incident and he had featured prominently as a bit of a hero. The scenes of crimes people had been to the site of the shootings and taken away the personal effects from the car. As Maddy's mobile kept ringing they answered it and informed Bear about the incident. This was done after they had checked him out. The fact that he was with the English police made this much easier. Bear immediately made arrangements for his son, Harry, to look after Maddy's animals and set out to be at the hospital as soon as he could. Lucy had nothing on her to indicate who her next of kin was so they had to wait for her to come out of the deep, drug induced sleep that would help her to heal and distance her from the nightmare of the hijack.

Having satisfied himself that the friends were being well looked after Robert McHeath set off for the police station to make his report. This done he then retraced his journey to pick up his gear and went on his way. He drove thoughtfully back to his modest but comfortable home in Dundee. It was very masculine and by the time he had settled back in he wandered round the house wondering what differences a permanent woman would make to the place. He must be tired he thought as this was the last thing on his mind. He showered and went out to his favourite pub for a beer and a nice fattening Scottish fish supper. He was spare of frame so could afford the occasional foray into deep fried comfort food. He had arranged to see his sister the next day so he needed some sustenance to give him strength. He loved his sister but as she was the older sibling she was strong on 'bossy'. He considered it to be controlling whilst she considered it to be caring. The middle brother was often the peacemaker in these battles of will but the foundation of love and good nature between the three of them never let these spats get out of hand. His mother on the other hand was well into her seventies and as strong as an ox. She would welcome him home and try not to be affected by his single state. But then she would sigh and realise that her youngest son was a tightly buttoned down emotional time bomb and was best left alone. She had tried and failed to introduce him to eligible women. She now passed the baton to her daughter. A figure, she considered, well able to fill her own substantial matchmaking shoes.

When Lucy woke up it was well into the evening and the soft light gave a strange hue to the ward. Some lights had been turned on and there was a general buzz in the background. She struggled to sit up and felt very heavy headed. For a moment she had no idea where she was then gradually the nightmare of the day came back to her and she cried out for help. A nurse came hurrying up and held her hand soothing her with indistinct words until she calmed down again. "Where's my friend? The one who was shot. Where is she? How is she? Please tell me she's ok."

"Now then, my dear, calm down," the nurse continued stroking Lucy's hand with her own, "Hush dearie," her soft accent was redolent with a soothing balm and Lucy turned her head to look at the ministering angel. "Thanks, yes I will calm down but please tell me about my friend."

"Well my dear I have it on good authority that it was only a minor wound and she'll be just grand after a wee while." Lucy visibly relaxed at this news and appeared to sink into her pillow. "You have a good night's sleep and then you can see her in the morning." She tutted and clucked

113

as she made Lucy comfortable and then left her to her drowsy thoughts and blessed sleep. Lucy slept a deep and renewing sleep, which could have had something to do with the sleeping draught she had been given, and awoke early the next day to find a policewoman and her daughter next to her bed, waiting for her to face the day.

Amy hugged her mother and kissed her cheek, "Oh Mum, what scrapes you do get into. How are you?" Amy brushed her hair from her forehead as if she were a child. "Amy, my love, you ..." Lucy smiled and cried and reached out thin arms to her rotund and beautiful daughter. "Hush Mum I'm here now. It'll be ok, you'll see. Angus will drive us home and you can rest. The kids are dying to see you." Lucy beamed then remembered the policewoman, "Why are you here? Do you need to talk to me about yesterday?"

"Yes Mm but we can wait if you'd rather until you get to your daughter's house."

"Oh please that would be better." Relief flooded through Lucy but then the policewoman added, "If you will just briefly say what happened we can fill in the blanks later." She was well aware that even a short time lapse can dull a memory, especially one that has suffered a shock as profound as this one. "Your daughter will stay, we've had a chat, we won't tire you too much, then you can visit your friend. We've already spoken to her." Lucy stumbled through the events of the previous day and sat back exhausted on the rather uncomfortable hospital bed. Amy decided to take control and asked the policewoman to let that be for the time being. She gave the address near Dundee where they would be and suggested that her mother got dressed before going to see Maddy.

Maddy had had a reasonable night. She was pumped full of painkillers and sleeping pills and so awoke to a bright summer's morning streaming through the grubby hospital windows. It was a depressing scenario that did not add to her feeling of well being. Her head was heavy and her mind slow, the after effects of the drugs leaving her dull in spirits. The police had wanted her to recall all the events of the day before but her sharp mind was not willing to go back to the trauma just yet. Her answers were hesitant and unsatisfactory. The doctor in charge of her case decided that enough was enough and asked the police to leave her for a few hours. It was a young and thrusting detective constable that was collecting the statement and he was reluctant to let go. For a few seconds there was a personality tussle between the doctor and police, fortunately for Maddy the doctor won the day and she was left in peace. Bear had arrived at the hospital the previous evening and made straight away for Maddy's bedside. After he had sat and watched her for a while he had left her in a deep sleep and checked into the local guest house. He arrived in the ward just as the policeman was leaving with a face of granite. The young man did not like being thwarted.

Bear had decided to take charge of Maddy until she was better. He had also come to a momentous decision about his future in the 'job'. He was in his very late forties and had enough of the stress, both mental and physical, that it put on him. He would talk to his boss and determine a get out strategy, the sooner the better. He would then try to persuade Maddy to... well there was time enough for that discussion. Today was about reassuring this rather lovely lady that he was there and would take care of her for as long as she wanted. He was also in a prime position to help shield her from jumped up detective constables. What hadn't featured in his euphoric calculations was that this particular detective constable was the son of the local superintendent.

It is a good thing that mankind often travels hopefully in blissful ignorance because if it was always clear what was in store people might never take that first step.

CHAPTER TWENTY
A Passing

It was ten days after Ronnie's death that George had managed to arrange her funeral. The days following her death had been a blur. He continued his own treatment for his cancer which caused him much pain. Without Ronnie somehow the pain seemed worse. Jane had tried to be all things to all people. She had been the prop that George needed, her husband, as usual, was busy at work and was working up to a brilliant deal that could not be put off even if his step-mother-in-law had died in tragic circumstances. Jane forgave him all his absences but she insisted he took time off to attend the funeral. Their children too would have the day off school to support their grandfather. Jane was a tower of strength. It was, however, a hollow tower and inside she was crumbling. It was a testament to her acting skills that none of her nearest and dearest knew anything of her inner state. Her children had been too young when their grandmother died but this was their first real brush with death since then and it needed sensitive and sensible handling if death were to be accepted as an inevitable part of life. After all, their grandfather was not to be long before his grave also beckoned to him.

Jane knew that she would suffer later, but for now she had to be the efficient rock to which they all clung. She had helped her father go through his and Ronnie's address books and invited all the people they thought would want to either attend or send messages. They anticipated that there would be about two hundred people who might try to come to the funeral. Luckily the parish church was a large Victorian monstrosity that held nearly three hundred. The caterers were booked, as was the local hotel, the proprietors of which were good friends and fellow Rotarians. She would have a good send off. George had helped their local rector write a eulogy for his wife. It was a difficult task as the temptation was to either become maudlin or over long. How to reflect a life in a few hundred words? This was George's dilemma. In the end he opted for brevity and sincerity. He would add one of her favourite passages from *Cranford* by Elizabeth Gaskell. It was the scene towards the end of the book where two old maids were chasing the sunshine as it warmed up the carpet in an effort to protect the floor from sun damage. This had always surprised him as it was totally at odds with how Ronnie had been in her life. "Life's too short to chase sunbeams!" This had been a familiar saying of Ronnie's but the book had been one of her favourites and she had read it many times. It was as though the totally different world of the Cranford ladies acted as a balm on her self imposed whirlwind of a business life. For some people of course, a short life chasing sunbeams would seem like paradise.

He and Jane had made so many 'phone calls that he had become as an automaton. People expressed their 'sincere condolences', their 'sorrow', their 'deepest sympathy' and every variation in between. He was not unappreciative but he stopped listening and just made noises of polite acceptance. He hardly knew with whom he spoke. Ronnie and he had discussed how he would like to 'go'. George had been adamant that he wanted to be cremated and then scattered over their garden. They loved their time in the garden together and as was their way, argued as much as they agreed on what to do when and what to put where. He had an especial Horse Chestnut tree that was a particular favourite and Ronnie had agreed to sprinkle him there beneath its branches. During their chats about his passing they had touched but briefly on hers. "George, in the unlikely event that I go first do not bury me 'neath the sod'. Promise me. Do what you like with my ashes but do not bury me." He had agreed and not pursued the conversation as it was a circumstance so unlikely that he had dismissed it from his thoughts. Now he had time to reflect

George had decided that his special tree would be good enough for both of them. She had been a free spirit and she would be happy there. Jane had suggested a casket that he could keep but as soon as she had spoken she realised that there would be no need as he would follow her in a matter of weeks. She bit her tongue to stop herself from crying and bustled about cooking her father a dinner he would probably not finish, or even taste. Jane kept a list of everything she had done, including all the likely pitfalls as she was only too well aware that she would have to go through this again and she could expect no practical help from her husband.

The school friends had all been notified and had sent beautiful letters of condolence and happy memories. Lucy's had been particularly sad and included the line, *"Dear George, … I thank God she is now at peace and with her beloved son. We all relied on Ronnie's sense of fun and her ability to make us laugh with her dreadful jokes. Perhaps we didn't always see the deep rooted hurt that never went away after your tragic loss."* Maddy had sent a card with a type written note as she still could not write with her damaged arm. It seemed so impersonal that George was a little hurt, deep down he knew he was being unreasonable. Jane in her new found respect for the women who were her step-mother's oldest and closest friends tried to make him understand but he was not to be comforted. Beth called personally with a card and an arrangement of flowers and seemed to Jane to be the one other person who could bring her father out of his deeply grieving shell, albeit a temporary relaxing of his guard but it was a welcome relief to her. Liza had written with great warmth and spoke of their schooldays when, *"…Ronnie stopped the awful bullying I received at the hands of the games mistress. She was an Amazon! I shall miss her so dreadfully…."* What Liza did that Jane so appreciated was to write to Jane separately and offer any support she might require. She even offered to come up beforehand to help with any arrangements. This generous spirit so touched Jane that she secretly broke down and wept. It is so often the kindness in extremis that breaks the dam of emotion.

The morning of the funeral saw the local community decked out in their finest black mourning clothes. Cars were parked everywhere and anywhere. The traffic warden was not on duty that day so there were no irate mourners at the end of the day. Beth was the first of the friends to arrive and take her seat half way down the main aisle of the church. She sat, dressed in darkest grey, and looked as insignificant as she could. It was her way of blending in until she felt confident enough to shine. Liza and Edwin soon joined her and their ample frames almost filled the pew. Edwin looked as uncomfortable in a suit as it was possible to be. Liza was stunning in flowing black satin and chiffon. The summer sun was warm enough to make it comfortable in the cool church so nobody shivered, except with emotion. Liza's hat was a triumph of the milliner's art and suited her pretty face. Maddy and Bear arrived next and sat behind their friends. Maddy's arm was in a pristine sling which made a stark visual contrast to her smart black suit. She looked pale under her make up and leant often on Bear's arm for comfort and support. He looked as though he were her bodyguard, ready to fend off anyone with evil intent.

What none of the friends expected was to see Lucy at the funeral. She had become lost in her daughter's care and none of them had heard whether she would attend. Her frailty was so etched in their minds from their last meeting that it had not occurred to them to expect her. Thus it was a pleasant shock to see a determined Lucy walk into the church holding her son-in-law's arm. Her daughter held her other hand and they guided her to the same pew as Maddy and Bear. Ronnie's coffin was smaller than any of them expected it to be. She had seemed so large in life that she couldn't possibly have fitted into that small space. This exaggeration of size was a testament to her forceful personality. As the coffin was brought in to sit in sad isolation at the front of the church, Jane wheeled her father in behind it, in his wheelchair. He could barely stand now and his frame was spare and unclothed in flesh. It was clear to all who were there that his time was very near. The service got under way to a packed congregation and all were surprised when the moment for the eulogy came and George was wheeled to the front of the main aisle.

119

He tenderly touched the coffin and turned to face the assembled crowd, "Dear friends, when my first wife died I thought I would never again find happiness in a partner. Ronnie swept into my life and made me whole again." George continued to outline their life together and tried not to become too sentimental. The people listening were astonished at the strength of his voice. It was incongruous coming from such a wasted man. Some wondered if he would last the day he seemed so frail. As he finished with a quotation that summed her up for him there was not a dry eye in the house; "This is from Lament by Thomas Hardy written about his first wife; 'How she would have loved a party today! Bright hatted and gloved, with table and tray and chairs on the lawn her smiles would have shone with welcomings …But she is shut, she is shut from friendship's spell in the jailing shell of her tiny cell.'" He turned to touch once again the coffin as he spoke the last words indicating her tiny cell. It was done. He could say no more. Tears streamed down his face and he crumpled. Jane took him back to his position by the front pew and held his hand.

The service was over and the coffin had gone to the local crematorium, accompanied by immediate family only, to be burnt. The wake was held in the opulent rooms of the local hotel. All was perfectly organised with discreet waiting staff moving silently among the guests. It was that time in proceedings when relief starts to take over and people begin to chatter and laugh and recall happy memories. Maddy and Bear were ensconced in a corner with Maddy seated as she still felt somewhat weak. Liza and Beth were standing talking down to her whilst Edwin went to arrange some chairs for them. Lucy had taken herself off to the ladies room where she could feel some space between her and the crowds. Amy and Angus were outside breathing the polluted air from the traffic and longed to be back in Scotland. They had left Lucy with her friends and felt no sense of alarm for her. She had said little about John during the last ten days but shivered every time his name was mentioned. Amy realised something had gone on that her mother could not yet bring herself to confide to her. Time would bring it all out she had no doubt. Patience was what was needed now not well intentioned bullying.

The conversation between the friends moved back and forth, concentrating on Ronnie and their memories of her. There were lots of, "Do you remember ..." comments and the small group dwelt on their schooldays with brief mention of their many reunions. It was some time before Beth started to miss Lucy. "Maddy, what time did Lucy go to the ladies?"

"She's been gone ages." This second remark was from Liza. Maddy paled even more than usual, "Go and find her you two. There is so much you don't know. Make sure she comes back here with you. I'll fill you in when we are all together. Hurry." Beth and Liza hurried away. The ladies room was occupied by a couple of other women dressed in mourning but neither of them had seen Lucy. She was not there. Liza even shouted at the cubicles and banged on the shut doors, "Lucy? Lucy? Are you in there?" Nothing came back except several muffled, indignant and embarrassed versions of "No."

As they left the toilets Liza said, "Where the hell is she? And what happened in Scotland. We haven't had the full story yet." Beth more calmly added, "No. I imagine it goes back much further than Scotland." The two 'detectives' searched the usual places in the hotel then went back to report failure to Maddy. Maddy was now clearly alarmed, "Have you looked outside you two? Keep looking." Away they went and this time searched the hotel gardens more thoroughly. Bear refused to leave Maddy's side until she begged him and reassured him that she would be all right and that she would not move. She felt so weak that she couldn't bear the thought of moving anyway. Her injury coupled with the death of her friend and all that had gone on since that fateful picnic at Lulworth seemed to have added emotion onto emotion so she didn't know what to grieve for first.

Beth and Liza walked round a corner of a hedge into a secluded part of the hotel grounds and saw Lucy being held in a vice like grip by an, as yet, unknown assailant. They cried out and rushed to help her. As they neared they saw it was her husband who held her and he was carrying a knife. He had it pointed straight at her stomach about six inches away from her. The pair stopped dead in their tracks. John's face turned to look at them and they saw it was suffused with hatred. Into this gruesome tableau came Bear who had come into the quiet area from a different direction. Thus it was that John did not see the new intruder. Beth had started to back away so that she could go and summon help. Liza moved forward to block John's view of her friend's intended departure. Bear signalled to Liza not to give him away by the time worn gesture of putting his fingers to his lips and shaking his head.

Beth managed to back off from the scene before John could utter a word. She hated leaving the group in various stages of terror but knew she had to get help. She raced round to where she thought Amy and Angus were, "Amy, its your Dad. He's got a knife. He's going to kill her. Please get the police and ambulance. Hurry." Amy took a brief moment to take all this in then said, "I'll phone. Angus, you go with Beth. I'll be there as soon as I can. Don't let him hurt Mum." Angus grabbed a large looking man who was standing outside the hotel, smoking. "Come, there's a crisis, please help." Such was the large range of friends that both George and Ronnie had acquired through their life in business that the man Angus drew into their drama was a magistrate who had been a Guards Officer. Used to dealing with many kinds of crisis, he had overheard and was already putting out his cigarette and calling for back up on his mobile 'phone.

So it was that within minutes of Liza and Beth initially arriving at the scene the crowd had increased to Liza, Bear, Beth, Amy, Angus and the magistrate. Within ten minutes the local police had arrived and there was an ambulance standing by. Liza had tried to stall John by talking to him. She was good at talking and he was temporarily distracted, although not enough to take his hand bearing the long bladed knife away from hovering near Lucy's stomach. Bear was inching his way round to where he could 'take' John. Amy and Angus arrived and joined in the exhortations to John to leave Lucy alone. To each effort at distraction from all the onlookers John replied to Lucy as though they were the only ones present. "So, you've brought all your friends with you have you." "You bitch. Why bring our daughter in to your scheming." "You devious cow, now our son-in-law will think I'm an evil bastard. You planned all this. I ought to finish you off right now." Lucy tried to speak but her mouth was so dry she uttered an ugly sound then stopped. Her face showed she was clearly in pain where John had firm hold of her arm.

The magistrate spoke using his best court voice, "Now then sir. Why don't you put that knife down and let's talk this through?" John glared at him. "I am sure we can sort this out in a more comfortable setting, just let the lady go."

"You're not a lady though, are you Lucy? You're a conniving bitch. Tell this, whoever he is, tell him. Go on." With this he twisted his grip on her and made her wince even more. As the police gathered slightly more tightly round the central characters, moving cautiously closer without seeming to move at all, Bear had got within striking distance of John and was about to tackle him when Lucy fainted, John turned and saw Bear. He recognised this great oaf as the one who had caused him much embarrassment the day Lucy left. It had taken him hours to extricate himself from the local detectives. John swung the knife away from the limp Lucy and lunged at Bear. The police were on him in a moment. Bear fought to keep the knife away and John was brought down. As Bear looked down at his arm he noticed blood dripping from somewhere but he felt nothing. He lifted his sleeve, saw a nasty gash and said, "Bugger."

Maddy and Jane stumbled into the arena and tried to make sense of what their eyes told them. Jane, exhausted with the physical and emotional exertions of the past weeks, shouted at everyone, "For God's sake this is a funeral. Have you no sense of propriety."

CHAPTER TWENTY ONE
Reflections

It had been a month since Ronnie's funeral. Lucy, Amy and Angus were safely back in Scotland. Maddy and Bear were happily back in Surrey with her animals. Liza and Edwin were busily dealing with a very good summer season down at the gallery and farm. But where was Beth? She was not in her house. Outside that place so full of memories and anchors that it had at times seemed like a prison was a board that said, 'FOR SALE'.

Beth had decided to sell up and move down to the West Country. She, as yet, had no idea exactly where she wanted to go but she knew she must move from the stifling suburbia that had nearly strangled her. She was a good cook and very practical. After a lifetime of number crunching for the local bank she needed and desired a complete change. She had given in her notice at the bank and they had asked her to delay that for a month longer than usual as they were making swingeing changes. To delay her departure would help them and they offered to make it worth her while financially. This she agreed to so that in two months from now she would be free of the bank and all the years of abject boredom. She had taken some more time off that was due to her and she headed for a haven that had impressed her very much. She checked into the Majestic Hotel under the safe banner of Marjorie and Alfred. They were pleased to see her and made her welcome. As it was nearing the height of their season she had a smaller room than before but it was well appointed and all she needed. It seemed that she had taken the last of the rooms, the hotel was full and Marjorie and Alfred were kept on the go from morning to night. They had seasonal help but it was still a very busy time.

Marjorie and Alfred remembered the women from their time of the Lulworth Cove picnic. They had mulled over the rescue many times with the coxswain of the lifeboat that rescued them as he, the coxswain, was distantly related to Alfred and was a frequent visitor to their hotel. James Trevelyan was a sailor born and bred. He had lived all his life in the county of Dorset and ran a small chandlers business as well as a charter boat service. It had never made him rich but it had made him happy. To be associated with seafaring folk of all ages and gender and persuasion was his idea of heaven. They swapped stories and information, goods, money and advice. Friendships were made on no more than a discussion about sheets, cleats and hawsers. He knew the sea around the southern shores as well as any. Any crew sent out with him on a rescue trusted him completely, literally, with their lives. He had been defeated only a few times when the sea claimed its victims. These he felt keenly but he had never failed in his duty to go back out the next time he was called.

James, Jim to his friends, was well into his fifth decade and was a widower. His wife had been a trouble to him in that she nagged him unmercifully about giving up the sea. In the early days of their marriage he had been so in love that he would have given up anything, anything that is except the sea. It was in his blood. His father and grandfather and his grandfather before him had been sailors. Jim and his wife argued incessantly about the unreasonable nature of her request. What gradually emerged was the fact that her grandfather had been killed at sea and she was desperate not to lose her own husband in such a way. The tragedy of this was that she lost him to her own anxiety and fear. It was eventually an unhappy union. This unhappiness made the grief when she died altogether more intolerable as it was suffused with guilt that he had not loved her more.

The ten years since her death had brought no new companion. He had kept all at arms length, even his son and daughter. They met regularly and enjoyed each others company but he was a closed book emotionally, except when at sea, then he became alive. There was one further exception who could open up his shuttered heart, the one other person who could enter his world and tease him and cuddle him and love him unreservedly and that was his granddaughter. It was a touching sight to see the older man and this little toddler walk by the sea. He would tell her stories about anything and everything associated with his life at sea. He would embellish where necessary to make her laugh or gasp with delight and fear.

Beth had been at The Majestic for a few days and had been looking round at all the local estate agents and had scoured the local papers for suitable jobs. She had been busy and happy and full of hope and anticipation. So it was a jolt to her feeling of well being when, one evening, she was sitting in the bar enjoying a glass of wine before her dinner, she recognised the coxswain of the boat that had rescued her and her friends. In truth she had been putting off her other mission in this part of the world. She had intended to seek out the crew and apologise and make a donation to the Royal National Lifeboats Institution. This particular evening, there he was, she could never forget his face as she had cowered under his glare when he had told the women how stupid and foolhardy they were that day. She very quickly drank her wine and went up to the bar where he had just sat down to enjoy a pint of Alfred's best. "Excuse me, I , um, you probably don't remember me but.." Jim looked round and looked and said, "No, I don't." Rudely he turned away and carried on drinking his beer. Beth went very red and hesitated. She didn't know whether to carry on or slide away in embarrassment. Marjorie came to her rescue. "Jim, don't be so rude. This lady was one you rescued down at Lulworth Cove about five weeks ago or so. She probably wants to thank you or something."

"No thanks needed. I'll go out when I'm called and do my duty. No need for anything else." Saying this he turned and saw that he had been rather brutal in his handling of this woman as she had positively shrunk inside her clothes and was turning away. "I just wanted to thank you and your crew." Beth stumbled out the words then with more dignity than she felt she drew herself up to her full height and said, "You may not appreciate my words but please tell your crew." As she turned away she looked back and said, "I'll send a donation to the RNLI but it will be for your crew's honour not yours." Shakily she walked out of the bar and up to her room where she collapsed shaking onto the bed. She had no idea why his rudeness had affected her so badly. She was used to rebuffing angry people at the bank. Perhaps it was because she had rehearsed the speech in her head so many times that she was disappointed not to have received a warmer acceptance.

It was not long before there was a tap on her door and she opened it to see Marjorie standing there with a tray of supper for her. "Sorry about Jim, he's a gruff old misery. Please don't let him put you off. Have your supper up here tonight but I'll expect you downstairs in future. Hold your head high Beth and he can't hurt you. He's hurt many another unfortunately. Haven't time now but I'll tell you his story tomorrow when things are a bit quieter. Sleep well." She shut the door and walked away to finish the dinners and give Jim a piece of her mind. She was too late for that because Alfred had scolded Jim for being rude to the guests and so Jim had taken himself off. "He'll be back tomorrow night. He won't miss the jazz night, He never does unless he's called out. Don't worry Marj. We'll sort it."

"OK. I wonder why Beth is here now. She said it's just for a holiday but Jean at the estate agent said she's been asking about property and there's lots of local papers in her bin every day turned to the jobs vacancies. Putting two and two together I think she's thinking of a fresh start. I must find out more from her when I've got time." "Marj now don't go interfering. Let people alone." Marjorie's only response to Alfred's entreaty was a smile as she tapped her nose in a sign of secrecy.

Beth woke up with such a happy heart that she wondered why. Then she realised that the confrontation with the lifeboat people had been weighing her down. Now it was over and she could get on with the rest of her business down here. She really liked it but knew that it takes a long time to get to be accepted in a new place. That morning she decided to tell Marjorie what she was up to. It might be nice to have an ally and anyway she needed them to take messages about her house sale back home. Once she had told her new found friend (who had received the news with great and genuine delight) she felt relieved and decided to walk along the coast and just drift. It was a beautiful day with just the right breeze so it was not too hot. It was well into the afternoon when Beth stopped to sit on the cliff path and reflect on the events of the past few weeks. Lucy was making good progress in Scotland with her family. She had a letter from her and she was getting stronger and more confident. John had been arrested. It seems that Cynthia had found a younger and richer man and dumped him just after Lucy had gone to Scotland the first time. Having been on his own he had decided that Lucy was the cause of all his ills and had sought her out. His task was made easier by Jane. She had not known that there was a rift and so had left a message about Ronnie's funeral on his answer machine. He had known that Lucy would go if she could and so had turned up with a view to taking her home. When she refused to even talk to him he got a knife from the hotel kitchens and had a 'red mist' moment.

Beth lay back on the sweet smelling cliff top grass. "Wow" she thought, "What a life Lucy has had. Not one to be envied." Hers on the other hand had been predictable and dull and safe. Her own fault no doubt but she wished for some adventure, as long as it was a safe adventure. She was not brave and daring but she was bright and kind. People like her just did not have adventures. She sat up as the sun went behind a small cumulus cloud and noticed two people heading in her direction along the cliff path. A young dog was running ahead of them which suddenly disappeared over the edge. The man of the couple tried to look over to see and possibly rescue the dog but he slipped and also disappeared from sight. The woman was distraught and when Beth ran up to her was almost hysterical. "We've only just got him, please do something." This was said amid gulps and sobs. Beth rang 999 on her mobile and asked for help. Once she had done this there seemed little that she could do. She was trying to calm the woman down and make her wait but the woman seemed to want to go where her companion and puppy had gone. Beth tried to physically restrain her but she was young and strong. Beth didn't think she stood a chance of stopping her but from somewhere she found the strength to hold onto the woman who was becoming increasingly volatile, "Let go of me you bitch, bitch, bitch." With this last word she collapsed and sat on the cliff top sobbing. Beth was affronted as she was only trying to help. Mentally she switched compassion from the woman, who she now decidedly did not like, to the puppy and the man. She wondered where they were and edged forward to try to see where they were.

As Beth slid towards the cliff edge she wondered at her own lack of care, she had left the woman to fend for herself. If she went over, so be it. She could just see a man's leg hanging over a sort of rocky shelf; clearly he was not dashed on the rocks below. The leg was moving and so she had high hopes he was not dead. Perhaps the puppy had suffered the same fate and would be rescued. Beth brought herself back to the safety of the grassy path and turned to tell the woman what she had seen. The woman had passed out and was flat on her back. Beth remembered some half forgotten first aid she had been forced to go through at the bank. She struggled to get the young woman into a sort of recovery position. Finally she got her facing downwards and up on one arm. It was a timely act as the woman was then sick all over Beth's trousers and shoes. "Well thanks a bunch for that." Her disgust showed in her speech. A rather stentorian voice offered, "Don't blame her it'll be the hysteria." Beth swung round to see a policeman on a motorbike just behind her. Why and how she hadn't heard him she could only wonder. "Thank god you're here."

The policeman got off his bike and immediately went towards the edge as far as he could without going over, "Charlie delta to Charlie fox, I'm at the scene. One woman unconscious, one in attendance, haven't had a chance to speak to her yet. We are two miles east of High Point on the cliff top." He broke off his conversation into his radio, "Go over there did they?" He pointed to the exact spot. Beth nodded and pointed,

"Yes, first the pup…" she got no further, "Just a minute madam, yes they went over, if you pick us up from the helicopter, one is in green and the other in black." He stopped speaking and then turned to Beth, "What did you see?" Exasperated, first at having her idyll interrupted, then at being insulted and the vomited on, then the final straw was to be shushed by the policeman when she was only trying to help. "I was trying to tell you." She paused, "Come now madam this is an emergency."

"I know," she almost shouted at the man, "I saw it, first the puppy then the man. She," Beth indicated the prone woman "was hysterical. I looked over and…",

"That was rather fool hardy madam." This censure was almost too much for poor benighted Beth, "I was very careful Officer, I'm not a fool." She started to walk away, "Madam I need your name and …" "Yes, yes, all right. Look I've tried to help and just got insulted." Beth stopped and sighed the largest sigh and gave in. "Officer, just ask me what you want to know." This had all been but a matter of moments. The rescue helicopter was over head and things were starting to happen. They had been joined by others. All was action and calm efficiency. Beth was obviously in a state of shock. She had not noticed any of the forces gathering and building up to a rescue. She sat down on the grass and was immediately covered with a blanket by a kind paramedic who had noticed the signs of shock. The compassionate woman, who when praised would say she was only doing her job, comforted both Beth and the formerly hysterical woman. This she seemed to accomplish with hardly any effort and both women were quiet and calm within minutes.

An hour later it was over. The man who had fallen had sustained a broken leg and was being transported to hospital. The puppy was unharmed but shaken and was back in the care of the woman. She held onto the puppy so tightly that it struggled and struggled until she was given a piece of rope by the police and told to get a lead for it as soon as possible. Statements had finally been given to the police motorcyclist who had been first on the scene. Beth was checked over and declared fit. As she was still rather numb another police offered her a lift back to the hotel, which she gratefully accepted. As she sat in the lounge of the hotel, drinking a strong coffee laced with brandy (one of Alfred's specials) she reflected on her spoilt day. It was beautiful weather, Dorset was at its loveliest with her green hills and dramatic unforgiving coastline and she wanted to drink in all of it. She felt cheated of missing even one part of one day. Up to this moment Beth had known she was searching for something and had thought it may be found in this peaceful part of England. With a Damascene revelation she now knew with utmost certainty that she had found where she wanted to be. Her exercise in trying to find somewhere to be at home and at peace now had new force and determination. Like a zealot with a newly confirmed faith she set about finding a new home and fresh employment with renewed energy.

That evening Beth was in the bar and was talking to Alfred about her plans. She had previously hinted at her intentions but now she shone with a new light. "What sort of work are you looking for then?" Alfred's enquiry was not just polite interest. He and Marjorie were struggling with casual labour and the success of The Majestic was increasingly putting a strain on both of them. "Oh I thought I'd see ..." Alfred couldn't wait, "We need help here d'you see?" Unusually for him he seemed embarrassed, "I expect you'd want more..."

"No, no don't apologise. I'll try my hand at anything. What did you have in mind?" Unseen Marjorie had come up behind Beth, "Anything and everything. Can you cook?"

"Yes and I'm not bad at figures." She laughed, "30 years in a bank. Must've rubbed off." Marjorie hugged her and Alfred joined in. "Let's talk in the morning. OK?" "Right. How about another glass of wine to celebrate?" Beth agreed and it was the start of one of the most pleasant evenings she had in a very long time. She didn't even mind when Jim the coxswain came in and congratulated her on her part in the cliff rescue. He was still gruff but no longer rude. Perhaps it was the wine on top of the brandy but Beth was dancing on air and felt a match for any bluff seaman that night.

CHAPTER TWENTY TWO
Devon Again

Liza and Edwin settled into life in their Devon idyll very quickly after the first shock of Liza's outpourings following the reunion picnic. They had hardly had time to assimilate the awful news and revelations when she suddenly took off to stay with Beth which had ended with Ronnie's death. It was all too much and so, clutching at a kind of normality, Liza and Edwin became exactly what they had been. Outwardly they were a happy hardworking loving couple; inwardly a mass of seething unresolved issues. The season was too busy for much heart to heart talking. Tom had finally got proper joint custody of his children and was almost back to the happy son he always had been. Somehow this made Liza more discontent. Edwin, being the sort of person for whom no discussion was bliss, was shocked one evening when Liza informed him that her demands were still on the table.

"But Liza love I thought you ..."

"No, Ed you don't think."

"But darling I ..." Edwin dried up. He was once again lost. After years of confidence and apparent happiness, he knew not how to enter his wife's world. Suddenly he could take no more, "I'm off. Tom needs a hand. Do what you like." He stormed out leaving Liza in tears, of anger.

This was not what she had hoped for. She wanted to take Edwin with her on her journey of discovery but she now thought he would be a most unwilling partner. Another thought struck her, she must act now or the moment would have gone. She made a 'phone call.

Lucy took the call and listened to her friend's voice describing a wonderful offer. "Was she ready? Did she think she could cope?" Thoughts raced through her like quick silver and she prevaricated, "Liza, you must give me time to think it over. Its been one hell of a year." She rambled on, "John's case comes up soon and I must go to it. He must not get the better of me any more. No more running away. I'll call you when I've decided." This was a new Lucy, a strong Lucy, a Lucy who had nearly suffocated in her marriage and who was not going to be brow beaten again, even if it was by a friend with good intentions. Lucy turned to her daughter and said, "God I feel good," smiling she hugged Amy then left the room. As Liza put the 'phone down she muttered, smiling "Well, well, well, well, well, she's cured." With that she went to make peace with Edwin and try plan B.

As Liza approached Ed he looked up, "No more. I'll take no more today."

"Ed, I just…"

"You can just want on your own. I don't know what you do want. At the moment I don't care. Leave me alone." This was not going how Liza had imagined. She had always had what she wanted. Ed had denied her very little. Whatever they could afford she had. She went off for a bit of soul searching. Perhaps Beth would be able to help, she was always a good listener. As she dialled Beth's number she remembered she was away in Dorset. Beth hadn't been very explicit but she supposed she needed a holiday after the last few weeks. Well, Liza thought, after all the years of devotion. It had been a tie and a mill stone but she had never once shirked from her duty and she considered that Beth had loved her mother although she'd been a trial in the latter years. Liza suddenly felt very alone. She had everything, so what was missing. Was it really an adventure in South America or something deeper? Did she still love Edwin? What a silly question. Of course she did. Didn't she? Liza wandered over the farm towards the river that ran through their pastures. She sat down and felt the water cool the air as it played over the river bed. The summer evening was drawing in as she sat and contemplated what a horrid ungrateful person she had become. Edwin had given her his all. Still she wasn't satisfied. She'd become a bossy, interfering, ungrateful old has-been.

She fled back to the barn where she'd last seen Edwin, eager and very anxious not to lose him. Somehow someway she would fulfil her early dreams but not by losing Ed. She had to tell him before it was too late. Her plump little body moved with the grace of a young gazelle although rather more wobbly as she entered where Ed and Tom were discussing the next day's tasks. "Ed, Oh, Ed, I'm sorry." She crashed into her husband, took him off balance and they ended up in the muck and straw. As they sat up covered in cow dung they started to laugh as they realised what fools they were. Tom said nothing as he was too hysterical to speak. "Ed, I'm going to write a book. Then we'll go to South America." Whether Ed's sigh was one of relief at not having to trek the world to find what he had in Devon or that he had his wife back he wasn't sure. He just felt relief. He didn't believe for a moment that she would write a book but he would patronise her and wait until she decided on something else to occupy her. At that moment Liza gave in to the final compromise. Keep Edwin and what she had or give it all up for a long buried dream. Liza kept her dream buried. It would eat away at her but she would stamp and rage and then give in again.

Liza walked back to the house to have a bath and get rid of the smell of cow. As she walked she knew she had capitulated too soon and too easily. Ed would always get his way because he had no imagination to even try something different. He would be lost. Liza sighed a deep heartrending sigh and wondered achingly if the next generation would remain unfulfilled or would they have the courage to reach for the moon. "Now Voyager" with Bette Davies came into her mind. She thought about reaching for the moon but instead had settled for the stars. The moon would have to wait.

CHAPTER TWENTY THREE
Maddy's Dilemma

"What a start to the summer!" Maddy was sitting in her garden with faithful Nimbus by her side and the ever more faithful Bear cooking up a storm on the bar-b-q. He liked the challenge of providing decent bar-b-q food for a vegetarian. Maddy had revelled in being looked after but she was restless and getting irritated with her recent incapacity. "I was a fool to stop for that young addict," she spat the words out and they were full of self remorse, "I ended up getting shot and god knows what its done for Lucy. She…"

"Stop right there Mad!" he used his work voice, full of command and expecting to be obeyed, "You must not blame…"

"But I do and don't shout at me as though I was a rookie under your…"

"Well don't act as though you have no more sense than a roo…"

"I will not be shouted at I …"

"I shouldn't have given you that wine before eating its gone to …"

"No it hasn't I've been mulling this over for hours." Bear carried on cooking and said nothing. He took a long draught of his beer and glared at her. He had decided ages ago that he loved her but he found her independence a challenge. He was used to being obeyed and she was not used to taking orders. Why should she? She was a successful career woman with enough spirit and money to live well and certainly did not need to be treated to subjugation.

Bear found her difficult to read. He so wanted to take care of her but she wanted, what? He wasn't sure that whatever it was he could give it to her. Or that she would take it from him if he could. She suddenly added, "Then Ronnie. What an end! She was a mad driver you know. How the hell she was never prosecuted, well I do know." She paused, "Mason's look after their own don't they." She was looking for a reaction from Bear. He looked up and realised what she was fishing for, "Why don't you ask me out right."

"OK, are you a mason?"

"No." Bear thought for a while then said, "Would it have been a problem if I were?" Maddy decided that very simply she had to explain, "I was passed over for years in my first chambers because I was a woman and therefore not one of the chosen elite. It may be different now but it rankled and still does. So yes it would matter. I hate secrecy and I've seen it lead to injustice." Bear arranged her meal on the plate. Maddy continued, "It was a bit of a stumbling block between me and Ronnie." She sighed, "We decided not to discuss it." We've all been friends for so long but we've kept secrets from each other and I tended to avoid some of the reunions because I was at odds with some of them."

Bear asked, "How?" She seemed inclined to talk so he let her; he thought it might help her shake off this rather desultory mood. "Oh, that with Ronnie, then animal rights with Liza. Beth sometimes seemed to lead such a dull drudge of a life that I felt I could scream for her. As for Lucy, well..."

"I've seen it a hundred times you know," interrupted Bear, "its hard for a woman to get out of an abusive relationship. They seem to creep up on them then they are too tired or afraid to leave." Bear continued, "In the early days I found them the hardest to cope with." Maddy was about to talk but she had a mouthful of food so couldn't, Bear carried on, "Mum was a bit of a martyr."

The meal was over, the evening had started to turn chilly so they cleared up and went inside. Bear had stubbornly refused to say any more about his parents and Maddy was reflecting on how to broach the subject of her plans for the future. She wanted Bear in her life but at the same time she was scared of failure, she'd had so many. "Bear baby I think we need to talk about stuff." He kissed the top of her head and said, "Yes but not tonight, I'm going home for now and we'll talk tomorrow. There's something I want to show you."

"But I wanted to …"

"Well you can't. I'll see you tomorrow. Sleep tight darling." With that he went out of the door and left her speechless. "Damn and rotten blast!" Well, not quite speechless.

ii

Maddy woke up the next morning. She had slept but fitfully. After Bear had gone she had telephoned Liza who had been as helpful as a chocolate teapot and was herself in a state of frustrated euphoria. As far as Maddy could gather from her incoherent friend Edwin had stopped being a doormat and Liza had folded. She was going to write a book but not yet. Surprisingly, Liza seemed happy with this state of affairs. Maddy had asked, "What about your dreams and your longing for travels in South America?" Liza had given a most unsatisfactory reply of, "Oh well. We'll see. One day perhaps." After that Maddy had decided not to bother with her problems and rung off. After all what was her problem? She had a good man who loved her, of that she was sure. What worried her was her ability to commit to a relationship when all her others had failed due to her strong independence and purpose. Deep down she wanted a loving relationship but not at the expense of her own soul. She had seen too many women subjugate their own lives for the wellbeing of their family and friends.

She finally decided that today she would go in to the office and start to wind her affairs up so that she could fulfil her dream and move. She still harboured a dream of running an animal sanctuary. She would tell Bear this evening and then they would have a row and then they would break up. She would be single again and deal with all the inevitable heartache. She'd done it before and hoped that this would be the last time. Her reserves were quite low. She was very grumpy with the people in her office and they all decided to leave her in peace and let her work whatever was annoying her out of her system. The only person to try to engage in a meaningful conversation was her secretary. However, even the faithful and devoted Ann could not get through to Maddy and she eventually stopped trying. Years of devotion are not to be dismissed lightly and she could not resist buying her a sustaining lunch and coffee and leaving it for her when her boss had temporarily left the office for a brief moment. It was towards the end of the day that Maddy felt able to explain to Ann what was going on. She owed her that after all the time they'd spent together. Ann was not surprised and was not at all concerned about her own future. She was a brilliant legal secretary and would walk into another job tomorrow. Her parting shot to Maddy was out of character but hit straight to the point, "Whatever you do, be happy. Please give this one a chance, he's a poppet. 'Night."

"A poppet!" How on earth did she know Bear and what had he done to make her think of him as , "A poppet." Later that evening when she was getting ready to go out she rehearsed what she would say to Bear and how she would be as she walked away, yet again from another man before he stifled her.

Bear took Maddy to a restaurant that was famous for vegetarian food. It overlooked a mature and winding river from a vantage point on the green rolling hills that bordered the Surrey/Sussex borders. "Bear, I've got something to tell you and I..."

"Listen Love, I've something to say, let me go first."

"But, I..." she hesitated as she had built herself up to this point,

"Look Love, I need to get this off my chest before I explode."

"Well it'll be a toss up then who explodes first 'cause I'm the same, OK go ahead." Reluctantly she waited, her heart pounding with anticipation and sorrow.

"There's no easy way to say this." He paused for dramatic effect, "I'm leaving the force."

"Oh." She'd been expecting all sorts of declarations of love and such but not that. "Oh"

"Is that all you can say? Oh" He mimicked her tone.

"What will you do? Have you plans?"

He smiled and nodded, "Oh yes, I've already thought about it long and hard and..." Will you move away? Will it be far?" She knew she sounded a bit desperate but she was non-plussed to say the least. "I... I... thought you were going to .." She stopped as she knew she couldn't finish the sentence. "Oh I don't know what I thought," she added lamely. He was enjoying himself, rather too much for her liking, she liked to be in control and she realised she wasn't. He took a slow lingering drink of his wine and carefully put the glass down and twisted it in his fingers, "Actually I've bought, no, to be precise, I've put an offer in on a place in Wiltshire."

"Oh"

"That seems to be your favourite word this evening."

"Well I'm a bit lost really. I thought we had a good ..." she searched for the word, "friendship."

"Is that what we have?" Another dramatic pause then, "I thought it was a bit more than that."

"Well yes but with you going away I..." She could take no more, "Oh damn you. Whereabouts in Wiltshire? I've been looking there and..."

"I know." He laughed and decided to put her out of her misery, "Look I've been searching for the right place where we can set up your animal rescue place and live in a comfortable old farmhouse, its just been refurbished by the way and we could either live in sin or get married, what'd you say?" Silence. "Oh and by the way I love you, OK?"

Maddy now had to shift her whole thinking. This lovely man was offering her what she wanted and what she had worked for but he had taken the control away and that was scary. "Bear I love you too but I'm no good at marriage. I've failed three times and my other relationships, well, not a good record." She added in a fit of honesty, "I'm usually also in control, you've taken that away, whoosh" She imitated the action of

139

pulling the carpet from under his feet. She gulped her wine, coughed and then said, "Well I s'pose I could have a look at the place."

Bear sat back, the smile on his face could have been interpreted as a winning smile.

CHAPTER TWENTY FOUR
More Grief

Sometime in the middle of August, approximately two months after they had 'buried' Ronnie (well scattered her actually) Jane had to make the same long list of telephone calls, only this time it was to inform people that George had died, finally at peace with his condition, at home with Jane and the children around him. Jane's husband was rather busy and so couldn't be home for the last moments of his father-in-law's life. Jane would forgive him, she always had. Although it was the height of the season for Edwin and Liza they duly got in extra help for Tom and made the journey to Surrey to help Jane pay their last respects to a man whom they had known but little. In fact most knew him only by anecdote as Ronnie had not actively encouraged visits. She was not ungenerous but merely wished to keep her two worlds apart. She cherished her childhood and she cherished her school friends. She had been an Amazonian champion to them all in her own way. She could not let them in on her grief sodden life after the death of her son. It was too painful especially to those who knew her well and who would have helped her through. She just couldn't bear the role reversal that would have ensued. Beth and Liza understood this in her. Maddy and Lucy were just a little hurt by it. Through all the years of meetings and reunions no one said anything about this to her. They let her be who she wanted to be. Still they loved her.

Beth was the exception. She had left them alone when the boy had died but after a while she had visited quite frequently and was quietly a great comfort to both Ronnie and George. She made no demands and offered a good listener's ear for their stories. In truth they had offered her an escape from the tedium that had become her carer's life. On reflection she had few regrets but was rather subdued and had lost the ability to really laugh or express deep emotion. It was all too long suppressed. She was there at George's funeral alongside Maddy. Liza and Edwin were there and they were all half expecting Lucy to make a last minute show but she never turned up. On the 'phone she had been hesitant but had implied she would make the journey. The rest of the friends assumed that she just changed her mind. The August day was dull and overcast. A slight drizzle started as the coffin was brought into the church and it stayed that way all day. Packed to overflowing the mourners endured a lengthy eulogy from one of George's Lodge companions. It was a grand send off but not a glorious one. Jane was striking in her mourning clothes. Her husband had managed to find a slot in his busy schedule to make the service. During the 'wake' afterwards he was to be found talking on his mobile 'phone and making jokes about family funerals and their necessary interruption to his first love, his job.

Jane's dignity was remarked upon and at an opportune moment Liza cornered her and offered, "Jane my dear, I'm so sorry you've had to go through all this twice in one summer." Jane acknowledged her kindness with a watery smile. "Here's our card, call me anytime if you want a chat. We're going now, long journey you know. That motorway, huh." Liza made a face at the thought of the trek, patted Jane's arm and left. Edwin was pulled away from a very nice chat with Beth and they made for the West. Maddy followed soon after and made her excuses. "Must go. Lots to sort out. I…"

"What are you up to …?" "How are your plans …?" Both Beth and Jane asked at the same time. Maddy walked away with an airy wave saying she would be in touch soon and not to worry. Beth parted from Jane saying, "Sorry Lucy couldn't be here but she probably couldn't bear the thought after what happened at Ronnie's." Jane nodded and Beth added, "Call me. Don't be alone. Use my mobile though, I'm rarely home these days." She almost skipped out of the hotel lounge, not seemly perhaps but it was how she felt, liberated.

Jane sat down that evening. She had no parents of any kind now. She was a wife and mother and her husband spent all his time and energy at his job. He hadn't made love to her for months. She wondered about Ronnie's friends. She had no such group to which she belonged. One girl friend from school and a couple from university were her sum total. She envied them their loyalty and their mutual acceptance of each other. She had always been rather judgemental about people and she had begun to realise that it was her fault she felt so alone. Even her husband preferred to spend time away. Well she was never one for self pity; she would rectify the situation as well as she could.

CHAPTER TWENTY FIVE
Lucy Learns to Trust

It wasn't just the last few months that had knocked the stuffing out of Lucy, it was the seemingly endless years of subservience to John. On reflection it could be adjudged her own fault but when one is in that situation it creeps up and suddenly the will power goes and fear takes over, making one immobile. These were the explanations she was using to try to explain to Amy and Angus why she had not left before. "Mum, yes I know but we tried to tell …"

"I know Love, it's so difficult …"

"See here Mother," Angus never called her Mum, that was reserved for his own rather austere but loving mother, "You'll never have tae put up wi' him again. We'll see ye all right."

"Angus, you have made me so welcome. Thanks. I think I'm ready to face the world again. I've been out and got a job." As the faces of her nearest and dearest registered alarm she quickly reassured them, "It's only part time and very local. I'm helping with the local literacy group for people who have trouble with the language. Adults. It's all set. I start tomorrow." Still they seemed unconvinced, smiling Lucy looked so much more alive they sighed and hugged her. Amy wasn't the only one with tears of joy and relief coursing down her face.

Duly the next day Lucy reported for work and was immediately drawn into excited conversation with an older woman about the local carnival and how she was helping with a float and wasn't it good to have the old festivals resurrected and how grand it was to live in such a wonderful place as this. Lucy was breathless just listening to her. However she was warm and what if she was a little bit nosey about the new helper. It was to be expected. Lucy had agonised for nights about what her story would be should any inquisitive person start to probe. She had run through complete denial to open admission of all that had happened. Obviously the line to take was somewhere in the middle. She was no longer in denial about the past and had received great help from Amy's doctor and his psychiatric counsellor. She was already walking taller and straighter, not slinking about hoping not to be noticed. Her face was fuller and younger and she was beginning to feel more confident. Maybe she was still rather fragile but that would pass and she would be, no, not her old self, but a new self, one rediscovered and bright. The older woman took her under her wing from the start and soon Lucy and Mrs M, as she was known, became firm friends. Gradually Lucy's story came out in dribs and drabs and Mrs M's heart went out to this brave ghost of a woman whose shadow became ever firmer and more tangible with each passing week.

The adult pupils loved Lucy's gentle approach to their learning needs and under the strict supervision of the supervisor helped them to establish a link with the language and grow in confidence. In truth it was a mutual caring.

It was nearly October and the harvest celebrations were well into the planning phase. The local area held a service and harvest thanksgiving supper, not as well known as Burn's night maybe but still, much welcomed as a break between the now distant summer holidays and winter gloom. Mrs M, always much involved in the community and the local church, was spearheading the organisation this year and she persuaded Lucy to offer a dish of her own choosing towards the supper. When she arrived home, following this conversation with Mrs M, Lucy spoke with her daughter and expressed her anxiety about such a public display of confidence. She didn't know whether she was up to the task or not. Everything she had offered John, both in terms of cooking and indeed herself, were rejected on the grounds of 'incompetence'. The worst times were when he just laughed at her for even suggesting that they might make love as they had done when they first married. Subsequently her need for tenderness was subsumed by a desire to survive.

"Amy?" Lucy whispered to her daughter who was sitting and reading in a rare moment of calm in a household full of busy people and two energetic children. Why she whispered she didn't know but it seemed appropriate. Amy put down her book and smiled a tired smile at her mother, "its ok Mum I'm just taking a breather. You ok?" Lucy sat down and sighed, "Sorry Love I just have to find some more confidence somehow." They had all suffered a huge blow that morning when they had news of John's sentence from the court. He had been bound over to keep the peace and had been given a probation officer to whom he had to report every week for six months. It was lenient to say the least but the judge considered he had suffered provocation. He had undergone a psychiatric report which was unclear and confusing. Lucy had read all the reports and proceedings as supplied by her solicitor. It appeared that years of abuse and rape and subjugation was as nothing to the establishment. The judge was of the old school and was heard to remark, "Well the woman's out of it now. She ran away after all. Might have had a guilty conscience you know. Why lock a fellow up because he chose the wrong wife." Luckily no one associated with Lucy heard this or murder may well have been committed on that judge.

Now the family had to get their lives back on track and live with the idea that John was a free agent once more. Amy had spoken briefly with her father after the trial and had made it very clear that she was not going to be torn between her parents and that she would always look after her mother. She had seen at first hand the damage he had caused Lucy and was, herself, a little frightened of him. "Thank god," she thought, "Angus is the antithesis of his father-in-law." Amy had told her mother the bare facts and omitted his final words as they parted, "Well Amy. So be it. But she's a liar you know. She's given me hell over the years. She owes me." With that he had turned on his heel and walked away. Amy shivered as she remembered and decided not to alarm her mother any further. She

146

had confided in Angus who agreed that the best course would be to say nothing. So, just as Lucy was beginning to function as a whole person once more she desperately wanted to fade again into the shadows in the hope of going unnoticed. Of course, Mrs M would not allow that, she had taken a liking to this southerner and decided take her under her wing. Thus it was that she had invited Lucy to cook for the harvest supper and for her to start to be part of the local community.

"What on earth can I cook that won't be laughed out of court?" The familiar expression had taken on a sinister meaning and she gulped with fear as she uttered the words. It would be a while before those reactions faded and could be dealt with easily. Amy smoothed her mother's sleeve and said, "Let's have a cuppa and go through my cookery books. You were rather good once you know Mum." Lucy agreed and they spent a happy afternoon going through some delicious recipes. Most were too elaborate for Lucy's taste and so in the end they decided on a straightforward lemon meringue pie. The supper was ten days away and so Lucy spent the next week practising until even the children were a little fed up (literally) with the different variations that Lucy tried to make it special. As the evening approached she calmed down and made a delicious lemon pie. Amy, Angus and the children were also to be at the supper and so Lucy felt encouraged by their presence. They set forth on a journey that was important to Lucy's recovery and re-entry into the 'normal' world where your loved ones don't beat you up and try to take your very soul.

It was Mrs M herself who welcomed the family group into the hall and told them where their places were. They wandered over to the table and immediately the children saw their friends and were off to chat and moan about the 'grown ups'. Lucy took her pie to the kitchen where Mrs M was in the full flow of her organising frenzy. She loved it and all was going well. Lucy put her pie where she was told and went to leave. "Lucy, my dear, don't go, I've just lost Andrea for the moment will you," she interrupted herself to give instructions to another woman who was dithering, dithering was not on Mrs M's agenda, "Rose, No, dearie me, the other way round, hm," she waved her hand towards the vast area of worktop which was covered in so many pots that Lucy wondered at how they would ever get order out of such chaos, "first the rice then the sauce, oh dear, dear, dear." Mrs M turned from the benighted Rose heaved one huge theatrical sigh then continued with Lucy, "please dear, will you put one each of these water jugs on the tables then we're fine I think." Lucy started to panic, her face froze and she started to shake, "Now then my dear," Mrs M had a keen eye for others and their condition, "you'll be just fine. One step at a time and you'll be OK." She smiled and gave Lucy a little push which was accompanied by a friendly pat on the arm. Lucy tried smiling in return and set about her simple task. Amy had expected Lucy to come straight back and had come looking for her. She was a bit anxious and over protective and was astonished to see her mother apparently so confident. She watched from the kitchen doorway as her Lucy braved the crowds. It was as she was putting the last jug on one of the tables that she looked up and saw a vaguely familiar face. It was a friendly face but also one that was associated with great fear. Robert McHeath had come along to support his mother in her efforts to bring the community together. He loved his mother but was well aware of her interfering nature where other 'lesser souls' were concerned. It was because he did not want to hurt her that he had therefore devised many ways to avoid the matchmaking schemes she had presented him with over the years. As with many loving relationships, honesty ran a poor second to humouring the beloved.

Lucy paled and stuttered a greeting that sounded more like a grunt to Robert. He knew exactly where he had seen Lucy last and that was in the cottage hospital where she was sleeping soundly recovering from her shocking entry into Scotland's border country. As she turned away he asked, "How's your friend? Is she well recovered now?" Politeness dictated that she answer so solicitous an inquiry, "Yes, mm yes thanks. She's all better now. Small scar." Robert insisted, "And you? Are your scars deeper?"

"I really don't think that it's ..." Lucy was about to be discourteous and so stopped floundering into an embarrassed hesitancy, "I've to find my daughter now. You … you were … kind that day. Thanks. I must go now, find my seat." She fled from his presence as Mrs M came up behind her and said, "I see you've met my son. He's the itinerant one, can't settle. I told you about him?"

"Oh. Ooh. Mrs M, excuse me I must sit down."

The supper was declared a success and it was followed by local people showing off their party pieces. There was the young girl who played the violin. She played such a haunting air that most were reduced to tears. An old man got up and recited from Walter Scott's Ivanhoe. People were reduced to tears as before but for a different reason. The old man spat each time he came to a letter 's' and so, cruelly but hilariously, people mimicked him and found him amusing. He knew of his slight impediment and joined in with the laughter, but only after he had finished with Scott. Mrs M encouraged a middle aged woman to sing a Gaelic lullaby and so on until all who wished to had performed and been well or sympathetically received. It finished with Robert being persuaded to recite a poem. Surprisingly he chose Wordsworth's reflections on Tintern Abbey and was rewarded with warm applause. The local minister finished the evening with a short speech of thanks for the harvest and a prayer. Robert looked for Lucy and her family after this but they had slipped away without notice as Lucy was as pale as ever and looked as though she might faint.

Back in Amy's sitting room she had been revived with a tot of brandy. The colour had come back to her cheeks and she suddenly sat up and made an announcement, "Coventry cathedral. It's all about reconciliation. That's what I need. Selfish I know but that's what I need."

"Mum, not with dad, surely after …"

"No Amy, not with your father, I'm tired not insane. No with the young man who held us up, I need to see him and find out why. It'll be good for me."

"Aye, you're right enough. I'll drive you. You'll not go alone." Angus spoke with calm authority, and when he saw the look of horror on his wife's face he added, "She'll be fine wi' me. It's a need in her, can't you see that darling." Lucy thanked him then told them about Robert McHeath and how he had twice been on the scene when she had felt threatened. She still didn't know how he had been present in so timely a fashion at the hold up and now she vaguely wondered why she had been so incurious. She would ask Mrs M when she next saw her. This new enthusiasm for sorting things out must mean she was on the mend, from the inside out. She felt very good. She hoped she would still have the courage in the morning when the brandy had worn off.

The next day Lucy was due to help out at her weekly session with the literacy group. She had no formal qualifications for teaching but as she became more confident she was increasingly used by the leader as a main helpmate for the seriously under-confident who used the centre. She walked in with a hammering heart as she knew Mrs M would want to talk to her about her son. Lucy had absolutely no idea that Mrs M's son was the man who had been a kind of saviour to her and Maddy at the hold up. Mrs M drew Lucy to one side as soon as she entered the centre and asked if they could have a chat. "Lucy my dear, Robert told me all about your dreadful experience on your way to your daughter's. You poor wee thing." She paused, something Mrs M did very little of in her busy daily life, "My dear you have had a ghastly time of it. You've hinted only at your former life. Don't be afraid to embrace your new life here. You didn't deserve the cruelty. You did not bring it on yourself." She emphasised the word 'not' in such a forceful manner that Lucy jumped. "Mrs M, you're very kind. I didn't realise your son was who he is. But, last night made me realise that I've got to go back and find that young man and get what the American's call some kind of closure. My son-in-law is going with me. He's a good man. I'll be back when it's all over. Will you keep a place for me here? You've made me so welcome."

"Oh my dear, of course. You take all the time you need. This is only voluntary you know." After a searching look at Lucy Mrs M reflected, "'tis a brave thing you intend, you know. Ring me if you need a comforting word. I've grown fond of you, lassie." Lucy was too choked to reply properly so she did an unprecedented thing and gave Mrs M a hug.

Not many people had the courage to be so familiar with this eminently capable woman. The gesture touched Mrs M and she returned the hug before she said, "Now then, you'll have me in tears soon. Go now and be strong my dear." Lucy smiled a watery smile and briefly wondered when she would be able to go for any length of time without filling up. Tears had been close to the surface for a long time. It seemed that lately she had let them all out at once. She thought it odd as she felt as strong now as she had for many a year.

When she returned home she found that Angus had taken time out of his work. He was owed some holiday and so the next week had been booked as leave and they would go back and find Lucy's closure. Lucy rang and told Maddy what she was up to. Maddy was horrified. Lucy silenced her with a memory, "Mad, remember Coventry cathedral? The amazing sense of forgiveness and reconciliation. Well I don't know if the young man will even see me but for my own sake I need to at least try. Then I can move on, just knowing I've tried. Mad, I'll ring when it's over. You ok?"

"I'm fine Luce. Bear and I are discussing future stuff but I'll tell you more when I know. OK? Take care of yourself. Bye." Amy had agreed that Angus was the best person to accompany Lucy the next week. Amy would stay and keep the house and children going in as normal a way as possible. So it was that after making arrangements and lots of telephone calls Angus and Lucy set off the following Monday. Lucy with a hammering heart screwed her courage up and told herself a thousand times that this was the right thing to do, a good thing. She fervently hoped the young drug addict would see her and not be too unpleasant.

CHAPTER TWENTY SIX
The Majestic Hotel

Marjorie and Alfred had been at full stretch for months now and finally it was autumn. There were still a few regulars who came when the high season was over. This part of Dorset attracted a lot of people who were probably well out of the need to holiday during school holidays. Beth had become a regular down there. The last few weeks had been especially trying for her as she went back and forth between her house in Sussex and her new life in Dorset. Marjorie and Alfred were now firm friends and she cooked for them when they needed her to and her cuisine was getting a reputation in the local area. She liked to cook with fresh local and seasonal ingredients. There had been a few tussles with visitors who had asked for the more usual food that is served everywhere. Alfred had used his very good disarming charm reserved for awkward customers. People went away feeling that a minor triumph had been achieved but on reflection they all realised they had been given what was available and not what they had initially hoped for. Few went away hungry or discontent. So life slipped into a different pattern for Beth. She sold her home and found a charming cottage that was built in the nineteenth century. She had only a quarter of an hour's walk to the sea but she could smell it in the air whenever she went into her small garden. It was very overgrown and she decided to wait until the spring before she did anything about it. She wanted to get the interior done first.

She had a tiny gathering of people for a housewarming. Liza and Edwin came up for the party and stayed in the Majestic. Maddy popped in for a very brief visit on her way to somewhere or another. She was very discreet and when she had gone Liza and Beth had no more idea of what she was up to than before she came. Bear was not with her and she fielded questions about him with great skill. Marjorie and Alfred came and one or two regulars at the hotel who had become very fond of Beth over the past weeks. James was one of them. As soon as he accepted that Beth was not after him and was quite content with her lot he relaxed and they joked and teased each other with increasing ease. If Alfred and Marjorie still harboured a hope that the two of them would pair up, they never said a word out of place. This was probably due to Alfred's putting his foot down with a firm hand and telling Marjorie "to leave folk alone to manage their own affairs."

The bank where Beth worked had let her go with a rather grudging acceptance. She had been there so long they thought she was part of the furniture. They gave her a farewell party and some fripperies. They obviously had no idea what she would like and she realised that she had only one firm friend there. All her own age group had long since moved off, either to have families or to greater and better things in the bank. She would not miss the daily boredom. What had once seemed a safe haven, a harbour from the stormy seas of being a 'carer', had long since palled. Often she had wanted to do something so outrageous that she would shock some of her less pleasant colleagues into some kind of reaction, other, that is, than their mocking of the poor creatures who went overdrawn or who failed to keep up payments on their loans and so forth. Beth had never joined in but had always withdrawn into her work considering it a safer haven than making waves of disapproval. She left her home with a little more regret. It had been solid and dependable and now she was selling it to strangers. She hoped they would look after it and love it as she had once. Beth had sighed a big goodbye sigh to the house and driven away. She didn't look back. It was unlikely she would go there again. She wouldn't want to see what the new people had done to it. If the house and garden seemed neglected then she would be upset and if it was well cared for she may, just may, be somewhat sad.

No, she had chosen her new path and she would stick to it. She might deviate from it if the path became too difficult but she would then choose another, but it would not be a backward path. There was no happiness in looking over one's shoulder. Happiness was to search for that which was formerly missing. She had a vague idea what that something was but she could not or would not put it into words in case she frightened it away.

Her small pension from the bank was enough to keep body and soul together. Her new house had no mortgage on it and so she was secure. Beth was used by Marjorie and Alfred as a cook in the high season but, friendly though they were they could not justify engaging her when the season was over. What was she to do in the long winter that lay ahead? Explore.

Beth woke up in the middle of the night and sat bolt upright. Yes, that's what she'd do. The idea had come from nowhere but it made her feel on top of the world.

The next day Beth set about her task with enthusiasm. She would try to research old Dorset recipes and put them into a book. At the same time she would talk with Marjorie and Albert and see if they wanted to put on regular Dorset fare. There was a modern movement afoot that liked to 'go back to finding regional roots'. Beth was interested in cooking, she was interested in local colour and tradition and she had time on her hands. All in all she was very pleased with herself. She wrote to all her friends and asked them to keep an eye open for any recipes that they might come across, or information, pertaining to her quest. Her next step was to go and see Marjorie and Albert. She thought they might help and be enthusiastic. After that she would tackle the museums and libraries and then try to talk to local groups such as the Women's Institute. She had no truck with their organisation and had run a mile in the opposite direction when they were mentioned. Her mother had been a member and she had considered it too insular and rigid for her taste. Now she would use them and try to keep an open mind. Her mother had regularly gone to their meetings until she was too ill to attend. She had once asked Beth to go in her place and give her prepared talk which was on the exciting topic of 'Ten exciting things to do with candles'. Beth had refused having first convulsed with laughter, in which, after a moment's reflection, her mother had joined her. It was a rare and happy memory for Beth and even now made her smile. However she would put that thought away otherwise she was not sure she could concentrate properly.

"What a good idea? Don't you think Alfredo my love?" Marjorie was very encouraging when Beth had settled in their lounge, been given a cup of coffee and a Danish pastry and the third degree about just everything and had finally got out what her mission for the next few months was to be. Alfred, who liked his food plain and simple and 'not mucked about with' was more cautious, "Well, Beth, I um I ...," he cleared his throat and started again, "look, its like this, people know what to expect when they come here, honest British food with pizza and pasta and chips and lasagne and ..." he tailed off, thought about what he had said and then roared with laughter, "We've got a lot to thank our Italian cousins for haven't we?" Beth and Marjorie laughed with him and then he added, "Look, we'll see what recipes you come up with and then discuss it again, we make no promises." Marjorie cut across his last few words, "Beth, we'll see. But we'll probably give it a go. Don't worry about him. His mother never cooked anything other than jellied eels and fish pie."

"Now then Marj don't go on about the old girl, I always had a good dinner even if it was a bit samey."

"Yes, well she wasn't so bad I s'pose. Taught me a thing or two."

"Did she, like what?"

"Well, nothing really I was just making Alfred feel better. Come on let's go into the kitchen and look at menus I've got planned for next season anyway." As Marjorie and Beth left the lounge Marjorie turned and threw an order at Alfred, "Bar needs your special touch dear, give it a good going over there's a duck." Alfred duly rolled his eyes heavenward and did as he was bidden and the discussion was over, for now.

"Marjorie, which is the best library do you think? I'm going to Dorchester County Museum but I don't think there'll be much there."

"Wool's not bad, it's a bit small though. Dorchester I s'pose is the one. Talking with the local womenfolk will probably be a bit more authentic. I'll ask around if you like."

"Thanks Marjorie. D'you know you've been good for me. I hope to repay you one day."

"Don't be daft, we needed you this end of season and we're grateful. Only sorry we couldn't keep you on. We can call on you next spring can't we?"

"Of course. Hopefully we'll have some proper Dorset food by then."

Beth decided to fully embrace the electronic age and buy a new computer and get back on line. She thought she could increase her research capabilities that way. Meanwhile she set off for local libraries and museums to try to find out what she could about her chosen subject. She knew she would be a little bit disappointed if someone had recently done such research and beaten her to it, but still she set off hopefully. As she was walking away from the Dorchester museum, where they were very helpful but the research unfruitful, so far, Beth decided she would go to the rather old fashioned but charming tea shop just round the corner. Just round the corner, however, was a rather bluff sailor who had his head down and was walking in a charging bull motion, trying to avoid a certain middle aged woman who had been convinced at one time that they would make a perfect pair. It had taken him months to extricate himself from her determined approaches. He cannoned into Beth and took the wind right out of her. As she clutched her chest, both in surprise and pain, she muttered, "Oh, hello James, you've winded me." That is what she meant to say but it came out as, "Bloody hell that hurts." James stood motionless and speechless as he saw the pain on her face, "Sorry, Beth. You ok?"

"Uh, no, I'm not" Beth realised this was rather blunt so she added, "But I'm sure I will be, just need a cup of tea or something." She assumed he would help her to the tea shop which was within arms reach, she was wrong. "OK there's one just there, I'll be off." Beth couldn't help her next retort although she fully intended to say it only in her head, "Miserable devil." When she realised it had been said out loud, she put her hand over her mouth first with embarrassment then with amusement as she watched James turn, look shocked and then laugh out loud. Such a laugh it was, a thing quite rare but worth waiting for so Beth joined in and they staggered into the tea shop together and sat down. James ordered tea and toasted tea cakes. The ageing waitress knew him of old, "We don't see you in here much nowadays. Bin keepin' well 'ave you?"

"Yes thanks Silv. How's Ted? OK?"

"All right apart from every part of him, misery that he is." The waitress laughed and added, "But then he's my misery and that's my lot in life. I'll get your tea." She walked away, with her waitress's stoop firmly pronounced, and gave him a parting knowing wink.

There was an awkward silence then they both spoke at once, James immediately stopped but Beth carried on speaking. It was as though once she had formed the idea she had to get it out before her courage failed, "Look here James. Marjorie has told me about your..." she hesitated, "circumstances. I understand ..."

"Do you? How could you?"

"Well I'm trying to at least. Look here..." She started again, "I'm not looking for, well, a partner or anything like that. There was a time that I ... well enough said on that score. Anyway I've come down to Dorset to start the next phase of my life. It's been a trying few years and I deserve, yes," she added with emphasis, "deserve a fresh start." She paused and he said nothing so she carried on, "That day you rescued us seems to have been a turning point for all my friends. One of them is dead and the rest have had some pretty horrendous things happen to them. Yes they have." Another pause which, again, he declined to fill. "You're very difficult to talk to. I don't mind a friend but I don't want anything else. Why can't we just be friends? You don't have to keep avoiding me." James looked startled, "But I don't, I ..."

"Yes you do. We seemed to be OK then suddenly it seems to me anyway that whenever I go into the hotel to see Marjorie you scuttle away hoping I won't talk to you. You came to my house warming then, nothing, running scared I'd call it!"

"Well Alfred said ...,"

"Oh I see. He's an interfering old ... person." She calmed down the noun that was on the tip of her tongue, "He just wants us both to be happy. Just as he is with Marjorie. Let's call a truce and at least be polite. You know you want to." Beth's smile could be very disarming when she tried and he gave in to her warmth. "Yes it would be nice. Let's have tea and talk about your latest venture." When she looked quizzically at him he added, "Beth, there is nothing, nothing that Marjorie and Alfred keep to themselves unless it is intensely personal." He smiled and said, "And even then they use their discretion." Silv watched her old friend and his new lady and smiled and spread the gossip as though it were of national importance. Which of course it was, to her.

Beth and James parted amicably and with a renewed comfort in each other's company. The air had been cleared and they both rather tentatively thought that they had laid the foundations for a good friendship. Marjorie and Alfred would be happy in one way but sad when they realised their matchmaking dreams were fruitless. James had offered to look out his mother's old recipes. She had been Dorset born and bred and like many ladies who had been through the Second World War had kept both a diary and a collection of recipes. He even had, he vaguely remembered seeing somewhere, some of his mother-in-law's recipes. Perhaps he had given them to his daughter. They might as well be used and useful rather than gathering dust in a cupboard. An afterthought hit James as he drove home and that was that if he was seen to be friendly with Beth the others might leave him alone. Actually they mostly did but just one or two never gave up hope of warming his soup and his bed.

Beth had no idea of James' turn of mind she just welcomed the thaw in his attitude. She felt that she had done enough for the day and made some sundry purchases and went home. She was rather keen to go for a walk along her favourite cliff path, she wanted to clear her head. It had been a morning of highs and lows and she needed the exercise. She hoped she hadn't made a fool of her self with James but she was tiring of his awkwardness. Their mutual friends, Marjorie and Alfred, were becoming embarrassed by his inability to be at ease with her. Well, whatever the outcome she had done all she could. Walking always put things in perspective.

Her computer was due to be delivered in a few days and she would then be able to get on and search a wider field. She understood computers to some extent through the work at the bank and she was looking forward to emailing her friends, Maddy and Liza. Lucy was not on line but maybe she would join in. The possibilities were endless. As she strolled over the cliffs in the late autumn sunshine her mind was in another place. Her reverie was interrupted by a sharp barking sound. She briefly thought that another dog had gone over the cliffs as the one earlier on in the summer had done. She still felt a slight chagrin at the ungrateful way the woman had berated her. Shock does strange things to people but even so she hadn't deserved that. She looked for the source of the noise and saw a poorly bedraggled fox terrier chained to a cliff top bench. Further inspection brought no people into view. She cautiously approached the dog and went down on her heels to gain its trust. The dog was pathetically grateful for any attention and whimpered and licked Beth's hand. Realising that the dog had been abandoned she unhooked it and picked it up. It was probably full of fleas or worse but she couldn't leave it and it was too weak to walk.

The local police were sympathetic but matter-of-fact about its future, if it wasn't claimed in two weeks it would be destroyed. Beth had no intention of getting a dog but it seemed that a dog had 'been got'. Molly moved in and Beth was never alone again. Rather exorbitant vet's fees coupled with 'necessary' dog paraphernalia made a hole in Beth's monthly budget but seeing the instant trust in Molly's eyes, she caved in and they were an item.

The cliff walk became her regular route and she briefly thought on an old adage of her aunt's, "Things happen in threes you see if they don't!"

CHAPTER TWENTY SEVEN
Liza and Edwin

November was a gloomy month. It had been a rollercoaster year. Liza had lost a good friend in Ronnie. Her dreadful experience in dealing with John at the funeral had made her appreciate the transient nature of life. She had feelings of dissatisfaction that had spread tentacles of unrest through her world following Lulworth Cove that had not gone away. Liza really had little idea of how to deal with it all. She had stopped goading Edwin into arguments. She had stopped interfering in Tom's life now as he seemed much more settled. His access to his boys was regular and usually fulfilling. Liza and Edwin consequently had regular contact with their grandchildren and that hitherto bitter gap in their lives was once more filled. As Liza went about her chores in a rather desultory fashion she pondered on her two failed goals this year. One was the holiday adventure in Peru and the other was about her writing a book. She fully understood the impracticalities of suddenly going off to South America. She was cross with herself for being so understanding. Edwin had heaved a great sigh of relief when he realised that life had returned to normal. Sure enough it was sometimes clear that Liza was unsettled, but the more he worked the less he seemed to notice.

Increasingly nothing was right for Liza. She had tried and failed to get things sorted but the more she tried the more she seemed to be cast in the role of 'nagging wife' or worse still a 'malcontent'. As she felt things slip away from her, the person inside, she reacted badly. She was therefore deservedly to be labelled ungrateful or selfish. This made her more unhappy than ever. She was convinced that no one understood. She started to believe that and no one could help. Love, distant practical love from Edwin, was certainly not going to get through to the layers of pain hidden underneath the years of emotional padding. She decided that all was definitely not well and so she went to see her doctor. His first reaction was, "Uh oh another middle aged woman who is menopausal and discontent. Anti-depressants will do the trick." When Liza opted not to take his pills; he wrote her off and suggested she find some alternative remedy. "Well Mrs … I've heard that St John's Wort is good for," here he interjected a dry laugh, "well let's say 'feeling a bit low' shall we. All good chemists stock it nowadays." Liza sat and squirmed, "Look here Doctor I …"

"Yes, yes, well try to get a bit more exercise. You'll feel better soon. Come and see me again if it doesn't work out." His parting shot was, "We can always try the antidepressants you know. You'd be surprised how many people are on them. You're not alone." As Liza waked out of his surgery the one thing she did feel was alone.

At supper that night she told Edwin what had happened and his response was, "You're not depressed are you Love? We've had a good year. Tom's sorted. That's nice isn't it?" He finished his meal and sat back tapping his stomach; "that was good." For the second time that day Liza felt patronised and a non-person. Silently she got up and for once didn't attempt to clear the table. She glared at Edwin and then left the room. Soon she was on the 'phone to Beth, "Beth, I'm in a muddle. I know you've not long moved in but can I come and stay? Please?" Beth sighed inwardly but agreed. So it was that Liza went to visit Beth and unfold her current nightmare. It took Beth no time at all before she realised Liza was desperately unhappy. Try as she might she could not get her friend to talk to her husband. Edwin rang daily but there was always some reason for him not being able to talk with Liza. Beth started to run out of excuses, "How many times can you be in the bath Liza? Talk to the man. He cares for you." Liza's only response to this was, "In time. Not yet." What irked Beth was that Liza seemed to take over her life.

She walked Molly, she became friends with Marjorie and Alfred. Much to Beth's chagrin she even got James to open up and chat and laugh. Beth once again was being sidelined and reduced to onlooker in her own existence. A shadowy thing that went unnoticed while a brighter star shone in her firmament. After a week of intense activity and frenetic socialising Beth called Edwin and asked him to come to talk with his wife. She felt that if he didn't come she, Beth, would explode.

Edwin arrived in the teeth of a howling gale one dark November evening. Liza was completely unprepared for his visit and Beth was crushed when she saw the look of betrayal in Liza's face as she received the full glare of her displeasure. "Liza, I … couldn't keep lying to him. He's your husband. Talk to him. He's suffered now for a week. Tell him how you feel for God's sake." Liza did not answer she merely turned from her friend and slowly took her husband out of the room and up to her bedroom. Beth shivered under the hostility and decided, despite the weather, to take Molly out in the car to The Majestic. Hopefully there she would receive a warmer welcome. She knew Liza and Edwin would need time to resolve their 'issues' and Beth reasoned that they would feel freer with her out of the way. The rain blew in sideways as she struggled into the car. As Beth drove along the tiny coast road she fought to keep the car straight. Suddenly the car groaned and stopped. "No, no, no." Beth tried to start it but there was no life in it. She had just had it serviced and so she had no idea what may be wrong with it. She was about a mile and a half from the hotel and so she decided to walk the rest of the way with Molly tucked into her coat. Molly thought this was great fun and snuggled down to enjoy this latest adventure. Beth had a torch in the car and so for a while she was able to see where she was going. The torch had not been used in anger for months and the battery had no life in it and soon she was walking in the dark.

Molly was fine as long as she was with her mistress. She was also warm and cosy. Beth was not. Battling the high wind and rain she soon lost her bearings. She was convinced that she was heading in the right direction but after a while she thought that the road didn't feel right under her feet. She had strayed onto a metalled path which was breaking up. The sound of the sea was ever closer. Beth stopped by a scrawny hedge and sheltered for a while wondering what to do. She would 'phone Marjorie and ask for some help. Where had she left her mobile? A vision of her 'phone nestling in the pocket of her car door flashed before her eyes. "Of all the stupid things ..." She started to speak to Molly as that gave her comfort. "What are we going to do little thing? I can't let you perish out here after all you've been through. Give me some inspiration." Molly's answer was to snuggle down even further out of the wind. The storm raged on and Beth decided that she would retrace her steps and try to find the hotel. After all she had driven the road many times.

An hour later, Liza and Edwin had had a good heart to heart. Liza had cried and told Edwin that she had to make changes or she would suffocate. Edwin had had time to reflect on what he knew in his heart he should have done long ago. He had become complacent. His small victory in getting Liza to drop the adventure idea had caused him nothing but trouble leading to this latest separation. He knew he had to let her go to win her back. He could not and would not go across the other side of the world. It wasn't in him. What he could do though was encourage Liza to go with a friend and pray for her safe and happier return. This is the basis of their discussion which took place amidst tears and a loving embrace. Feeling better than she had for a long time Liza and Edwin went downstairs to talk with Beth, only to find her gone. Edwin came in from looking outside, "Her car's gone. Where the bloody hell would she go on a night like this?"

"The Majestic."

"She seems to have taken Molly too." Liza interrupted her husband with, "Oh my god it's all my fault. I gave her the evil eye when I realised she'd called you."

"I know I saw it. It gave me the shivers and it wasn't directed at me. Though p'rhaps it should've been."

"We've got to find her. I feel so bad Ed. Come on Love."

Edwin's four-wheeled drive was more robust than Beth's tiny car and so they battled more successfully against the storm. It wasn't long before they came upon the abandoned car and were increasingly fearful as they examined it and found it empty. Liza 's often repeated, "Oh no its all my fault," didn't help Edwin as he tried to keep calm, find Beth and sooth his wife at the same time. He snapped finally, "Shut up for pity's sake shut up. You're not helping." Liza responded as though slapped in the face and sat upright and made more of an effort to look out for her friend. She had treated her shabbily and wanted to make amends. About a mile past the broken car they saw a bundle by the side of the road. Sitting beside the bundle was a tiny figure. This tiny form was howling. The pathos in its voice would have melted the hardest heart. They rushed to pick Beth up and realised she had fallen and hit her head. How she had not crushed Molly was a miracle. They gently put both the pathetic creatures in the car and drove as fast as the storm would allow to the hotel. As they approached the hotel they noticed that there were no lights on. All that they could see were the faint flickers of light that comes from candles. "Great there's been a power cut." This from Edwin. As he swung into the hotel driveway, "Thank God we've made it." A tree, which had stood for hundreds of years, decided it had had enough and crashed to the ground pinning the vehicle under its vast branches.

CHAPTER TWENTY EIGHT
Lucy Confronts A Demon

As Angus drove ever nearer to the prison, Lucy's determination seemed to falter. She had been silent for much of the journey and Angus had happily settled into a rhythm that allowed him to contemplate all manner of things that normally he was too busy to consider. When Lucy spoke therefore it brought him back to reality with a bump, "I…I'm not sure Angus. I mean if I … or what if he ..?" She tailed off. Angus gave her a moment to recollect her thoughts; he knew she would try again. Lucy took a deep breath, "Angus," she almost shouted so determined was she to stick to her resolve, "I am going to try to see him but I worry that all the forgiveness in my head will just disappear when I meet him."

"Aye, well, I'll be with you. I'll not be far. Trust yourself, you've become so strong these last few months." Lucy sighed and sank back, relaxing, "Thanks."

When they arrived at the prison reception they were asked for the documentation given by the prison service to allow then to offer to visit. The officer looked askance at them and asked what they wanted to visit him for. He emphasised the word 'him' as though he were scum. Lucy tried to explain, "Officer, I … I was a victim when …NO." She spoke with great determination now, "No I am not a victim, I was once but no more. He held me up, when I was travelling with my friend and…"

"Well, you'll not get to see him t'day. He's decided that he doesn't want to see you."

"But I don't understand," Lucy persisted, "I've come a long way to see him and they said it would be OK." The officer relented and stopped being officious, "Look miss he's been put in solitary for now for his own protection. Ring tomorrow and see how things are." He turned away then thought again, "An' if you'll take my advice you'll think twice about seeing him. He's no good to you." When Lucy looked enquiringly at him he added, "We need tae get him off the drugs."

"Oh, I see. But it's for me you see. I want to move on and need to see who and what he is."

"Aye well, try again if you must but you'll no see him today."

This conversation, varying only in delivery, was the reply that Lucy and Angus got for the next day as well. That night Lucy sought fresh courage for her task and looked at the icon she had bought when she and Maddy had visited Coventry Cathedral. She always had a symbol of the 'cross of nails' with her. It made her humble as she thought of the almost instant forgiveness of the people of Coventry, or at least one member of the clergy, who started the rolling ball of reconciliation and forgiveness. As she remembered the feeling of peace and light that had pervaded her soul that day she considered the ordeal that lay ahead. This young man was just the start, she had made up her mind to seek out John and forgive him. That would be a harder thing to do. The hold up was not personal, John's treachery was and that hurt much more deeply. However, she knew that for her own sake she had to try.

On the third day the young man relented and they gained access to the prison and were taken to a safe room to await the offender. A police officer and a prison officer were also in attendance as this meeting had been attained through the new initiative that allowed victims to confront their attackers. The word confront was not the one used but that in fact is what happened. Often the villain was unrepentant but those that were gained hugely from the encounter. The police officer had no hopes of this one being any benefit at all. That's why they had tried to put Lucy off when they realised that delay was inevitable. When they saw her determination they gave in and strongly persuaded the young man to see her. They were trying to protect her but now the new strong Lucy didn't want or need protecting, she wanted 'closure'. The man they brought in was hollow eyed, very thin and in his early twenties. He sat down without a word and glared at Lucy and Angus. He picked his nose and snorted, still he said nothing. Lucy began, "I've come here to try to understand why you did what you did to me and my friend that day." Her attacker looked at her and then said, "Who the hell are you?" The prison officer intervened at this non too promising start, "Now then, you know very well who this lady is. Be civil." The last command had a weight to it that the young man obviously respected, "Aye, sorry." Lucy felt this was encouraging, "Are you sorry for what you did that day?" He looked at her and saw a thin middle aged woman. He did not see the person just a stereotypical image. He had been encouraged to go through this programme but he didn't care a bit about this woman or her friend. His main task that day was to get away from his 'suppliers'. Going to prison had seen to that although they had long tentacles and may yet manage to get to him.

He wanted this over with and to get back to his cell, "Aye. Sort'a." With a flash of revelation Lucy understood that this man had no interest in her forgiveness and that she was there purely for herself. This thought made her feel very uncomfortable as she truly wished to forgive him. Once started she couldn't come away without finishing the task so she offered him what she had come to do, "You may not want it but I forgive you for what you put us through. I can't speak for my friend only me." With that she stood up and made to leave the room. He glared at her for a while then spoke with a soft defeated voice, "It was no personal. You're like my auntie; she never gave up on me, till she died. Thanks for coming but," he paused and took a deep breath, "I'm lost you see, the drugs, they're too deep. Just don't think about me." After that things happened very quickly as he was ushered out and then she was led out and within no time at all she was back, outside and walking towards the car with a very relieved Angus. "Angus you're a dear for bringing me and for your patience. Amy chose wisely when she chose you." Angus blushed and smiled but said nothing. They drove back home with Lucy wondering how she was going to tell Amy that she had to reach closure with John. Amy no longer spoke with her father and had often offered the opinion that she wished she were a love child from someone else. "Mum, are you sure you didn't have an affair with a rich count and I'm the result?" Lucy's reply to this joke between them was a smile, a sigh and "If only, oh if only."

Angus had rung Amy after the encounter, "Well love she seems philosophical about it. She's done what she came to do but I don't think it went as well as she'd hoped. He's an undeserving bastard." Nice as Angus was he had no illusions about drugs and pushers and habitual criminals. He thought Lucy's attempt at 'closure' was brave but misguided. He liked his mother-in-law and hoped that this would be an end to it and that she could move on. Amy told her husband, "Well when you bring Mum back I've arranged a small party for her. I think she's up to it now don't you?" Amy didn't wait for Angus to reply she just carried on happily, "Just Mrs M and a few from the centre, plus some others."

"Well don't make it too big love it's been quite draining for her."

"Ok, I love you, drive carefully. See you in a few hours." As Angus drove them home he glanced at Lucy who had fallen asleep and her face amazed him. She seemed so peaceful, perhaps confronting the bastard had done her some good after all.

They arrived home late in the afternoon. Amy greeted them with the news that they were having a small celebration that evening and for Lucy to get some rest as she was the guest of honour. "Mum, you deserve a treat and I've only asked a few people who have got to know you and they all think you're super." Amy rushed on talking about the party so that her mother would have no time to dissemble. "Off you go mum, I'll bring you a nice cup of tea and then you can get up and have a leisurely bath and make yourself gorgeous. Wear that new dress we bought the other day, its soft heathery tone suits you down to a T." She enveloped Lucy in a massive hug and pushed her towards the stairs. In a daze Lucy did as she was told and slept for two hours. The sleep was nightmare free and deep. She woke up feeling as though a huge weight had been lifted from her. "Wow," she thought, "what a journey. Now where's that heavenly bath oil?"

Lucy emerged ninety minutes later looking and feeling refreshed and in control. She'd not felt like this since, goodness knows when. Probably when they all left school and they'd hugged and laughed and were so full of the expectation and excitement of adulthood. She spoke softly to herself, "One step at a time Lucy old thing, one step at a time."

Amy had surpassed herself with an understated feast of salmon and champagne. She knew that this party would have to be low key as her mother was very unused to the limelight. Mrs M and the regulars at the centre were there as were a few neighbours, good friends of Amy and Angus and Mrs M's son. Robert had asked his mother if he could accompany her. He had briefly outlined his two previous and very brief encounters with Lucy and he just simply said, "I'd like to get to know her." Mrs M grinned until she could hardly contain her enthusiasm, "Oh Robert, Robert, my dear boy I…"

"Mum for goodness sake," he laughed, "Just contain your soul in patience will you. I know full well what you're thinking. I just like the look of her that's all."

"OK, come with me I'll just have to call Amy and make sure its all right but I'm sure it will be." After Mrs M put down the 'phone she turned to Robert and her face turned pale and she asked, "Robert, were you in any danger. I mean a gun!" He had wondered how she would take the news but it was soon smoothed away and anyway he knew she knew that his work had taken him to some hairy places in the world. She was not a worrier and for that he was grateful.

As Lucy entered the sitting room she saw the familiar faces of the small group of friends she had made since her flight to sanctuary. Amy guided her mother to the centre of the room and Angus put a glass of champagne in her hand. Her grandchildren gave her hugs and went skipping out of the door to the conservatory where they'd pledged to be good and from where they could observe the grown up party. All was excitement and laughter. Amy made a very short speech as to why they were having this party. "Thanks for coming all of you. This is for Mum. She's made a huge journey to get here, both physically and emotionally. She's just done a very brave thing. We won't dwell on it but I'm very proud of her." She raised her glass and said, simply, "To Mum." Everyone joined in and Lucy went very pink and answered, "Thank you. You've all made me very welcome." Then the party started in earnest. The background music Any put on was from Tchaikovsky's Swan Lake, one of Lucy's favourite pieces. Lucy felt on top of the world and mingled with growing confidence. Finally she moved on to Mrs M and there was Robert smiling a hesitant smile. Hoping to be accepted and quite unsure of his inclusion in the select gathering.

"I never had the chance, properly, to thank you for **your**," Lucy stumbled, "Er your fortuitous um…" she dried up. Talking to Robert seemed to make her a little nervous and he mumbled in return, "T'was nothing. I just happened to be painting and saw it all happen from the hill."

"Oh I've wondered often how you happened to be there." Lucy suddenly smiled at him and put her hand on his arm and said, "I'm glad you're Mrs M's son. She's been a godsend to me." They carried on with their conversation and time flew by. There seemed to be no one else in the room. "Look. I'm monopolising you. Have dinner with me next week and we'll talk some more. I think Amy wants you to circulate some more now." He had spotted Amy talking with his mother and looking anxiously their way. He picked up his plate and headed for the buffet to eat some more of the delicious food. He very much liked this woman but his inner man told him he was hungry. His first plateful had been taken with politeness in mind. Now he'd been accepted by the 'guest of honour' he felt able to have some more.

The next morning when Lucy and Amy had finished clearing up and putting all the best glasses and china away Lucy dropped two bombshells into her daughter's world. They were sitting in the winter sunshine, strong coffee in hand when Lucy said, "Amy, I do appreciate all you've done for me. You're lovely. I'm going to have dinner with Robert McHeath next week. He's nice." Amy was delighted and said so. Lucy let that sink in before she added, "I'm also going to see your father if I can." Amy was horrified, "Mum, you're an idiot. He's not worth it."

"Ssh Amy, I need to try for my sake, not his. I need to go and see if I can forgive him. I was weak but now I'm strong." Amy continued to try to persuade her mother about the folly of this proposal. Lucy was adamant, "Unless anything drastic happens to change my mind I shall try to find the emotional wherewithal in the Spring. Don't worry Love I will plan it all before hand." With this Amy had to be content.

CHAPTER TWENTY NINE
Maddy Runs Away

Maddy had taken months to clear her office and had dragged her feet with regards to finding somewhere to live. Bear was losing patience and had set up and lost several opportunities for properties in the country where Maddy and he could settle and indulge their passions. He had not proposed marriage to Maddy as he thought she would run scared. He knew her track record was not good. His wasn't so wonderful either. They both needed time but Maddy was always avoiding his suggestions and she had taken an inordinate amount of time in handing over her cases to her successor. She would miss the bustle of the office but she was tired and her arm still hurt on occasions. It had been a bloody six months and now in mid-winter she was setting about finding a place to live at the worst time of year. Bear was still her loving friend but she was scared of failure. She did love him and she was quite convinced that he loved her, but the question that constantly went through her mind was, "Was it enough?" His son was a delightful human being and they got on really well. He was so much like his father it made her heart ache when she saw them together, getting on better then ever.

Bear had to be away on a course for the whole of January. He was used less and less in an operational capacity but he was quite brilliant at running courses. Maddy never asked about his work and he rarely said anything. Years of caution meant that his reticence was automatic. Maddy didn't mind this so much, it was his assumption that she needed looking after that grated. She wanted him, very much, but as an equal partner, not as a bodyguard. His natural propensity for protecting the weak had turned into guard dog status following her ordeal with Lucy in the Border country. Maddy needed space to think and so she took the opportunity when he was away to go away on her own for a break. She told no one where she was going. She took her dog with her, her cats were looked after by her lovely neighbour, and off she set for Cornwall. She rented a cottage there that allowed dogs and she spent a glorious few weeks, on her own, walking by the rough and invigorating seas. The last summer was full of light and dark. It all seemed to go wrong after their reunion at Lulworth Cove. She would contact the others when she returned and suggest that they meet there again and perhaps lay a few ghosts. Certainly the ghost of Ronnie would be there. She was a strong presence. Maddy supposed she should think of her in the past tense but her death had not made her a lesser spirit, just an absent one.

As Maddy walked with Nimbus over the cliffs and along the shores in the stormy January weather she reflected on all she had done. Her life had been full of highs and lows just as anyone else's. She thought how people grow and how their lives are shaped by reacting to circumstances. Certainly her clients were mainly people for whom the world seemed to be an alien place full of people trying to trap them. Their own inadequacies helping them to feel victimised. She had always been an active woman meeting problems head on if not going out and searching for them. She had lived a full and varied life. Her three husbands were all quite nice but so totally wrong for her. None of them wanted a clever resourceful woman, they had wanted to be cared for and cosetted. This was not Maddy's style, unless of course you were a creature that needed protecting and saving from inhuman acts of cruelty or neglect. It was a time of welcome solitude for Maddy and she revelled in it. She recharged her batteries and felt well and relaxed. Her arm would probably never be quite right again but it was certainly stronger. Now she had to decide what to do about Bear. She loved him, but always she asked herself the same question, "Was that enough?"

The weeks in Cornwall had been good for her. She loved the wildness of the coast, especially round the Lizard. Its rough majesty filled her with excitement and she felt alive. However, like all good things, one can have too much so after a month she packed up and went home. She had run away to see what she could find deep within her and she had found it. She longed to tell someone and so on her way home she decided to call in on Liza in Devon. Liza had welcomed her call and had made a sumptuous tea, which of course included the famous Devon cream.

Maddy had not spoken with Bear for a month. She had left a message on his answer 'phone to say where she was going but that it was unlikely she would call him. She had finished by saying, "Anyway Bear, you'll be busy and won't have time to miss me so I'll call when I get back. Have fun. Lots love bye." Bear played this message over and over again to see if he could determine how things might work out for them. He was used to being in control and was uncomfortable that he didn't seem able to get inside the head of this lovely woman. Dissatisfied, he put all his energies into running the course and tried not to think of Maddy. He knew in his heart that she was working things out and whatever she decided would affect their life together dramatically.

Liza welcomed Maddy with open arms. As they walked round the farm and Liza showed Maddy what changes they had made since last she was with them Liza tried to pick up on Maddy's mood and Maddy likewise tried to do the same with Liza. Finally they sat down to high tea and the conversation drifted into companionable silence. Maddy had eaten her fill and sat back and looked at her friend, "Liza what's wrong?" She was used to asking direct questions and didn't elaborate. "What d'you mean? I'm fine."

"Liza, I came to see you in hospital, remember? You rambled quite a bit you know." They both thought back to that awful time when Liza had gone to stay with Beth and she had worked some stuff out with Edwin. The truth was Liza felt horribly guilty about Beth and had yet to work out a way to make things up to her. "Look Liza, Beth will be all right in the end. The doctors assured us…"

"Oh I know," Liza interrupted, "but I feel so awfully ashamed. I was so selfish. I keep thinking of that little soul, Molly, sitting by Beth in the road that night and I can't help wondering if she's not a better friend to her than I'll ever be."

"Now stop it. You're being a bit self indulgent you know."

"And when that tree crashed on us it was, oh, god I can see it now." She shuddered.

Maddy tried a different tack, "I understand that Marjorie and Alfred looked after her until she was able to go home. Molly's been a godsend all right and that chap James seems to have been rather attentive too." Unfortunately this made Liza feel worse, "But I should have looked after her. It was my fault she was there in the first place." "Now, this is just too much guilt. Liza you were injured too. Edwin's just got back to, well almost, full fitness. He'll always walk with a limp now; you've got enough on your plate." She could see that Liza was reflecting on this and carried on, "Interesting how Molly was the only one unharmed. Beth thinks it's because she had already suffered enough and that the fates wouldn't let her suffer any more. Touching faith. Look let's call Beth now and see how she is."

Liza hesitated, "I've not..."

"Liza you must have called her!" Maddy was shocked.

"Well no I couldn't bring myself to ..."

"Right then, now's the time. I won't let us break up now after all we've been through. Where's your 'phone?"

As Beth's 'phone rang she stretched out her hand to pick it up and saw the scars on her hand and up her arm. Inwardly wincing at the ugly sight she answered the call.

"Beth? Its Maddy. I'm here with Liza. How are you?"

"Maddy, how lovely. I'm getting there. I've had a lot of help here, considering I'm a new comer they've been marvellous." She paused then added, "How's Liza?"

"Feeling bloody about you and she wants to make amends. Here she is."

"Beth, Oh Beth, forgive me, I'm such a selfish bitch. I'm a coward too 'cause I haven't rung. Sorry old thing."

"Liza you idiot. Yes, you were selfish then but you were confused and yes, I do forgive you. How's darling Edwin? He saved me. I'll never forget that."

"He'll always limp but he's getting his strength back. My god we were lucky that night, a few inches either way and we'd be singing with the angels now."

"Yes or dancing with the devil, perhaps. Eh?"

"Beth! Thanks. You're a true friend. I won't forget either. See you."

Maddy felt as though she had at least done some good here and now decided that it was time she was on her way. "You going Mad? But you haven't said what your deliberations have ..."

"Ah, well that will have to wait until I've told Bear. I'll ring and let everyone know," She smiled and added, "In the fullness of time. Take care and stop with the guilt. Love to Edwin. Bye" With that she was off. Liza waved her friend goodbye and stood for a while reflecting once again on how their lives had all taken such dramatic turns since Lulworth Cove. The heavens must have been angry that day to have caused such chaos. She didn't really believe in a god but she regularly had doubts about absolutely everything. They had been forced to examine the metaphysical poets at school and had consequently had long earnest debates about the meaning of life, the universe and themselves. Maddy had always outwitted and out debated them all but somehow they had rarely altered their views, just conceded points. Ronnie was the most determined to do well and had a hunger for success that the others seemed to lack. Success that is in the commercial sense. Liza thought of Ronnie and how she'd died. She also thought of how she, Beth and Edwin had nearly died too. Something had saved them, was it fate, god or just happenstance. Beth believed in a god. Edwin was not known to have considered it at any length. He was Welsh Chapel and had a soft spot for unadorned services with lots of singing. Whether he truly believed she doubted that he knew himself. Where had the time gone?

Why did they stop debating such weighty issues? They had all been so caught up in living and earning a decent standard of living that they had forgotten how to question the mighty topics, usually reserved for academics. Perhaps she would get back to some kind of study. It might ease the ache she had within her. She decided that the ache might be a feeling of failure because she had sold out to a good life instead of a challenging one.

Maddy had no such thoughts as she drove away. She was occupied with how she would tackle her Bear. He was a difficult character and she had not met anyone before who had matched her in spirit and strength of mind. Whether they would make a good team was another matter. She had to see him and talk with him. She hoped that her month's silence was not an obstacle to being with him again. He could be unpredictable.

CHAPTER THIRTY
Beth Revisited

Dorset, once thought of by Beth as a nice quiet place in which to put down roots and to recapture some tranquillity in her life, had flung one challenge after another in her direction. She went through them in her head as she sat looking out on a stormy February day. The view from her cottage was usually peaceful and renewing but today it brought back all the horror of the November night that nearly took her life. Perhaps it was the storm but she thought it most likely to be a result of the recent call from Maddy and Liza. She had some resentment towards Liza. She had harboured a feeling that she had been ill used by her friend. Most of all she felt troubled and sorry for their plight.

Molly sat by her armchair in her soft bed and Beth's hand strayed absentmindedly to stroke her ears. Her mind went back to the stormy night and how she had wandered lost, dazed by several falls, in the wet as she fought the howling gale force winds trying to find sanctuary. Molly was tucked into her coat and the last memory, before waking up in hospital, was Molly licking her face as she lay in the mud. Marjorie and Alfred had heard the mighty tree crack and fall and rushed out to look on the scene. They had been horrified to see a vehicle underneath and from then summoned all help. The emergency services were very late in getting to the injured parties as the roads were treacherous. However, they managed it finally and found what at first appeared to be a hopeless case of three fatalities. Gradually the miracle of the night unfolded and after two hours all of the occupants were free. Liza was the least injured and suffered cuts and bruises and shock. Edwin had sustained a broken leg and hip but had turned after the crash to help relieve the pressure from a large branch that lay across Beth. Liza was trapped but less badly hurt. The darkness had added to the fear and all had to wait, in pain, for the rescue. Edwin's back began to give way as he fought to keep the enormous branch from crushing Beth who was still and twisted.

Marjorie and Alfred made the trio as warm as they could and spoke words of comfort throughout the ordeal. They pushed blankets in through the damaged windows so that the effect of the sodden branches was lessened on the poor trapped creatures. Suddenly Marjorie heard a small whimpering sound coming from under the vehicle and as she bent down a bedraggled Molly crawled out, bloody but unbowed. She caught her up in her arms and wrapped her in a blanket too. Such was the little dog's desire to reach her mistress that she struggled to leap out of Marjorie's solid arms and find Beth. It was both pathetic and touching. James had been dining at the hotel that night and he too was in attendance and brought all his practical knowledge to bear but in truth there was little anyone could do without special equipment. When the rescue teams arrived the small group, Marjorie, Alfred and James were suddenly no longer helpful but reduced to the role of onlookers. All three casualties were eventually taken to hospital from where Liza was discharged the next day. She went to stay in the hotel whilst Edwin spent another week in the hospital before being transferred to one near his home.

James wouldn't let anyone look after Molly except him and he took her to his chandler's store where she sat in her basket and watched every move he made. Every afternoon James, Molly and James' granddaughter would walk along the harbour and up to the headland. Marjorie was rather put out as she was quite keen to have Molly, "No Marjorie, you've got your hotel, she'll not be in the way with me at the shore." He had been so adamant that Marjorie had given in straight away and immediately started thinking more matchmaking thoughts. She was incorrigible and always travelled hopefully.

Beth spent three weeks in hospital then another two at the hotel being pampered by Marjorie and Alfred. She'd been home for several weeks now and James had regularly come over to walk Molly and sit with Beth. Christmas had come and gone hardly noticed by any of them. They chatted inconsequentially or said little. When there was silence it was warm and accommodating. Beth still had nightmares about the storm but they were so vague she couldn't put her finger on exact moments. One afternoon she had slept and awoke to find the light had gone. The cottage was in darkness and the fire had gone out. Shivering she stumbled to find the light and then went to re-light the fire. There were no logs in the basket; she couldn't find the matches anyway. Beth wandered about getting more and more frustrated. She couldn't take any more and she collapsed sobbing into her bed. She'd had enough. How long could she fight? She felt she'd reached the end. What was it all for anyway? She looked after her mother, she'd worked hard all her life and now, when she had a chance of comfort and pleasure she was laid up with a scarred arm and back that constantly gave her pain. Now she had no fire and she was tired and hungry and sorry for herself. She let go and cried until there was no more crying in her.

James approached the cottage and was surprised to see that there were no lights on in the sitting room. He knew she would have to be at home as she had ventured out very little since the accident. He wanted to take her to dinner at the hotel as a surprise. He went in via the back door calling her name and Molly ran out to meet him. A muffled voice from the bedroom called down and after a while Beth appeared. She was crumpled and tear stained. Her hair was awry and she looked defeated. She looked at her visitor and went up to him and put her arms round him and hugged him. They'd had no physical contact up to now and he was rather bemused. However, in a flash he understood, he wrapped her in a huge friendly embrace. She put her head on his shoulder and whispered, "Thanks."

The moment was over in seconds but its restorative power was magical. She smiled and said, "I've been having a crisis. Its over now but ..."

"I know darling. You've been through a huge ..."

The silence grew as they both took in the use of that one word. Beth's face suddenly shone and she looked young again, "My Jim." They hugged again and this time the love flowed between them. They didn't kiss they just clung on as though they might lose each other if they let go.

Marjorie and Alfred expected the pair in for dinner as James had hinted that he might try to persuade Beth out for meal. There were a few stalwart walkers in for an evening pint and bar meal and so Marjorie was kept quite busy for a while. When she had time to look she noticed that James and Beth had come in and were sitting at a corner table looking at the menu. Alfred was standing talking with them and all of them were grinning. No one had said anything out of the ordinary but Alfred was sensitive to atmosphere and he had noticed little things about the two of them that made his heart glad. He took their order and almost floated to the kitchen with the order slip.

"Marj, Marj. I think, you know what I think?"

"What's happened? You're like the Cheshire cat."

"Oh, Marj. I think..."

"Yes, you said that," as she could stand no more she almost shouted in frustration, "You think what?"

"Jim and Beth! The long wait's over." Tears of joy leapt to Marjorie's eyes as she grabbed Alfred's arm in exuberance, almost cutting off the blood supply in her ecstatic grip.

"Champagne?"

"No, let them be. We don't want to frighten them away. Its taken long enough.

So it was, thanks to Alfred's 'sensitivity' that Beth and Jim enjoyed the first taste of togetherness under the watchful and restrained eyes of the hopelessly romantic pair.

CHAPTER THIRTY ONE
Liza's Continuing Dilemma

As she waved Maddy goodbye, Liza turned and walked slowly back to her kitchen. Instead of clearing away the debris from the meal she sat down, with yet another cup of tea and sank into a reverie. Maddy seemed to have turned her life around and she thought she knew where she was going. Liza hadn't heard from Lucy for a while but as she was safely within the loving care of her daughter she didn't waste too much emotional energy on worrying about her. Beth was another matter but that nice couple at The Majestic Hotel seemed to have taken her under their wing. Liza had been mortified by the accident and wished she'd had the courage to ring her earlier. Maddy had made that happen. Liza reflected that Maddy had always been a fixer. Even at school she had been the one to get people to talk and make up when foolish quarrels had divided their tight group. Ronnie had been the protector but it was always Maddy who 'fixed' things. Just as she had now waltzed into Liza's life, unannounced, and fixed it for her to breathe again. Fixed it for her to feel that she could repair the friendship with Beth, which was very precious to her.

The stony road, full of potholes, which had characterised her emotional state in the past year, was finally reaching some kind of resolution when the accident happened. Everything was thrown into sharp focus and she clearly saw where she ought to be. Obviously her place was with Edwin and the farm and helping with all the business things, just as she always had done. But oh, where were her plans and dreams? What price now her adventure, her longing to go off and do something, explore South America, visit the ancient Peruvian masterpieces? As if in answer to her silent musings Edwin limped into the kitchen and sat down, sighing as he did so to relieve the pain in his leg.

"Maddy gone?" The enquiry hardly needed an answer as he could see the remains of tea and the empty chair.

"Yes, she seems to have made up her mind which way to go with Bear but she wouldn't say which way that was." Liza automatically got up and put the kettle on to give Edwin a restorative 'cuppa'. With the practise of years he swept up a scone and jam at the same time nodding to Liza that he would like some tea.

"Bear's a secretive devil. I tried to get him to open up at Ronnie's funeral but he kept avoiding my questions. You seem a bit unsettled old thing! What'd you say to having a meal out tonight? There's a special seafood night on at the Royal Oak. Fancy it?"

As Liza passed behind him to make the tea she caressed his head and said, "That'd be nice. Tom too or just us?"

"Just us. We need to spend some time together."

This concern for her wellbeing was almost the last straw for Liza as she had been thinking very selfish thoughts. She knew Edwin needed her now more than ever but she still hankered after … what? She'd pulled herself together after running away to Beth's. She'd almost broken down but didn't quite go the whole way. As she decided she ought to be grateful she also thought that she couldn't even have a breakdown properly. Perhaps she was just an ungrateful woman going through the last stages of the menopause and that one day soon she would wake up and realise what life was all about.

The Royal Oak was quite crowded as their seafood nights were very popular. Edwin had only got a table because he knew the owner very well. Liza and Edwin had a nice if somewhat snug corner table, well away from the routes to the kitchens and the toilets. They sat back and enjoyed their cool white wine as they waited for the famous 'platters' to be dished up and brought with great panache to their table by the eccentric 'Gaston'. No one knew if that was his real name but he used a French accent that would not have been out of place in a 'Carry On' film. Liza seized her moment as Edwin sat in fevered anticipation of a gastronomic masterpiece, "Edwin my love. You know all the things we've discussed over the last few months. I know we've come to lots of decisions but I…"

With unusual insight Edwin interrupted her to say, "You want to go to Peru don't you darlin'? I'm a lot better now. If you could postpone it for twelve months it would be a help but if you can't then so be it. I can't bear to see you continually trying to pretend you're happy."

Liza smiled a watery smile, "You do know me very well but this time I was going to offer to wait until you felt able to come with me." Edwin went to interrupt but she ploughed on, "No please let me have my say. I'm a selfish old woman sometimes, yes I feel unfulfilled deep down but I gave up a lot of stuff a very long time ago. I've been harbouring silly childish dreams and instead of growing up I've resented it. I don't want to go without you. I love you, your chest may have slipped and your hair gone west but you're still mine." She smiled at him to take away any uncertainty that may have caused.

"Well, I don't know if I'll be able to this year. I've got to see another specialist and…"

"Yes I know so what I've decided to do is an OU course on South American studies."

Edwin looked at her with astonishment as she continued, "Not a degree, not at first anyway. I'll just go for a course first and see how it goes. Its been so long I don't know if I can do it. But I want to try. Or we could do it together, what d'you say?"

They decided to walk round the farm before they went to bed. Full of good food and wine they strolled, hand in hand, as they had done years ago when they were young and newly guardians of the land. Liza was about to expand on her plans for intellectual fulfilment when Edwin suddenly stopped and creased up, "Oh my god Liza, tha pain, its almost unbearable. Help me." The last plea was enough to break her heart. She had always been the one who was looked after and cared for with great tenderness. She knew in a flash that he was her destiny and she was his. She helped him gently to the ground where she made him comfortable. She put her coat over him to keep him warm and ran to get help. Puffing and exhausted she cannoned into Tom who was making his last rounds before sleep and told him what had happened to Edwin.

Liza and Tom spent an anxious night in the hospital waiting for doctors to tell them what was happening. Edwin was sedated and happily was unaware of the great distress that his wife and son were suffering on his behalf. Liza thought that he would be permanently disabled from this latest problem. Tom thought so too and his thoughts turned to the enormous help his father still was with the farm and how he would cope without his amazing strength. They had called Liza's other children who were variously coming down straight away or the next day. Liza sat by Edwin's bed where he now was sleeping peacefully and cried silently while she watched her mountain of a husband laid so low. Tom, ever the practical one, bustled about getting his mother coffee and talking to doctors whenever he could find one to stay still long enough to answer questions. One young registrar finally took them to one side to tell them the results of their investigations.

Liza looked at the young doctor, "when did doctors and policemen start looking so young" she mused. When did they get to be the middle aged people that others dismiss as 'has beens'? The doctor spoke on but Liza heard next to nothing of what he said. She was in shock and as she gradually and very gracefully, for a rotund person, slipped to the floor in a faint, Tom held her gently while the doctor summoned help. This was turning into a rather bad night.

CHAPTER THIRTY TWO
Reunion Time Again

The 'phone calls had flown back and forth between the friends about where to hold this year's reunion. They all agreed in some measure that a lot had happened since last time. As is often the case with events of great enormity the passing remarks they all made were of a light hearted and frivolous nature. Maddy had urged Lucy to come down from her "Scottish holiday". Beth had told Liza to, "Stop living off the fat of the land and come and stay for the reunion." Nobody told Maddy what to do, that was the way it had always been. They had decided, without dissent, to meet again at Lulworth Cove. Another picnic was planned and they were all given tasks as to what food to bring and so forth. No one ever stuck to the plan but it was nice to have a plan. They all agreed that the first week in June would be best and so as the date grew near the friends had to decide how to tell the rest of the group just what was happening in their lives. Everything had changed and they had all made plans to step outside the box of comfort that they had been lying about for years. Whether their friends had been fooled by their distortions of the truth was another matter.

i

How would they react without Ronnie? Beth gave much thought to this as she prepared some of her more unusual Dorset recipes. She had tied to recreate some dishes that she'd found referenced in the local library. She thought she may as well try them out on her friends before

186

launching them on the unsuspecting public at The Majestic. There were very mixed feelings as she packed up the picnic hamper. Ronnie had always had a good appetite, what her grandmother would have called a 'good trencherman'. Beth still packed a lot of food but wondered if most of it would come back. Poor Ronnie, she so enjoyed their reunions. Maddy had missed quite a few but she had promised to be here again this year. Maddy hadn't mentioned Bear in her last two or three conversations. Maddy still hadn't moved away from her urban life despite her many protestations that she needed to bury herself in the country and do good works around animal welfare. Of all the group it seemed that Maddy had least reason not to fulfil her dreams and yet also appeared the most reluctant to get going and make things happen. Well they could all tackle her about it at the reunion and get her to open up.

How was Beth going to mention Jim, her coxswain? They had reached an 'understanding' and after a shaky start with Jim feeling overwhelmed with conflicting feelings they had settled for a life together. That was as far as they had got in their negotiations. Jim had his chandler's shop and boat hire business and Beth was really ensconced in her plans for resurrecting Dorset recipes and maybe writing a cookbook about the dishes. She had promised Marjorie and Alfred that, given her health had returned in full measure, she would help them out with their summer season. Alfred was still unsure about the local recipes. Born in London he could understand his mum's cooking everything that went with 'mash' but was reluctant to offer what he termed 'odd sounding' meals. "Tried and true, Marj, that's what our punters expect, not strange things out of the ark." Marjorie was torn between her husband's intransigence and their new friend's enthusiasm. "Well, Alfred, let's make it a theme night, say every Sa..."

"Friday. Friday nights. That's what we'll do. If it doesn't work we can have other themes. Brilliant. I knew I'd come up with the answer." Whistling Alfred went about his daily chores with renewed vigour. Marjorie throwing the towel she was folding at him and with a fond, "You idiot," went on with the laundry.

Maddy had decided not to tell her friends about the complications of her life at the moment. Until she was sure, she needed time to reflect. She had never been one to talk things through with anyone, she was a woman who had, hitherto, always known her own mind. This time it was different. Bear had been patient. She knew he loved her, but she always came back to the same idea that haunted her far into the night, "Was it enough?" With failed relationships littering her life's path she was wary to the point of obsession with not making yet another mistake. She just did not have the emotional energy to have any more failures on her mind. What was the alternative though? She loved Bear, she loved her animals, she wanted to work for any cause that saved human and animal suffering but she doubted her ability to lift herself from this emotional torpor. Ronnie's death had been a huge blow to her world. They had not met very often in between the reunions. Of all the friends they had not been the closest but even so Maddy felt increasingly bereft. What she had considered a stability had gone and her world was no longer certain. They were all on the edge of slipping into the twilight zone. 'Fifty may be the new forty' but some days she felt removed from the world of the young.

She had booked into The Majestic as last year and was slightly surprised by the warmth of her welcome. She hadn't realised that Beth had made such an impression and had become so integral a part of her new home. She had fitted right in as if this was where she was always meant to be. God how she envied Beth that sense of belonging. That welcome in another's world which had always eluded Maddy. The envy was only temporary as she knew what sacrifices Beth had made for her mother. She looked at how her own life had developed and found that she had mostly enjoyed it. Mistakes were just a part of her search, her searching for what she had never had at home. Acceptance! The word hit her like a train. Acceptance, she had always struggled at her work to fight for this cause or that. She had made it difficult for people at work to be her friends. She was driven and had only just come to the understanding that what she wanted was to be accepted for who she was and not for whom her parents wanted her to be. Wow! On reflection it seemed to be a simple resolution to her many hours, days, no a lifetime, spent in trying to work out where to go from here. Her parents were both dead and would never give her the recognition that she had craved. Strangely, now she had worked it out, she came to the conclusion that she didn't need their approbation. She felt serenely calm and decided to go down to the bar of the hotel and have a glass of cool wine. This was a celebration. She finally realised where she wanted to go and who she wanted to be, just her.

iii

Liza felt a sense of deja vue as she prepared for her journey the next day to Lulworth. It all seemed so familiar because it was. This is exactly how last year's reunion had begun, hopeful and full of promise. The weather forecast was as good if not better than last time, it seemed they were in for an early heatwave. How marvellous to be able to talk about the weather. As changeable as it was it was a constant source of comment. She had packed some Devonshire goodies, full of cholesterol and no doubt very bad for one but that is what she did and she loved it. Judging from the way her friends devoured her contribution they thought little of the dire warnings constantly in the media. How would she hold her head up with everyone else, seemingly, moving on and becoming what they had always wanted to be? Beth, now she was immersed in a life that gave her much fulfilment. Lucy appeared to have found a niche that gave her love and comfort the like of which she had not known for many years. Liza always wondered why she had not left sooner. She had little understanding of those with no self confidence. Maddy had a gorgeous man and a future that promised to make all her crazy dreams come true. Animals, yes they were important but it was family that made the world safe and true. It was family that gave the values for living that set out right from wrong. Ronnie! What a life she had led. Dead now, dead as the lamb she had cooked for lunch. What was it all for? Beth knew. Maddy knew. Even Lucy was finding out. Here was she, Liza, the successful business entrepreneur, farmer's wife, mother and grandmother envying the others their crack at living.

As these thoughts swam through Liza's head she came to the realisation that she was rather jealous of their lives. She had plumped for looking after Edwin over her fulfilling her dreams. On reflection it had not been a difficult decision. She had thought of many ways such as distance learning and single adventure holidays but when it came down to it she didn't have the spark. She lacked, what was it she lacked? Why did she feel cheated when all that she had cherished was there in front of her? Edwin was actually getting a little better and needed rather less of her time. The second spell in hospital had pulled the whole family up short. They had gathered round his bedside fearing the worst but the blood clot had been dispersed and he was finally allowed home to be on permanent medication. Their relationship had subtly altered and now she felt that his dominance and leadership was drifting to allow her to have more of a say. She was loved and she loved in return. Many would envy that state and she knew she was being ridiculous but still her inner self nagged at her and left her incomplete and discontent. As she packed the car for her journey she told herself off, "Liza old girl, you're an ungrateful cow. Be happy and content." She waved goodbye to Edwin and set off.

iv

"Lucy, Lucy, Lucy. Why do you have to go? Why do you have to visit that man? He's given you nothing but grief for years. He should be locked up by rights."

"Robert, thank you for caring but its something I just have to do. I don't know how to explain but I'll try. You didn't know me when I was in despair. Maddy drove me here to my daughter's and I was all set for a collapse. I'd allowed myself to be a victim and now I look back it hurts to think of what I'd become." Robert made to reassure her but now she'd started Lucy wanted to get it off her chest.

"No, please let me finish. Its hard enough. As we drove up here I felt an overwhelming need for some spiritual guidance. I'd heard of Coventry and its role in reconciliation but it was only a vague notion. Anyway Maddy took me there and everything changed inside me. Not immediately you know but my healing started then and hasn't stopped. It's for me to at least try to forgive John or at least get some closure. I'm not sure myself if I can forgive him but I think I need to see him and find out."

"I've become rather fond of you since we met. There was something about you, even when you fled from those drunken …"

"Please, let's forget all that. I rather, um, like you as well but I can't be moving on 'til I've nailed the past, so to speak. Say you understand. Its … you're important to me too."

"Lucy, will you make me a promise?" Robert pleaded with her but before she could answer he carried on, "Lucy, my life hasn't been the most straightforward. There's more to tell yet. Now is not the time or the place but please promise me you'll come back and give me a fair hearing?" He took her hand and caressed it.

Lucy, still unused to any such tenderness from a man trembled and, God forgive her doubting soul, she took her hand away. Instantly she was sorry as she watched the pain in his eyes as realisation dawned on him that she still had much to heal before she could trust. He was sad. He'd hoped that the weeks and months of their careful friendship, no one could yet call it courtship, was enough to show her his true mettle. He withdrew and very gently took his leave. His parting shot was one of patience with an undercurrent of dismay. "I'll be here if you ever come back Lucy. Remember though, I'm only human."

Robert left and Lucy sank to the sofa cradling her head in her hands and wept. She had just blown away a lovely man, with whom she could have a wonderful life, she loved him as she had never loved John but something held her back. She considered through her misery that she

191

probably was just not worthy of his attention. She sat bolt upright and almost shouted at herself, "No, that is the old Lucy, the new Lucy is worthy of any one. What have I done?" She ran after Robert who had backed out of Amy's driveway and was preparing to go on his lonely way when he saw her rush out of the house and run towards him. "Robert, please wait. Robert, Rob …"

He was out of the car, hurrying to her and swept her up in his arms before she could get another syllable out. "Oh whist, hush, shsh." He comforted her with his embrace and hoped that she had run after him for this and not just because he'd left his hat behind or something similar. He didn't wear a hat but the bizarre feelings that swamped him at that moment had sent his mind into odd places full of insecurity. "Come back love please, come back?" Lucy pleaded.

She'd called him love, Robert felt on top of the world. Within a few minutes they were back in Amy's sitting room, sitting together on the sofa and holding hands.

"Let me explain, or at least try. Robert, I sometimes slip back to that frightened apology of a human being. Its very rare now but it does happen. I'm scared of being happy. You are so dear to me. Come with me down to the south coast and be there when I've had my reunion. My friends are so important to me and I want you to meet them. You could come and pick me up and meet them then. I'll do the John thing on my own. I don't know if I'm big enough to forgive him but I must lay some ghosts. Just to be able to walk away with my head held high will be enormous, and so important, for me." It is not certain how long she would have carried on talking without stopping for breath but Robert decided to kiss her. Lucy went very pink, smiled and kissed him right back. There were not two happier fifty 'somethings' in the whole of Scotland.

v

Thus it was that the four friends prepared to gather once more for a reunion. One of their number thought that this may be their last

192

reunion. Their lives all seemed to be diverging in a way that they had not done so in the past. Perhaps it was the upset of losing Ronnie. How they would handle that would be a testament to their abiding love for one another.

CHAPTER THIRTY THREE
A Detour

John had made a new life for himself. After the debacle with the funeral and being dumped by Cynthia he had decided to start again. He had not moved house but he had changed jobs and was now a consultant. It seemed to bring in the money but there were days when he wondered what on earth he did to earn his money. He advised people, who should know better than he, on local political issues. He was not one to look a gift horse in the mouth and so he patted himself on the back and carried on, much as before, believing that the world owed him a living and that Lucy had been the one at fault in their marriage. If only she had been a better wife. If only she had supplied more of his needs then he would not have been unhappy and would not have resorted to anger through frustration. Yes, it was certainly her fault and that was the end of that.

Robert and Lucy were booked into the Majestic for two nights, the one preceding and the one following the reunion. So it was that on the night before the reunion Lucy walked down the familiar street that had been her home for so long. Familiar yet alien it produced a desire in her to turn the other way and just keep walking. It was a warm early summer evening. People were coming home from work and there were children riding their bikes up and down the road and over the pavements. Teenage boys skateboarding and narrowly missing pedestrians gave it all a feeling of normality. Lucy had insisted that Robert stay in the car at the end of the road and wait for her.

Lucy's determined steps faltered as she approached the house where her degradation had taken place. The horror of some of the worst times flooded over her. She started to sweat and her throat went dry. She tried to summon up the overwhelming feeling of peace that she had felt in Coventry. Unfortunately there is no magic in faith. She felt alone. John was at home and opened the door to a ghost. The source of all his troubles. He recovered his equilibrium fairly well and used his well known sneer accompanied by, "Well, well, well. Look who it isn't. Come crawling back have you?" He folded his arms in a blocking gesture. He thought it made him look in control. Lucy thought it made him look ridiculous. From that moment she knew that she had him beaten. She realised that he had not and probably never would change from the cowardly bully that he had always been. She wasn't ready to smile at him. She was in fact shaking from head to foot but inside she was strong. The moments dragged by. John didn't ask her in, he just stared at her, challenging her to make her move. He genuinely thought she had come back to him. Her words, when they finally came out were a shock. Lucy took a deep breath, "John. You are a mean bullying bastard. I'm not ready to forgive you. I have a new life and you are history." She turned on her heel and went to leave. She could manage no more. It was tame compared to what she had rehearsed but it was enough. Clearly it was too much for John as he leapt out of the doorway and grabbed her arm. "Wait. You have the nerve to talk about forgiveness you … you … bitch, you utter bitch you …" He was incandescent with the old rage. As he started to shake her she fought back. She kicked and swung her free arm to hit him but he was still stronger than she was. She thought that perhaps this was the worst decision of her life to come back and treat him like a human being. She was failing.

It was the boy on the skateboard who saved her. As she had walked into this nightmare he had almost knocked her down. She had sidestepped with a little hop to avoid him and smiled at him, when in truth he expected yet more abuse from the adult world, he surprised himself by smiling back and grunting, "Y're ok?" He stopped and saw the arrogant git, who usually shouted abuse at him and his friends, beating the hell out of this tiny woman. His sense of comradeship swung into action and he called his skating partners over and they walked up the path in force. "Leave her mister." "You fucking bully, let her go." "Here, mate, have a go at someone your own size." "Fuzz is coming." John's world was crumbling down around him. Who were these louts to talk to him on his own patch? Robert had come round the corner and was on the scene in an instant. He cradled Lucy in his arms and looked at the scene where the rather large teenagers were holding John in vice like grips. They seemed to be enjoying themselves. For once they were on the good side and the police couldn't tell them off or move them on. Robert took control and said, "Hold him lads. The police will be here in a moment."

Domestic violence is not popular with the police force. It is a tricky road to tread. However, this time a sympathetic couple answered the call, as did a paramedic response unit. The female policewoman and her male colleague took statements from all present, arrested John for assault (eventually he would be charged with breaking the terms of his suspended sentence as well). Lucy was cared for by the paramedics but she refused to go to hospital. Robert handed her into the car as if she were porcelain and fussed around her. He drove away having first made sure that the lads who had helped did not go unrewarded. One of the mothers of the boys had come out to see what the commotion was and she went back inside her house with renewed respect and pride in her rather wayward son. "I couldn't and didn't forgive him you know." Robert didn't reply. "I just couldn't."

"Lucy, if I speak now I'll say awful things like 'I told you so' and 'why didn't you listen' etc." Lucy put out her hand and touched his arm. "I know love."

"People like him don't change. He's a bastard and will always be predatory. God you're stubborn. I'll have to learn to live with that I suppose." They drove on to the Majestic in a silence filled with promise but marred by shock and pain.

CHAPTER THIRTY FOUR
Lulworth Again

Beth was the first to make her way to the spot on Lulworth shore that they had occupied last year. She had a cool box full of experimental recipes that she fully expected her friends to pick at, be polite, then eat everything else. She'd spent some time the previous evening talking with Maddy in the bar of the Majestic. It seemed so odd to be where they were last year but with everything so changed. Maddy had subtly altered and had withdrawn from the open confident person she had been. Still outwardly buoyant Beth noticed a certain reticence when it came to revealing her current plans. On the subject of Bear she would say absolutely nothing. They had all thought Lucy was due to stay at the Majestic but as she hadn't turned up they considered that it had been too much of a journey for her and that she was still in Scotland. Unusually Maddy decided to turn in early and so Beth spent a little more time talking with Marjorie and Alfred then she too went home. Last year they had all arrived bearing secrets and that had turned the day into a watershed for them all.

This year the June day had started with a little sea mist then at about eleven o'clock the sun had broken through and the warmth had given Beth a new feeling of hope. Strange how a small thing like sunshine altered everything. But then of course the sun shining was not a small thing at all, it was essential. The media of late had taken up the story of global warming and was bombarding everyone with guilt about using the earth's resources and that it was all the fault of mankind. Beth was heartily sick of it all. Even when she had bought her cottage, only five miles from the coast, people had pointed out to her that in fifty years time it may well be actually on the shore line. Some had joked about it and others had spoken as if it were a dire warning. She had fallen in love with the place and that was that as far as she was concerned and if it didn't last another hundred years well then she was not going to be here and so why worry. Scientists were always changing their minds anyway and Beth had become quite cynical about their prognostications. She turned her mind away from weighty issues of the doom and gloom about the future and decided to concentrate on having a good day. It was going to be hard enough without Ronnie anyway. She spread out her blanket and sat down to wait.

The next to arrive was Maddy, she sauntered down to the cove and slowly made her way to where Beth was sitting. Maddy had a grin on her face that was so like her old self that Beth's feelings of doom were dispelled. Ignoring any attempt at polite greetings Maddy burst forth with, "You'll never guess who turned up last night, go on have a guess, who d'you think?"

"Well I can only assume it was Lucy. Was it? Is she OK?" As Maddy seemed in no hurry to tell she continued, "Oh for goodness sake Maddy, you'll drive me mad. Who is it? Is it Luce?"

"Yes of course its Luce but who has she got with her that's the question. Go on have another guess. Who d'you think?"

"Well it won't be a man for a start. She'd be mad to jump into another relationship so soon after that bastard John."

"Ah ha. You wait and see. If I tell you we met a chap on the way up to Scotland last year and he's lovely will you believe that Lucy seems to have fallen on her feet." Maddy wondered whether to tell Beth about the fracas yesterday with John but decided that it was Lucy's story and it must be up to her to explain. Beth thought there was something else but couldn't get any more out of Maddy. It helped ease the sudden silence when they both looked up and saw Liza struggling along carrying all sorts of blankets and boxes. As they got up to meet her and help her they noticed someone else just behind her, also carrying bags and a blanket. "Liza, you look well. How's everything? Who's this? Jane. Oh" Maddy finished rather impolitely. Beth took up the greetings, "Hello Liza. Brought too much food as usual. I'm sure we'll get through it. Nice to see you Jane. How are you?" Jane noticed the extra polite way that the greetings changed when they spoke to her and she felt a momentary tinge of jealousy. Friends like this didn't grow on trees and she had no one like it herself.

"I hope you didn't mind me coming but when Liza invited me it seemed like a lovely idea. If you'd rather..."

Maddy now felt bad and so over enthused, "Of course not, you're more than welcome. We can talk about Ron and we can all get drunk and grieve together. Its less than a year after all." She hugged Jane and so did Beth, though Beth was rather more reluctant. She was unsure if she liked Jane and considered Liza had taken a step too far in inviting her.

Outwardly the awkwardness was over now and they all laughed and struggled with the copious bags and blankets and cushions and fell over themselves to be jolly and comfortable. Liza looked relieved and a little guilty. "Jane dear, don't listen to this but I asked Jane to join us because she loved Ronnie too and her husband is useless when it comes to feelings and with George going as well, well I thought it'd be nice. For us all."

Beth answered, "Liza, you're a silly old thing. Of course it's a lovely idea and Jane you're more than welcome. The initial awkwardness was because we didn't know, did we Mad?" Beth had answered because she had felt negative about the intrusion and wanted to make amends. She was perhaps a little too hasty.

Beth had given the lead and Maddy, not usually the follower agreed, "Jane, welcome to our group. Its very exclusive. You have to be special to get in and that's why you're here." Liza was so proud of her friends she hugged her knees and stared wet eyed out to sea until she'd got hold of her emotions. Jane was quite emotional when she replied, "Ronnie used to talk about you a lot. You were so important to her. Especially after the accident, you know when they lost…" She couldn't finish the sentence. "Yes, we know. We all deal with grief in a different way. Ronnie's way was to go at life even faster. She thought it hurt less that way. It doesn't of course." Beth reflected.

There was a lull in the conversation. They all settled down in whatever fashion they found comfortable on the shore and waited. Lucy was a long time coming and so Liza and Beth decided to go and find her. Maddy and Jane, when left alone, were the least forthcoming of the group and so they fell back on polite conversation until Maddy, uncharacteristically, mentioned her current dilemma and her desire to run an animal sanctuary. Jane was immediately enthused and gave her encouragement to expand her dream. Jane recognised a fellow 'buttoned up spirit' immediately. As Maddy talked about both her dream and Bear Jane suddenly interrupted with, "Do you love him, and want to be with him? Its quite simple you know." Maddy hesitated then said, "Yes, I do, but …"

"There are no 'buts' if you love him and want to be with him. Love without the other is more difficult but, may I say, having known you for so little time I hesitate but perhaps its easier with comparative strangers." Jane took a deep breath and carried on, "You've been a lawyer far too long. You overcomplicate your life. Try to eliminate the dross and start with a very simple question. Be honest with your answers to yourself and then you'll get to the point much more quickly." Maddy still said nothing. Jane looked at her with great sympathy, "Maddy. Believe me life is too short not to take risks. I've put up with rubbish far to long myself. Go for it. Be happy. Ronnie admired you and respected you most of all. I suspect you thought differently."

Maddy faced Jane and without speaking gave her a hug. Jane felt welcomed and accepted. All Maddy said after a while was, "You're right. So bloody right." As Liza and Beth looked back down the beach they saw Maddy hug Jane and then there was a visible easing of body language and finally much laughter. Liza rather smugly said, almost to herself, "I knew it, I just knew it."

Beth put her arm round her friend, "Liza old thing. It'll be ok you know. It will. Eventually. You, more than any of us have a journey yet to make. Don't pick me up on my grammar either. You are so talented but Edwin needs you so much. Be a little more patient." Liza looked at her in alarm. It was as if Beth had read her very thoughts yet none had been expressed. "I'm not a witch Lize but your emails have been full of dashed hopes. Not carping but rather, no, very, sad. You have so much and want so much. That's not wrong but timing is important. Ronnie's dead and look what she went through before she died. George and she were almost estranged." Liza looked horrified as though Beth had fortold Edwin's demise. "No, No Lize I'm not saying he's going to die but he's not strong enough yet. He will be." As she spoke with such determination Beth wondered herself if she was a witch. Her father had often called her mother a witch but that was for a different reason. "'Nuff now here comes Lucy."

Lucy limped towards them across the shingle. She was smiling but clearly there was something amiss. They ran up to her, as well as any middle-aged, unfit women can across moving stones. As they embraced and greeted each other they all started to cry. None of them knew why but the tears were cathartic and they smiled through them all. "What a soppy lot we are!" Liza was the first to break away. Beth stood back and looked long and hard at Lucy. "Come and tell all of us about it. Whatever it is I guess you won't want to have to repeat it. Right?"

"Yes, Beth. Sound as usual. Come on then. Let's go and join the others. We've all got some explaining to do. Yes, and then we must start with a sort of remembrance. " Lucy seemed strong today. They had expected a frail apology of a friend considering the recent events. The three of them approached the picnic spot that seemed cosy and exclusive. Lucy accepted Jane's presence without comment and gave her a hug along with the others as though the younger woman already belonged. Jane appreciated the gesture and immediately fell under Lucy's spell.

Maddy took the lead, "Now we're all here let's start with Ronnie. Champagne I think." They all stood and raised their glasses heavenwards and Maddy spoke, "God bless you Ronnie. A friend in every sense. Rest in peace now. I hope you and George find your boy in eternity." The rest echoed, "Ronnie. Good friend. Rest in peace." They drank and all stared out to sea for a while, saying nothing but each thinking their own thoughts. Private thoughts that needed no sharing, no explanation, just for each alone. Maddy looked round at Jane and offered, "Do you want to honour your dad?" More champagne was added to each glass then Jane spoke, "Dad, you were a wonderful father. Thanks for everything. Ronnie, thanks for sharing your friends with me. They're diamonds, each and every one." She raised her glass to each of the friends in turn and drank their health. Someone needed to break the tension. That someone was Liza who as usual took the more practical and grounding role. "Well Jane, there's enough of us to share." Liza patted her rotund tummy and laughed. Simply and beautifully she had turned them back to the present and that was what they all wanted.

They settled once more into a tableau of conviviality surrounding the food and drink. Some picked at the food, others broke out more drink and they waited for Lucy to begin her story. Beth encouraged her to start, "Lucy, we've all got so much to update everyone with but you are the prize clam. What's been going on? Why are you limping? Who is the handsome stranger that Maddy told us about?" Lucy grinned and began her story.

CHAPTER THIRTY FIVE
Lucy The Strong

"Where to begin? I suppose you all remember Ronnie's funeral? Well I was obviously shaken up and still not in a very good place. I almost thought I'd brought it on myself you know." Jane interrupted, stricken with guilt, "Lucy, I am so, so very sorry. I had no idea that you had such a time with him and it was me that left the details on his answer machine. I hope you can forgive me?" Lucy didn't smile but she looked at Jane and said simply, "Of course." Lucy took a drink of wine and carried on, "I went back to Scotland and Amy and Angus were so cocooning that I felt I need never have to take a step anywhere on my own if I didn't want to. You know the rest through my infrequent letters. However there's stuff I didn't tell you. My time helping at the literacy group was made so easy by a lovely old lady, Mrs M. Remember Maddy, that chap who just happened to be on the spot when we were hijacked?"

Maddy gasped but said nothing, not wanting to break the spell. Lucy had never been this forthcoming. Holding centre stage was Maddy's or Liza's role, not tiny Lucy.

Lucy smiled an unconvincing smile, painful memories not far beneath the surface. She continued, "The one from the hotel? Yes him. Well Mrs M is his mother. I gradually got to know him and he sort of asked me to dinner. It was all lovely and gentle and friendship but underneath the chit chat was a bit of an undercurrent." Suddenly Lucy hugged her knees to her and rocked back and forth in a private moment on public display. "Go on for goodness sake Luce. Then what?" Liza could contain her curiosity no longer. She had no qualms about breaking any spell.

"All right. Well then I decided that my only way to peace, inside, was to make peace with my abusers. You know the drug runner and also...John." She said his name quietly as though he still had power to hurt her. "Shout it Lucy, shout it so that you get back your soul." The words inside her head came tumbling out and she shouted his name and flung him from her. "The hijacker was reluctant to see me but I did and forgave him. He wasn't interested although at the last minute there was a glimmer of understanding but he's in very deep, but actually I felt better." She looked at Maddy and said, "It was Coventry you know Mad. It had such a profound effect on me I had to try." Maddy replied only with, "Lucy you idiot. You're a good soul."

While the others digested this latest folly, as they saw it, of their gentle harried friend, Lucy stood up and opened her arms to the sea. "Its so good here. I feel alive."

"Never mind all that," Liza once again wanted to know the whole story, "What about John? Is that why you're limping today? What did he do to you? You didn't go to forgive him did you? Oh for goodness sake Lucy."

Rather embarrassed now Lucy tried to explain all that had happened. Beth was the only one who understood, "You had to try Lucy. Thank god you're ok."

"Thanks Beth. At least someone understands."

"We all do Lucy but we hate to see you hurt." Maddy was protective.

"Well its over now and he won't hurt me any more. You know those lads were brilliant. I don't think they've been on the receiving end of police praise before. Robert was great with them."

"When do we see this paragon? Is he coming down later?" Liza continued to push the group into some action. She was restless and wanted to have a walk. She was glad Lucy was now all right but she needed to get up and do something. Lucy caught the tone and decided she had held sway long enough. "Yes. He'll be down with Marjorie and Alfred later with some strawberries and cream. Their gift to us. Beth you've really settled here haven't you? They think the world of you."

Beth smiled at Lucy and also got up to join Liza. I feel like stretching my legs lets walk a bit. The group proceeded to break up for a while and some went for a walk, others wandered along the shore line looking for interesting flotsam. Jane and Maddy threw stones into the water and tried skimming. Jane won with a 'five bounce'. Lucy's arm hurt so she just watched and wandered along drinking in the air and longing for the time when she could introduce Robert to her friends. The three of them got as far as the café and found the old man there who last year had rented them his boat. They introduced themselves to him. "Ay I remember you all, 'cept this one." He indicated to Jane. "I'm a sort of newcomer to the group. It was my step-mother who was here last year and took the boat out to sea." The old man grunted, "Oh her. Mm." He looked round then added, "She's not here with y'all then?" Maddy took over in case it was too painful for Jane, "I'm afraid she met with an accident and died last summer." His reaction was unexpected, "Yes, she'd her last pages written all over her. I'm not surprised." He thought some more, "She'd lived that one, so she had." As the three women walked away from the café Maddy said, "Beth had that feeling too. Do you remember Lucy? What she said as we stood and waved Ronnie goodbye?"

"Yes, I only half believe in that sort of thing but, well its a mystery. There might just be something in it. He seemed totally unsurprised." By the time they got back to their picnic area they had decided that he was a soothsayer, a witch, a warlock and a medium. As they sat down Maddy added, "He could just be a good guesser."

Laughing they all sat down and rummaged for more food and drink. They sighed and chatted and laughed and felt good being together. They spotted Liza and Beth coming back and waved. When they'd all got comfortable again Lucy said, "Maddy, your turn." And so it was.

CHAPTER THIRTY SIX
Maddy in the Spotlight

"Truth to tell I've been in a bit if a state since last year. I think Ronnie's death upset me more than I made allowances for. When I tried to hand over my practice I vacillated until I must have sent my colleagues raving mad. I would have hated to work with me. When I came down here last night I had decided nothing. It was something Jane said that put things in focus." She stopped for breath. She been gabbling and snatching at her words until she was out of breath. This was not like her at all and the others were concerned at her lack of confidence. Jane offered, "Its sometimes easier to see clearly from a bit of a distance."

"Anyway I don't want to say too much except that I've treated Bear abominably and I hope its not too late. He bought me a farm you know, actually a small holding. I never even went to look at it. What a selfish cow!"

Liza interrupted with, "Buying something like land or a house is a joint thing. It's a bit arrogant if you ask me."

"Thanks Liza. That's what I thought but his reaction was so sad, I could have gone to look."

"Not if you weren't ready. We're bounced around by people all our lives we must retain some kind of control." Liza was in one of her 'don't mess with me' moods. So no one did. She carried on, "If he's the one for you Mad he'll wait. Maybe not for ever but its only been a few months. Ring him if you want to but stay in control."

206

Beth thought that Liza was bouncing Maddy into a corner so she intervened, "Mad, be patient. Bear seemed like such a nice chap. I'm sure you'll do the right thing when the time is right for you." To ease the sudden tension she playfully slapped Liza's wrist saying, "Liza stop running people's lives for them. You've got enough on your plate with all you've had to endure these past few months. Ease up old thing." Liza glared at Beth then realised that she was in the wrong and nodded her agreement. Lucy went over to Liza and gave her a hug. Maddy suddenly stood up and announced, "I'm going for a walk to ring Bear. I'll be back in a moment." She started to walk away then turned and said, "Jane, you tell them what you're up to. I know so I won't miss anything. Go on. It'll be all right."

CHAPTER THIRTY SEVEN
Jane Takes the Floor

"It's so great to be with you today." She paused to laugh, "That sounds as though I'm about to make a speech doesn't it?" In truth she was a little nervous as she would love to be accepted by them all as a friend. She had slightly envied Ronnie's link with such a bunch of people whose friendship was always true and forgiving. Jane had never had that. It had been Liza who had kept up a correspondence since Ronnie's death. Liza who had encouraged her to face her problems. Liza, who was discontent with her own lot but who had an empathetic understanding for another's problems. It was a gift that only she underrated. Jane continued, "My story is rather dull. The usual story I s'pose. I left uni and got a good job in marketing. I had early success. Dad was so encouraging." She wiped away a tear for her lost father, "He had to be both parents to me and tried very hard.., too hard, perhaps."

Beth interrupted, "Can you try too hard?" her wistful look held a world of wishing that her mother had understood her a bit better.

Jane continued emphatically, "Yes, definitely! He smothered a bit. I'm not blaming him but I sought a more detached husband and that's what I got. Our kids are great but we've just drifted. I'm absolutely convinced he's got a mistress. God knows why he's still with me."

Beth again, "Have you asked him?"

"No, I'm not sure I really care. I've done all the work with bringing up the children and the home. I've given up so many promotions because I'm part time." She put her hand to her forehead in an exaggerated gesture, "It's all me, me, me isn't it? Look this isn't a 'poor me' session. I just wanted to, um, say with Dad and Ronnie gone I've realised I've got a life before me. It's not going to be wasted. Sounds selfish but I'll always help my children but they won't grow if I've sacrificed everything for them. They've already become unaware of me as a person. That's all about to change." She took a deep breath and smiled thankfully at Liza, "I let it be known that I was available and a former colleague has offered me an associate post. I start next month."

This plump, pretty, dark haired woman was so clearly pleased with herself that she stood up and did a little hop for joy. Beth joined her and soon they were all milling around offering congratulations. No one asked about her husband. That was Jane's problem. He wasn't a bad man; he had just lost sight of his wife and family and had pursued other goals. These new friends would offer advice if asked but wouldn't give it unbidden. If they had known her a little better they might have done, but deep friendship like theirs takes time to 'bed in'.

Maddy rejoined the group and sat down. She looked upset and they asked her about the 'phone call. "Bear says he still loves me. He wants to talk but won't commit over the 'phone." In despair she added, "I've left it too late. He sounded distant."

Liza asked, "Where was he Mad?"

"Oh in a meeting or something." Maddy was exasperated and exasperating.

Liza told her so, "Maddy for goodness sake give him a chance. You've left it for weeks. Then like a bolt out of the blue you ring him and expect him to drop everything. Look Mad, your other husbands were all a bit weak. This one isn't. You walk all over the weak ones. Give Bear a chance. He's rather cute."

Beth added, "Mad, you're impossible. Bear's lovely. You love him, he loves you. Don't bully him. You're quite capable you know."

Beth remembered a time in school that brought an image of Maddy intimidating a girl who she thought had been cruel to the school cat.

They had all pulled her away from the frightened cat teaser. Maddy was a powerful force when roused, at least Moggins was safe after the incident. The girl avoided Maddy ever after.

CHAPTER THIRTY EIGHT
Liza Talks

"It will soon be time for Marjorie and Alfred to join us. I just wanted to tell you about my decisions before we get distracted." Lulworth was sunny and still. A few people were sitting on the pebbles and rocks near the slipway by the café but the group of friends were round the other side of the Cove and distant from any interference. A few dinghies were moored across the other side and bobbed about in the gentle lapping of the water. It was a unique place and suited the mood of the friends. The bay cast a spell on the five of them and they all felt sleepy and at peace. Liza spoke softly and slowly unfolded her plans for getting out of her rut, in time. "As you all know Ed's been very poorly since the accident, which looking back was all my fault." Beth opened her mouth to interject but Liza stopped her, "Don't Beth. I know deep down what happened. You suffered too. Well I've realised that my place is with him. He's a loving and good man and has never done me a wrong turn in our many years together. Whatever I've wanted I've had. Materially anyway. My problem I think stems from last year when everything kicked off and we lost Ronnie, Lucy had been through hell. Maddy was making changes. Beth I didn't know about yours until after but really my life seemed to be standing still." She paused but the others understood that she needed to get this out so they didn't interrupt.

"I love Edwin but I also have a burning desire to experience some excitement. Travel as well. I've investigated courses at the local university. They offer access courses with the option of time away in interesting places. I'm going to start South American studies in the autumn after next. I'm so excited. When I told Edwin he thought I was going away. Believe me I thought about that but I just love him too much to hurt him or leave him which is what I was thinking when I ran away to Beth's. Sorry old thing. I put you to a lot of trouble didn't I?"

Beth agreed, "Yes you did rather. I would never turn any of you away ever though, you know that don't you?" She looked at Jane and added, "That includes you now. Welcome to this very exclusive group." Beth still had reservations about Jane but thought that a few kind words would not go amiss in the circumstances.

"I'm so glad that you've sorted it all out. I worried for you this last year. You weren't yourself." Lucy spoke up. "Beth I know we haven't heard your story but the sea is so gorgeous now I feel like stretching my legs for a bit. Do you mind holding your story 'til later?"

"Not at all. It's a story soon told anyway. Let's walk."

So it was that the five friends sauntered along the shoreline and up over the cliffs at the eastern end of the Cove and stood on the headland and gazed contentedly out to sea. The sun was kind to them. A small sea breeze played with their hair and their clothing. Liza's baggy trousers billowed, Lucy's short summer dress danced about her small frame while Beth's marvellous gypsy skirt took the breeze and the brilliant reds and orange and lime colours swirled and gave her a carefree air. She looked timeless as she stood with her friends on the cliff. She mentally hugged her secret to her and wondered how they would take her news. They all marvelled at the beauty of the scene and chatted inconsequentially. Finally they made their way back to the picnic area where the remains of their day's grazing were picked over and they sat on the rocks and turned to Beth. With four pairs of eyes on her Beth suddenly felt a little shy. As she went rather pink Liza teased her, "You used to look like that at school when you fancied a boy. Who was that tall gangly chap who took you to the football match and thought the way to woo a girl was to get her muddy and drink pints of cider then make a grab for her behind the goal posts? You know he had red hair and huge teeth."

Beth sighed remembering the gauche young man who had set her teenage heart on fire then dashed all her hopes by going off with horrible Beverly whose father had a season ticket to the local football team. "Ozzy Otterbourne. I thought he was the 'end'." Maddy joined in, "That's right do you remember his friend, Clive something or other." She went giggly and added, "He was my first." She made a face of pure comedy theatre, "It took seconds." They laughed and Liza observed, "Difficult being teenagers isn't it. Boys and girls. God I wouldn't go back for all the tea in China." They laughed, reminisced and helped themselves to drink. Maddy prompted Beth, "Come on Beth, what have you been up to?"

"In short I've moved here and it's the best thing I ever did. I have made friends with Marjorie and Alfred who are the loveliest people. Oh and I've adopted a dog, Molly. She was abandoned and she's so cute." She stopped and drank an orange juice.

Liza encouraged her to continue, "Beth we know all that, you've sent all that information in your emails. There has to be more."

"Yes there is. I've started researching Dorset recipes. Everyone I've asked is most helpful and I've tried themes nights at The Majestic. They've had mixed receptions but we're going to keep on trying new stuff." Beth stopped again.

Lucy prompted this time, "And?"

Beth wrapped her arms round her knees and took a deep breath, "Well I went looking for the Coxswain of the lifeboat who rescued us last year to apologise and offer a donation to the RNLI. I found him, at the Majestic actually, he's a distant cousin of Alfred's. He wasn't very encouraging and I thought him a grisly old misery." She hurried on before she was interrupted again, "To cut a long story short, he's a widower, cautious of designing women and he was very unhappy. We got to become friends and when I was injured he looked after me and Molly and now we're, um, we're an item."

The friends, who had all hoped that she had found some well deserved happiness, could contain themselves no longer and whooped for joy and danced and hugged and laughed at the fates.

CHAPTER THIRTY NINE
Final Scene?

Marjore and Alfred walked towards the friends bearing a small dog and being trailed by a rather rugged middle aged man. Molly ran up to Beth and turned herself inside out with excitement. Beth greeted her by swooping her up and cuddling her. "What turned a grizzled old sailor from a confirmed bachelor to your beau?" Liza asked. Beth replied with great calm, "It's very simple. Sailors are very superstitious. I named this lovely little thing Molly and Jim's granddaughter's name is Molly. He thought it was a sign."

Alfred decided that he ought to say something as he was family, "Jim was just waiting for you Beth. Soon as we saw him with you we knew he couldn't help himself. He was so much grumpier than normal. He was just fighting the feelings and my Marjorie here was beside herself with excitement. I kept her back though." He added this last statement as though it were a rare and wonderful achievement.

Marjorie couldn't let that go, "I was only going to help them be together until they both realised the inevitable. That's all." Alfred put his arm round her and said, "Don't get the hump. Heart of gold my Marj, heart of gold." After thirty years together they could still seem to be the only people present in their loving world.

Lucy asked the obvious question, "Beth, did you know that...?"

"No I didn't. It was just happenstance. Kismet if you like. Anyway I intend to make him so happy that he forgets about being a miserable old sailor. He's very sweet really." The others looked at each other,

Beth was obviously very relaxed, and they had seldom seen Beth so happy.

Lucy had moved to take the hand of the stranger who hung back from the group. "Now we've met Molly and we've reacquainted ourselves with Marjorie and Alfred I want you all to meet Robert. Mad you must remember?" Maddy realised from her tone that she was asking for help, "Of course, nice to see you again. What a coincidence you being the son of Mrs M."

Liza added, "Yes we heard much of your mother and how helpful she was to our Lucy, here." She grinned at Lucy and continued, "But truth to tell we've heard precious little about you." She held out her hand, "Nice to meet you anyway."

Robert felt that this was Lucy's family so he thought he ought to reassure them that his intentions were honourable. On an impulse he took Lucy's hand and got down on one knee and asked, "Lucy, I want to be there for you every day. Marry me. I love you."

It took a lot to silence the friends but Robert had managed it. Lucy looked down at him and said very gently, "Get up please." Robert looked hurt but didn't move. A few stragglers had stopped to look at the group as though it was street theatre. For Lucy there was no one else on the shore, "Oh Robert, you idiot. Will you get up if I say 'yes'?"

"Aye, if you say 'no' then I'll be here when the tide turns and I'll drown in sea and sorrow." Lucy laughed with the sweetest sound that made her friends cry with love for her. "Mr Robert McHeath I will consent to be your wife but get up now as I don't want a soggy husband." Robert stood up and swept her into his arms and kissed her soundly in front of everyone. The small crowd clapped and went away feeling that life might just be all right after all.

All who knew Lucy's story were happy for her. Only Liza was uncertain about Robert's charm and ability to be good enough for her friend. But then Liza was uncertain about so much. Beth and Jane were genuinely delighted and Alfred produced another bottle of champagne from his basket and they toasted the happy couple in traditional fashion.

Another momentous reunion had come to an end. They had all gone back to the Majestic and were in various stages of departure. Coffee had been served and Maddy and Lucy were staying on for another night. Maddy had drunk so much champagne that it was the safest thing for her to do. Jane was on her way back home to deal with whatever the fates had in store. She travelled hopefully and with renewed energy. She would be back next year, if asked.

Liza drove home slowly and thoughtfully. She was going back to the life she knew. There would be no surprises. There would be no fresh excitement. Edwin would be there wanting comfort and reassurance and she would give it to him. As she parked the car she paused before she got out. She sat back and sighed. She wanted so much, did she have the courage to see some of her plans through. Her next sigh was a determined one. She would search out some form of extra study. She would expand her horizons and she would make Edwin believe that it was for the best. It would take all her ingenuity but it would be done. She got out of the car and walked through the door that led to the rest of her life. She entered with another deep sigh.

Beth took Molly home and prepared for the next adventure when she would become part of a couple. A novelty for her and one to which she looked forward with happy anticipation. 'Beth and Jim', 'Jim and Beth', how good that sounded.

Maddy lay in bed, her head reeling from too much alcohol, and rang Bear. He didn't answer his 'phone so she turned over and cried her self to sleep. She got up the next day with less enthusiasm than usual and got ready to leave. 'Would she be all right on her own? Would she have to be on her own? Would Bear respond and be her, what?' She paused in her thinking, what did she want? Well she thought pragmatically if she didn't know she couldn't expect others to jump on board her 'journey to the unknown'. She would come to next year's reunion. She would be the one to shock the rest. However she achieved that, it would be done. She longed to see Bear and sort things out but she couldn't make him talk to her if he had decided to give up on her.

She turned the car for home.

'If only they were young again, how different their lives might have been!'

"O God! Put back Thy universe and give me yesterday."
(Henry Arthur Jones and Henry Herman: The Silver King 1907)

The End

Printed in the United Kingdom
by Lightning Source UK Ltd.
129310UK00001B/277-318/P